AMITY
&
SORROW

AMITY & SORROW

A Novel

PEGGY RILEY

Doubleday Large Print Home Library Edition

LITTLE, BROWN AND COMPANY
New York Boston London

This Large Print Edition, prepared especially for Doubleday Large Print Home Library, contains the complete, unabridged text of the original Publisher's Edition.

Little, Brown and Company
Hachette Book Group
237 Park Avenue, New York, NY 10017

Little, Brown and Company is a division of Hachette Book Group, Inc. The Little, Brown name and logo are trademarks of Hachette Book Group, Inc.

The publisher is not responsible for websites (or their content) that are not owned by the publisher.

ISBN 978-1-62490-342-7

Printed in the United States of America

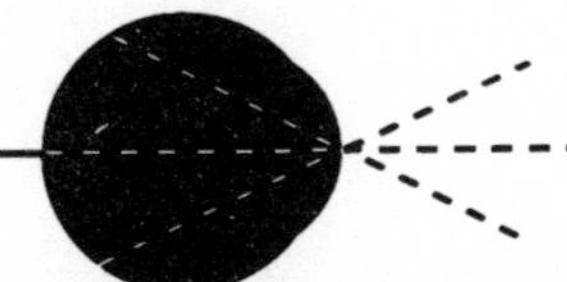

This Large Print Book carries the Seal of Approval of N.A.V.H.

For Graham

AMITY
&
SORROW

Two Sisters . . .

Two sisters sit, side by side, in the backseat of an old car. Amity and Sorrow.

Their hands are hot and close together. A strip of white fabric loops between them, tying them together, wrist to wrist.

Their mother, Amaranth, drives them. The car pushes forward, endlessly forward, but her eyes are always watching in the rearview mirror, scanning the road behind them for cars.

Amity watches through her window, glass dotted by chin, nose, forehead, and calls out all she can see to Sorrow: brown fields and green fields, gas stations and grain elevators. She calls out the empty cross of the power pole. She is watching for the end of the world. Father told them it would come and, surely, it will. They will see its signs, even far from him. Even here.

Sorrow has her head down and her back curled over so she cannot watch. She cups her belly and groans.

“Carsick,” says Mother.

Homesick, thinks Amity.

Their mother is taking them from their home and all they know, and they have no idea how they will ever get her to turn around and take them back.

When their mother took them, she ran them from the fire and the screaming, down the gravel path to the car, and Amity could see for the first time ever where the gravel path led, how it met a rocky trail, how it plunged through a band of evergreens to join a jostling potholed road that only smoothed when it came into town, the town she had heard tell of but never seen for herself.

But Mother said, “Heads down, daughters. Hide.”

Amity did as she was told, so she never got to see the streetlights or the shop fronts, the dark, quiet streets of evening, or the small families in small houses, doing whatever it was that ordinary town families did. She didn't see the metal shutters roll up at the volunteer fire station or the squat red engines emerge, though she did hear the sirens and see their lights flashing through her shut lids. She didn't see that the engines drove back the way they had come, covering the old car's tracks with their own toothy treads. She didn't see them struggle to get up the rocky trail and the gravel path, or try and fail to put the fire out. For there, in the car, there was only driving and darkness, the watching of their mother, the roads behind them and the sound of her sister, sobbing, as home stretched away from them, mile after mile.

Part I

MAY

1
The Red Country

Amity watches what looks like the sun. An orange ball spins high above her on a pole, turning in a hot, white sky. It makes her think of home and the temple; it makes her feel it is she who is spinning, turning about in a room filled with women, their arms raised, their skirts belling out like moons. She thinks how the moon will go bloodred and the sun turn black at the end of the world. She is watching for it still.

"Amity!" Her mother calls her back to earth, back to the gas station and the heat and the hard-baked ground, beckoning from beneath the metal canopy that shades the pumps. "Did you find anyone?" Amity walks back to her, sees that there is dried blood on her mother's face and figures she must have some, too, but neither of them can get into the bathroom to wash. The door is locked.

"I found a man," Amity says. "I talked to him."

"It's okay. I told you to. What did he say?"

The bathroom door is marked with a stick lady wearing a triangle dress. Locked behind it is her sister. "He said it locks from the inside. There is no key. It's a bolt she turned."

Mother slaps the triangle lady with the flat of her hand. "Sorrow, you come out of there right now. We are not stopping here!"

Amity pulls on her sleeve to cover her wrist, its bareness, the bruise blooming on the bone. All of this is her fault. If she hadn't taken the wrist strap off, her sister wouldn't have run.

"Where did the man go?" Mother asks.

Amity points at the flat of fields, where heat and haze make them shimmer like flu. She points to a yellow field, violent yellow, like yolk smeared across the land.

"You didn't go out there!"

"No!" says Amity, shocked.

• • •

Four days they drove, until Mother crashed the car.

Four days they drove from home to here.

Four days and the seasons have changed around them, the dirty ends of snow from home melting and running to make rivers, mountains flattening to make plain land, then fields. Four days Amity had been tied to her sister, to keep her from running, until the car hit a tree and spun over a stump and Amity took the strap off and Sorrow flew out of the car and ran.

The sky is spinning orange when the man comes from his fields. Dirt rides in on his overalls, spills down from his turned-up hems. With every step, it scatters like seed. "Hey," he calls to Amity and he raises his hand to wave. Then she sees him see her mother. She sees him take in Mother's clogs and long, full skirts, her apron and her cloth cap, as if he hadn't noticed Amity's own. His eyes follow the stripe of blood down Mother's face. "Hey," he says again and Mother nods to him, primly. "Closin' up now. Was there somethin' y'all needed?"

Mother looks at Amity. "I thought you

told him." Then she points at the bathroom door. "My daughter," she says.

"Is she still in there?" He pounds his fist on the stick lady, calling, "Come out of there, hey—what's her name?"

"Sorrow."

"Sorrow?" He squints and bangs harder on the door. "Sorrow!" He turns to Mother. "Maybe she's unconscious?"

"She's stubborn. How can you not have a key?"

"It's a bolt. Jesus!" The man rushes into a little shop and crashes around inside it, then he runs back out to his fields, darkening beneath the fiery sky.

Mother watches him go, saying, "Has he just run away?"

But he does come back, pulling up in an old Chevy pickup, its red paint turned pink from hard sun, and clambers down with a noisy box of tools. A boy jumps down from the truck bed to follow him, brown-skinned and lanky with a long tail of black hair that reaches halfway down his back. Amity steps behind her mother and grabs hold of her skirts to watch him.

The man and the boy jangle through the tools. They try ratchets and hooks, rasps and claws. They hit the door hinges with chisels, but they cannot lift it out of its frame for the bolt.

"Sorrow," Mother pleads. "Open the door." But not a sound comes from her.

Finally the man takes a sledgehammer to the doorknob. He batters away until he smashes it off and then there is only a hole in the door. The man calls through it, tries to stick his hand into it, but it won't fit. "You go," he tells the boy, but his hand is too big, too.

"You," he says to Amity.

Amity cowers until Mother pulls her out of her skirts. Then Amity creeps toward the door and bends to look in, sure she will find Sorrow staring back at her or her finger aimed to give Amity's eye a poke. But there is only darkness. She slides her hand through the hole, slowly, craning her wrist to find the bolt. "I'm sorry," she whispers. She turns it with a click.

And then she is being pulled back, out of the way, and the man and her mother are yanking at the door and it is opening. And only then is Sorrow revealed, there in the bathroom, there in her awful red glory.

The man goes inside to pull her up from

the floor, as if he doesn't mind the blood on the tiles, the blood at her hem, the blood on her skirts, or the blood in her hands. He catches hold of the bloody strap hanging from her wrist. "Jesus, girl, what you gone and done?"

Mother screams then, "Don't touch her!" And she rushes in to Sorrow, clogs slipping on the blood, and she grabs hold of Sorrow, to push her from the man. And the man grabs her mother, shaking her and shouting, "What's wrong with you, woman? What's wrong with you people?" And Amity is saying, "She's all right, she's all right now," and the man's saying Jesus, and her mother's saying don't, and then there's only Sorrow, rising up from the tiles and coming slowly to her clogs with her palms open, bloody, to quiet them all.

"Behold," she says. "Behold."

Two sisters walk, hand in bloody hand, through the darkness, following a man and a boy they do not know, being followed by a mother. They walk the path that loops away from the gas station and the dirt road and the stump where the car crashed, the path that leads them between piles of trash and junk and the far, dark fields. They cannot see what these things are, these shapes beside them, these washtubs with no bottoms, these bentwood chairs with no seats, these window frames and paint cans and stacks of tractor tires. They might be anything in this darkness. Maybe low, metal monsters, crouching in clumps and clusters to snatch at passing skirts with rusty claws. When they see them they'll know that this is a land that throws nothing away, a land once made of small family farms like this one, a land now surrounded by industrial-scale cropland, a highway, and hog farms. When the wind blows from the right direction, you can smell the stink of them; you can hear the squeal.

When they reach the house, the three females fear it. Not for the look of the place, a gap-toothed, rough-hewn, clapboard two-story, painted white a long, long time ago. Not for the four windows, up and down, dark and empty as sockets. Not for the porch that sags beneath it or the old, scabby tree that grows to the side of it, branches arching over to smother the roof. They would fear any house.

When the man pulls open a screen door

it groans on its hinges. When he pushes in the front door, so that all of them can see inside the dark mouth of his house, they shiver. They are forbidden to go in. It is a rule.

The man invites them inside, but they all of them shake their heads. To his offer of a bath or a coffee, Mother will say no, but she will accept a couple of his blankets, a tin bowl for washing, a plastic pitcher of fresh water. When the man says he can run Sorrow into town, see a doctor in the morning, she tells him, "She's fine."

"She ain't fine," the man says, head bent to look down the bloodied front of Sorrow and the wrist strap, dangling. "Why's that thing on her?"

"It hasn't hurt her," Mother says.

"I see you bleedin'. I see this strap on your daughter and I see all this blood. You can't tell me she ain't been hurt."

Mother shakes her head. "I haven't hurt her. She hasn't been hurt. It isn't the strap. There was—a . . . there was a child. And she's lost it."

The man takes a step toward her, hands out. "Sorry."

"No," Mother says. "Praise the Lord." A small cry escapes Sorrow.

"Jesus!" the man spits out and he goes into his house with the squeal of the screen and the hard door slamming. Mother stands, holding his blankets and shaking, until Amity takes them and makes a nest of them, there on the porch for her sister. Then Mother slumps down onto the steps.

Amity settles Sorrow down and lies beside her, to pray. She whispers, "When you pass through the waters, I will be with you." She waits for her sister to say the next line of it, but her sister only turns away from her, to hold herself in her own arms, as if she knows what Amity has done to her.

2
Marriage Bed

Where are you, woman?

On the porch step, Amaranth sits upright. She blinks into the darkness, then whips around to check that her daughters are safe in their blankets, all flung limbs and linens.

She shakes herself. She must not sleep.

Four days and nights she has driven and every mile, every hour, made them safer. She did not dare to stop. Every town they passed took them farther from home, but she cannot let her guard down now. He is right behind them. She knows it. Every car, every headlight behind them, was him.

I will find you. She hears him and her hands fly up to her cap, to cover her ears. She looks up, expecting to see him thundering over her, but finds there is only a leaf-bare tree and a thick spread of stars between its branches.

The voice is in your head, she tells herself. He is not here. The voice comes because she has stopped, because her eyes keep closing, sliding shut so that the world tilts her toward sleep. He is not here. He has not found them.

And yet, she must stand, pace the dirt yard before the house, and scan the dark for him, again and again, searching for the small red flash of brake lights, the sweep of his headlights, come to take them home. She has been watching for him so long she can't stop herself.

Even on her feet, sleep tries to take her. The ground rises up as if he has taken hold of a corner of it, pulling it toward him, hand over hand, like a rope or a bedsheet. *I won't ever let you go.* Once, it was all she wanted to hear. Once, she wanted to be so kept. His voice growls, hushed and soothing, so close she can almost feel his breath in her ear. She has to crawl back to the porch steps to keep from falling. And then she cannot help it; she falls.

She lies back on the hard porch steps. She feels herself rolling backward, curling into a ball, and her arms rising, as if reaching for branches. Her hands open, as if to catch its buds. She feels herself sinking, folding and falling, into the porch that sleep makes her marriage bed, where five hundred fingers coax her and claim her, pulling her flat onto clean, white cloth. She reaches for him and finds the brittle-boned arm of a woman. The plump hand of a young woman holds her own. She feels hair unspooled across her face: a blond braid, a gray curl, a chestnut hank that smells of wood smoke and of home. Long, slender arms wind about her to hold her. There are tears in her eyes and lips in her palms and she is cradled between them, snug and molded, rocked among women in their wagon of a bed. Safe. Silent.

And then he is there. Axis to their circle, pole to their spin. Center of the bed.

Husband.

He comes for her and wives part like waves. He feels down the length of her and holds her down. He rips her open before a hundred eyes. He breathes his heat on her skin and she unfolds for him, unbraids for him. Seen in the eyes of fifty wives, she unravels before him, coming undone in a tangle of thread.

Mine, he calls. And Amaranth is home again.

3

The Bluebottles

The room where Sorrow bled hums with bluebottle flies, eating. They cover every pool and shield every smear, turning Sorrow's red to an iridescent blue and black. Every stain of hers is transformed, vibrating and shimmering with a million wings and eyes.

Amity watches from the threshold of the bathroom door.

Is this a sign, she wonders—the end of the world, revealed to her at last? She knows you may not ask for a sign, for even the king of Judah was told that he might ask and he did not, and Father said it was for God to test man and not the other way around. She can only watch and wait for whatever she is given and even then it will be Sorrow who will pronounce it sign or no.

The fourth plague of Egypt was the plague of flies, but there are no flies in Revelation. She knows the world will end with the scroll that is opened and the seals that are broken. She knows her father will open them, every one, the white horse and red horse, the black horse and pale horse, the martyrs and saints and the stars dropping down. She has seen the martyrs and the saints, wrapped and spinning in the temple. She knows the timeline for the end of the world, but she doesn't know if they missed the signs that would come with the seals being broken, because Mother drove them so far and so fast. The flies and the blood might be a sign, but Sorrow is too sick and too sad to interpret and Mother has told her to wash them away.

The boy comes loping to the gas station with a hose and a plastic bucket. “What you doing?” he asks her.

Amity can only point at the bathroom and the hum of the flies in the blood.

"I got told to clean it, too," he says, nose crinkling. "Guess we're the ones who work 'round here." He drops the hose and takes an end to the side of the gas station to hook it to a spigot. She watches him working, how his over-big blue jeans hang off his skinny hip bones, how they pool overlong onto greasy-toed boots. When he hands her the spout end, she watches his dark brown hands and arms, how his sleeves have gone see-through from overwashing and his arm hairs are gold in the sun.

"Watch out," he calls, and he turns the hose on.

Amity takes aim at the bathroom door. She points the water at the walls and the floor, the corner sink and the metal toilet. She washes away the flies. She washes away the blood until the water goes pink then runs clear down the tiles, out the doorway, and into cracks in cement where the dry dirt drinks it down.

When the boy turns the hose off, it hangs limp as the wrist strap in her hands. "She okay now? Your sister?"

Amity can only shrug. She cannot speak to him.

"I was standing there," he reminds her. "I saw it."

"But you don't know," Amity says. Then she clamps her hands over her lips, aghast. Another rule, broken already. She had talked to the man because she was told to, but Mother didn't say she could speak to the boy.

"What's your name, anyways?" he asks her.

Amity stares at the boy, deciding if she might answer. He crosses his eyes at her. He sticks out his tongue. He pulls off his cap to waggle his ears at her while she wonders if every word spoken was like breaking a rule, over and over, or if a rule, once broken, was broken eternally. "Amity," she finally says.

"Amity? Like that horror town? What's it called?"

"I don't know about towns."

"You don't know much."

"I know plenty."

"Oh, yeah? Like what?"

"I know my sister's not having a baby now."

"Jeez Louise," he says. "You don't tell people stuff like that." He whips the hose out of her hands.

"You said you saw."

"Yeah, but it's private, that stuff. Family stuff—girl stuff. You don't talk about it after."

"Okay." Amity nods, absorbing the new rule. "What's your name?"

"Dust."

"Dust? Dust. Dust."

"Don't wear it out."

"What kind of a name is Dust?"

"What kind of a name is Amity?"

"It's an attribute," she tells him. "We're all attributes. What's dust? You can't be dust. I'd call you Honor, Honesty. Grace."

"Grace? Jeez. I'm Dust," he says. "It's a joke."

"What's a joke?"

"Polvo. I'm Pablo, but they called me Polvo. Means 'dust.'"

"What language is that?"

Dust squints at her. "Are you serious?"

Amity shrugs. She is always serious. "I don't think it's funny."

"No," he says. "Neither do I." He starts winding the hose back onto his shoulder, the water rolling out to write onto the cement. "Where do you all come from?"

"I can't tell you that."

"Well, you're learning something, anyways."

She nods. It isn't only that she isn't entirely sure herself where they've come from, but because she is certain it is a secret. "Where do you come from?"

He looks out at the fields then. "Dust," he says. Then he goes back to them, boots clomping, jeans flapping. When he turns back to look at her he can see she is watching and only then does she turn away from him, to look at the bathroom. Any signs that might have been here are well and truly gone.

Amity walks the looping path back, around the piles of scaffolding, the broken-toothed saws and wagon wheels, until she can see the house and the porch, where Mother waits on the steps for her, swinging the wrist strap. Sorrow sits bunched in her blankets.

Amity sets a bucket of water on the dirt.

"You took your time, daughter." Mother hands Amity the strap.

"I had to wait for the boy," she says.

"You don't talk to boys."

Amity hangs her head. Too late.

Mother turns to Sorrow, all smiles. "Are you ready?"

"For what?" Sorrow scowls.

"To get in the car. It's time to go."

"The car?" Amity gasps.

"Where else?" Mother says. "There's no magic carpet. There's no chariot of fire and horses to take us away."

"But the car, Mother," Amity starts.

"I'm too sick," Sorrow complains.

"No, you were sick. You're fine now," Mother says.

"I'm sick, I tell you. Sick!" Sorrow burrows into a blanket.

"Mother?" Amity says. "The car—"

"We can't stay here. We can't stop." Mother grabs Sorrow's blanket and tries to wrest it from her, but Sorrow clings to it. She dives for Sorrow's arm, to wrench her up, but Sorrow curls herself in, like a turtle tormented.

"Can't we stay?" Amity says.

Mother snaps around to her. "Of course we can't stay. What makes you say such a thing?"

"She says she's sick . . . and the car, Mother—"

"Didn't you see me?" Sorrow yells. "Didn't you see I was sick?"

Mother lets go of Sorrow. She puts her hands to her face and winces. She sinks onto the porch steps and takes her cap off, fingering the cut at her hairline and pulling on her pile of chestnut braids as if she wants to open her head. "I saw you, Sorrow."

Sorrow pokes her head out. "I'm still sick."

"Mother," Amity whispers. "Don't you remember the car?"

"Would you stop going on about the car?" Mother says.

Sorrow sits up. "You don't even know where we're going. What would Father say, dragging me halfway around the world when I'm so sick?"

"I don't know, Sorrow."

"I do."

Mother ties her cap back down, good and hard. "It isn't safe here, girls. We cannot stop."

"But how will we go?" Amity asks her. "You crashed the car and Sorrow ran. Don't you remember?"

Her mother tilts her head at her.

"It's a wonder you didn't kill us all," Sorrow says.

Mother looks from daughter to daughter, then she steps off the porch, wavering a moment, shaking her head as if to dislodge something, then she runs away. Runs away.

Sorrow watches her go, then she kicks off her blanket. She takes hold of her bloody skirts to flap them in the air, like a sheet on the line, until Amity can smell the meat and metal of her. "Did you clean that room out?"

Amity nods, sadly.

"I didn't tell you to."

"Mother told me."

"What about what I tell you? You should listen to me."

And that is her life, Amity thinks, suspended between the two of them. She wonders what would happen if Mother kept running. What would happen if she just left them here? And what would Amity do? Would she run after Mother or run away in the opposite direction? Would she run away from them both, or would she stay and wait with Sorrow until Father came, as he will, as he must?

"I'm sorry," she tells her sister.

"It isn't your fault," Sorrow says. "You're too stupid to know what's what."

"Maybe it's a sign," Amity says, thinking of the sea-red floor.

"You don't know what signs are. I tell you what signs are there." Sorrow lies down and Amity hears her say, "I was the sign. Me."

Amity wonders if her sister can remember what she did in the car, how she rubbed her hands together and put them onto Sorrow's belly, to boil up the pain within her, to still whatever was hurting her, to try to heal her if she could. She would do anything in the wide world for Sorrow. She slips her hand into one loop of the wrist strap and puts the other over Sorrow's, to tie them together, making her choice again.

4
Chickasaw Plum

Amaranth runs from the house on the hard red earth, around the pile of bedsprings and car parts, washing lines and aluminum siding, and along the fields where a farmer works a chemical sprayer, insecticide hanging in the dry air like a cloud. She doesn't stop for him.

She runs for the gas station, though their clothes are not made for running. Skirts twist and tangle, jam between legs. The bindings they wear beneath blouses are too tight to allow for deep breaths. Clogs rock over stones. She passes the gas station and the canopy's shade, the wet front of the bathroom, and turns onto a long dirt road that she can't remember driving down. She can only remember being followed, pursued by her husband and speeding to break free from him, his car bearing down on them, faster and faster. It is all she can remember.

Strips of wild scrub sit on either side of the road; beyond them, fallow fields grow grasses, tall and thistle-headed—spike-rush, prairie threeawn, devil's grass—baking brown beneath the vicious sun. She pulls her collars open as a bead of sweat rolls down from beneath her cap.

The car, she thinks. It is all they have—until she sees it.

The car, caught up on a black-bark tree, upside down and lying hoodfirst in its red-cherried branches. The trunk and back bumper have slammed into the ground. The four tires are upright and the undercarriage splayed, so the car is like a dog on its back, wanting rubbing. A branch has pierced the windshield and her hand goes to her head again. Glass sparkles from the road.

My God, she thinks. Sorrow was right. She is lucky. And she can remember it, all of it, swinging off the highway onto the thin road below it, sun in her face, and the road turning and churning into dirt and hedge and speeding to get away from him. Her daughters were screaming. She must have lost control somehow. She remembers the feeling of flying.

When she took his car, she hadn't known if she could drive it, remember the dance of pedal and clutch, of stick and steering wheel. She hadn't driven in so, so long. And now she could have killed them.

She crouches on her haunches in the road. She plants her hands on the dirt and feels certain she will be sick, from fear, from relief. She pants until she retches, shutting her eyes and hearing him, laughing.

She looks over at the trunk, upside down. She can't see how she'll open it, but she must. There are things inside that she must salvage, all she hoarded and packed. The full weight of the car rests on the trunk, but she tugs at the frame, uselessly. Beneath the car, flour dusts the dirt. Honey oozes, pooling onto dirty oats, and she thinks of the jars inside it, shattered and spilling now, soiling their bedding and clothing. She sifts the dirt for anything she can salvage: wooden matches, small bits of paper. She remembers that her wedding ring is in there, knotted into a handkerchief, the last thing she would have to pawn or sell when it came to it. She has to get inside.

The roof of the car, now the floor, is covered with metallic candy wrappers, bargain gas station treats on the road, for sweet mouths are silent ones. She jabs her hands between the seats to see if she can reach through to the trunk, but she only finds more paper, small white squares stuffed into every crack. She pulls them out of her way. And then she sees them for what they are.

Small white envelopes. Tithing envelopes.

The backseat is full of them. On each one you could read her husband's name and their address. You could see the sketch of a small, plain, barn-shaped temple, as it was before the fire.

Her throat tightens. Had her daughters found them? Had her daughters thrown them? Did tithing envelopes litter roadsides everywhere they'd been for the last four days and nights? Had they been tossed at borders and crossroads like crumbs for birds, for fathers, to follow?

Amaranth builds a fire beside the car from plaits of dry grass and a precious match. Into it, she feeds the envelopes, watching their church burn again and again. When the smoke is high and all the paper churches become ash, she sees a truck coming, heading straight for her. She stands and waves her arms to flag it down, to get help, to escape. And then she stops waving. Her hands drop. The truck is pink, a faded red.

The farmer swings down from the cab, engine running. "What the hell?" he says, rushing at her fire, kicking dirt at her flames. "What the hell, woman?"

"I'm sorry," she starts.

"Damn right you're sorry. Saw your fire four fields over. Take just the one spark to burn every damn crop of mine down. We have drouth here, woman, look about you. What you thinkin'?"

She looks at his tinder-dry fields. "I'm not thinking. Clearly."

"I'll say." He stomps the fire flat with his boots. Then he sees her car and gives a low whistle. He juts his chin at the tree. "Chickasaw plum there. Only tree on the whole goddamn road and you found it."

"Can you fix my car?" She puts her hand into her apron waistband and pulls out all the money she has in the world now. Her unfolding and counting have made the few bills left as supple as leather. She holds it out, but he shakes his head. "You have to fix it," she tells him. "You're a gas station."

"Maybe. Ain't a service station. Hardly even pump gas, now the highway's gone in. No one comes. Only folks like you, lost."

She squeezes the money in her hand.

"Where was you headed?" he asks her.

She cannot tell him. She doesn't really know. Turning away from him, she says, "I must have fallen asleep."

"Well, that's why the good Lord invented motor hotels."

She laughs. Of course she had slept, she must have. She would find herself suddenly awake at an intersection and wonder how she had come to it. She had woken at a suburban stop sign, roused by a car's insistent honking from behind. One time it was a long-haul truck that only narrowly missed her, asleep where she was in the middle of the road. Its lights full on in the darkness, the truck was an avenging angel, delivering justice. The driver stormed out, leaned his beefy face into her open window to tell her off, tell her she wasn't fit to drive and all that, but she only asked him what state they were in. The trucker stared at the sight of her two girls, tied together, honey smeared across their lips.

"Where you come from?" the farmer asks her.

She shakes her head. She dare not tell him. She shows him her money again. "Please help me. I don't know what to do."

"I'll tell you," he says. "Go home." He starts for his truck.

"But how?" She stares at her miserable handful of money. She stares at the last curl of smoke going out, drifting over the wreck of her car and his tree and out to the flat of his fields.

BEFORE: *The Leaving*

No one knew who fired the first shot.

No one knew who started the fire.

For weeks they had been fasting and watching, praying and waiting. Because of the patrol cars. When they arrived, the countdown for the end of the world began anew. Fear twined across their land and looped around the wives, pulling them tight to their husband, tight to their rituals.

By day, patrol cars idled on their gravel path. Officers drank from Styrofoam cups, radios crackling. By night, red and blue lights spun across the front of their temple while within it women were spinning like hoops, like wheels. Women spun in solo orbits, lost in chanting, lost in prayer, then they spun together in a wide circle that swung around the room, around the altar, and the hole in the floor that led to the room below them. When they spun they could forget patrol cars, forget that they were being watched and judged. When they spun they only thought of how the heavens turned above them and how God cupped them all in His wide, white hand.

"Who will be with me at the end of days?" he called from the center of the temple: preacher, father, husband.

"I will!"

"Me, Father."

"Me!"

"Who will see the might of the Lord against the fallen?"

"I will, husband."

"I."

"Who will rise in glory? Who knows now, in their hearts, in their bones, that the end of time is coming? Who will watch to see it come?"

"I will, I will," the wives called in response.

"Who will bear the Lamb?"

Her husband had been looking for signs

of the end for years now. Gossip from wives and news reports from the car radios that still worked only confirmed it. Millennium bugs and the towers collapsing had started a chain of evil, with earthquakes that split the land and unjust wars that split its people. They felt safe together and safe on his land, hidden like jewels. But more dark stories came with every woman. He told them the end was coming. Couldn't they feel it, every one? Soon, it was all he could preach or even think about.

He read them Revelation from memory. By then, it was the only Book he would speak, pouring the words of God out in hot, steaming bowls of wrath, while his face flickered red and blue, red and blue.

That last night in their temple, he called them to prayer and told each wife to wake her children, to bring them to the temple. "Husband," Amaranth said. "You have had them at prayer all day. They are terrified and tired. Let them sleep."

He gave her a look that rattled her teeth. "I will have my children at the end."

Women roused children from their motley assortment of sleeping places, from the cars and trailers and yurts and sheds that stood across the frozen early spring land. Sorrow was up, child no more now, but Amaranth had to shake Amity awake in the attic bed. "Bring down a change of skirt and petticoat," she whispered. Amity did as she was told. Amaranth ran through wives and baffled children and into the kitchen to pop spelt rolls into her pocket, dropping them onto the key that sat there.

In the temple there were candles lit in bobbins all across the planked altar, blazing in jam jars in each rough-hewn windowsill. Women brought their children in and all grew hushed when they crossed the threshold, stepping from the red and blue to the soft, pale light inside. Wives formed a ring about the room, encircling their husband and the altar and Sorrow.

He roared his Revelation. "Behold, I stand at the door and knock! If anyone hears my voice and opens the door, I will come!"

There, from outside the temple door, there came a knock. Wives screamed out. Children whimpered.

"This is a holy place!" he called. "No law or government will defile our church!"

Another knock came.

"Will I answer it?" Amaranth asked him, stepping into the circle. She saw how Sorrow gripped the edge of the altar with clenched fingers. "Husband, I will answer." She walked toward the door.

"Don't do it!" called a wife from the circle. "Lock it!" called another. The wife from Waco began to scream, uncontrollably, "It's a trap; this is how it happens!"

A baby began to wail and a mother bounced it, shushed it.

Amaranth reached to open the door and her husband called out.

"Stop! Hide the children. Hide them below. They will not take my children!"

Amaranth's hand froze on the door. Children were their glory, their purpose. How should they be hidden from police, as if they were shameful, as if they were not made, all of them, in their holy love?

He dragged the altar table back from the hole in the floor and lifted the hatch. "We must keep them safe," he said.

Women clung to their children, then bent to soothe them and explain. They dropped them, child by child, down into the hole, down into the dark of the room below. As for the children, they were happy enough, for down below there were piles of blankets, quilts to lie in and to jump on. There was food to last them for months of Armageddon, should it come to that.

Amaranth watched toddlers handed down by older children who swung in to follow them, but when Amity started down to the hole, she stopped her. "Stay with me," she said, and Amity nodded. She pulled her daughter toward the door to hide her in women.

The knocking at the door was a pounding now and Amaranth ran back to open it even as her husband shouted, shutting the hatch and moving the altar, candles swaying, "We will pray! You will pray!"

The women joined hands to make their circle. They began to spin their circle about the room. Amaranth opened the door on a chubby female officer in a navy polyester uniform. She had spoken with the officer before, but she did not smile or greet her.

The officer looked into the temple, to see inside the thing they had been watching from the outside: the plain wooden interior and the candles, the circle of women rushing by. She saw the officer startle at

Sorrow's open-throated, guttural cries and her husband's upraised hands.

"That the girl there?" the officer asked her, pointing at Sorrow.

And then she heard a shot ring out behind her. One single gunshot and women began to spin in a frenzy. Only the wife from Waco was still, gun in her outstretched hands. The officer crouched and grabbed for her own gun, shouting into her radio over Sorrow's prayers and the pounding of clogs, "I need backup!"

Amaranth scanned the room for daughters, for Sorrow, clinging to her father, for Amity, pressing herself against the wall. Amaranth forced her way through the spinning women, weaving among them, crashing into them, while her husband shouted, "I will break the seals!"

And then there was only grabbing and clutching and dashing and rushing and hands in her hands, hands pulling away, and the screaming of women, the silence of children, and the smoke and the flames and the driving away.

5
Stitches

Go home, he said. As if it were that simple.

Amaranth scoops the last pathetic handful of oats from the dirt beneath the car. She searches the scrub for something she can feed her daughters, any edible weed she might boil into a gruel. She looks for wild sorrel or chicory, picks dandelion and horehound. She snaps the pinkish tops of henbit. She pulls a Chickasaw plum cherry from the tree and rolls it between her fingers. When she nibbles it she finds it bitter and throws it down.

Go home, he said, when she has risked their lives to leave it, when she has hidden and lied and left, left her family and home and all the world that her daughters knew. This was her one chance and she has ruined it, squandered it. Less than a week from home and she has failed, utterly and completely.

He narrowed his eyes when she told him she couldn't go home, that there was no way of driving now and no one they could call for help. "No one?" he pressed.

"We have no phone," she explained. No phone, no electricity. They cooked with propane and heated their house and outbuildings with wood from their forests. They weren't on the grid and no local government knew who lived there or under what circumstances. That was how her husband liked it. She had liked it, too.

"There's gotta be somebody you can call," he said. "Somebody who cares you all are gone."

Amaranth tries to lever the license plate off with a branch. Police might find it and run it against their records. The tags were hopelessly out of date. Worse was the thought that her husband would find the plate and know for certain that they were there. What would he make of a farmer who had tried to help his family, who had seen and dared to touch his daughter, a farmer who had shaken her and told her to go home? What would he do to him?

The branch snaps. She has only managed to pucker the metal. She throws what's left of the branch with a shout and stomps back down the dirt road, pausing before the small shop. There will be food and drink inside it, and she thinks of all the gas stations she stopped in to fill their tank, how she stared at the packets of food while she waited to pay, the foam-filled cake snacks, the cans of fizzy pop from her childhood. She could take something for her daughters. She could even set money on the counter inside, so it wouldn't be theft. But she does not. Not because her children do not know this chemical food or that she fears its effects on them, but because she has seen a pay phone.

There, on the side of the gas station, above a water spigot, is an ancient pay phone. Someone has cracked the receiver and attempted to graffiti it with a marker. It takes her a long time before she can lift it to listen for a dial tone, convinced that the farmer has already used it, called the police to tell them she is there.

But no sound comes. The phone is dead. She hangs it up, grateful. And worried.

She stands at the hedge edge of the farmer's field and watches him working. He is a low shadow, flying across his fields on the back of a tractor, plowing ruts into dirt. In the distance is a grove of thin trees, grouped around a dry wallow. Clouds of red dust rise and drift, coloring the sky. She waits until he comes in for water. "Have you called the police?" she asks.

He opens the spigot on the back of his neck. "Should I?"

"Your pay phone's broken. Do you have another phone?" Water spatters off him. It dots her skirts. She catches it in her hands.

He shakes the water from his neck and hair. "What's it to you?"

"I need to know," she says, "if you've told anyone we're here."

"Who would I tell? What would I tell 'em?" He moves to the shade of the metal canopy and pulls a box of cigarettes from his jeans. "I had a phone. Had it ripped out some years ago. Got tired of people callin' me up, askin' for money." He holds the pack out to her. "You married?"

"No," she says, to the cigarette. Then, "Yes, I am. Married. Are you?"

He scrapes a match on the side of a gas pump. "Yep. My wife took off. Don't know where. So I know what it's like for your husband, you going."

"You don't. He's not waiting at home for me, I can tell you that. He's coming after me."

"You think so?"

She nods, her throat tight.

"He drink?" he asks her.

"No."

"Hit you? Hit your girls?"

"You don't understand."

"What's he done that's so bad? What's he done you can't forgive? You think marriage is some picnic? It ain't." He takes a long pull on his cigarette. "Maybe you done somethin', somethin' you think he can't forgive. And maybe he can't, but I'm tellin' you, he'd rather not be alone. You either made a vow or you didn't."

"I made a vow," she tells him. "I made a million of them. Don't you dare tell me how marriage works when your own wife left you."

He blows out smoke at her but she doesn't turn away. He stalks back to his fields, calling back over his shoulder, "I want you gone."

She soaks dirt from oats and watches her children sleeping. In the dark of night, she listens to him, in his house. The scrape of his chair leg, the endless scratch of matches being lit, aluminum cans being scrunched and tossed. She is waiting for him to crash through the screen door and sweep them all off his porch, back to the dirt and the road and the wreckage.

Are you married? he asked. He has no idea.

Lights switch on and off inside. She hears a brief burst of static, white noise from an old television, and a burst of recorded laughter before the volume is turned right down. And then it is silent, still, and dark. She can almost hear the house breathing with each breath that the man takes, inhaling and exhaling his smoke through window screens and the tree rapping on the roof.

She grew up in a small house like this, in a dark place with no streetlights, just like here. The land was hard and the people harder, but the sounds of night were of sand switchbacking beneath snake bellies, the cries of coyotes, the lonesome *who-who-who* of a horned owl from a Joshua tree. The rumble of her grandmother's empty-mouthed snoring, dentures foaming in a glass. In her bedroom, she would click her flashlight on and off, pointing light at the dark shapes of furniture and toys that she knew were creeping toward her every time she closed her eyes.

Her daughters have never known such silence and it makes their sleep fitful. The house she took them from was a clamorous one. Women moved from room to room along hodgepodge hallways, clogs thumping, skirts swishing, following the skitter of tiny feet, bare on boards, constant as rain. Doors opened, slammed shut. Children whined and giggled. At the very end, at its fullest, every bed and every room was full and no one wanted to be alone.

She doesn't know what to do with this silence. It rings in her ears, this lack of noise. It makes this man's voice all the louder. Are you married?

Yes, she is married and married again.

She is married fifty times, once for every wife. She was married to him first and last, married to him always. Each wedding is like a thread, sewing her down to him and to all of them—her family, their hard and strange ways—for eternity. She has had to run far and fast to pull herself loose from him, to rip those stitches, but still she can feel how bound she is, how very, very married.

She hears the man turn over in his bed, above the porch. She hears him smoke and sigh.

6
The Day of Washing

Come bright morning, Mother says it's time to wash. "Hands, clothing, hair, and faces!" she sings out. Amity sloshes back and forth from the gas station, hauling water and handfuls of grainy pink soap from the bathroom dispenser while Sorrow lolls on the blankets.

"Come and be washed," Mother calls, but Sorrow won't.

Amity whips her cap off and tugs her braids down. She cannot wait for her mother's fingers in her hair. Once a fire is built on the dirt and the water boils in the tin bowl, she lies back in her mother's arms and wonders if she was held like this when she was a baby, back before there were so many other little bodies who needed holding.

Mother lathers the soap in her strong, wet hands, making the world smell of marzipan. She picks apart Amity's greasy plaits and scrubs her scalp clean as a sheet on washing day. Mother smiles down at her and Amity basks in it, shutting her eyes to hold the picture, and she is suddenly glad to have left home and come here, glad to be held and seen.

"You look like a little seal," Mother says with a laugh. She rinses Amity's head, then pushes her away. "Come, Sorrow," she calls.

Amity runs, wet hair streaming, back to fill the bucket, but when she gets there, the boy is waiting for her, cap turned backward. She grips the bucket, thinking she should pop it over her capless head, and cowers from him in sodden shame. "Shut your eyes," she says.

"This some game?" He shuts his eyes as she hurries to the spigot to refill the bucket. "Keep your eyes shut," she tells him.

"What you gonna do?"

She creeps toward him and his face follows her, eyes shut so she can study him, the curl of his dark lashes, the whorl of hair at the hinges of his jaw. She moves close enough to smell him, close enough to breathe him in. And then he opens his eyes. “Gotcha!”

She shrieks and grabs his cap, flapping it at his face then jamming it over her bare head. It smells of him, like ten of him, like engine oil and dry grass and hot, wet skin. “No, I got you!” she says.

“What you gonna swap me?” The bucket fills and spills over, flooding the concrete. They both run for the spigot, to turn it off, his hand on her hand.

“Swap you?” she stutters.

“For my hat? What you got?”

“What do you want?”

He looks her up and down, from the drips her hair makes under his hat to the drops down her dress and her clogs. She sees him take in the rough weave of her fabric, shoulder to elbow, neck to calf, lined and creased as each garment is, taken in, let down, worn by Sorrow before herself.

He smiles at her. “When you got something I want, I’ll let you know.” And he whips his hat back. She shrieks and crouches into a ball, arms over her head. Then she gathers the bottom of her skirts and pulls them up, to cover her head. There may be no rule about showing pantaloons, but hair must be covered at all times. “Girls,” he says. “Sheesh.”

“You can’t see me,” Amity tells him.

“I see London, I see France,” he tells her.

“Who are they?” And at his laughing, she runs back to the house and to Mother, blind in cotton, bucket abandoned, kicking and tripping over sawhorses and pitchforks on the path from the gas station. She runs straight to her cap and slaps it on her wet head.

“Where is that bucket?” Mother demands.

When the water is boiled, Mother calls again to Sorrow, but Sorrow won’t be washed. She wraps her arms around the porch post and revels in her dirty skirts. Amity thinks of the berry vines at home and the mothers who picked them, the mothers who worked the presses, all splotched red and purple in the making of their jams and pastes and leathers. She knows something worse than berries has been picked in Sorrow and harvested.

Mother tugs at Sorrow's apron strings and Sorrow slaps away her hands, losing her purchase on the post. She scrabbles to regain it as Mother pulls open her overskirt. Sorrow twists away and Mother shouts at her, "Take them off!"

"No! Will you take everything from me?"

Mother calls for Amity to help her, while Sorrow yells for her to keep away. And then all Amity can do is take hold of her sister's hands and bend her head toward her as Mother grabs hold of Sorrow's skirts and pulls them down hard. Amity can see the blood caked on her linens, hard as scabs. Mother strips Sorrow, layer by layer, her overskirts and underskirts, her stockings and her bloomers, down to the stains on her skin. She doesn't stop until Sorrow is bare, her chest bound flat like any woman's, but naked below, whippet-thin with a thatch of red-stained hair. Sorrow folds her hands over her crotch and howls. She rushes back into the blankets, leaving Amity holding an invisible sister.

Mother scoops the skirts up and tosses them in the tin bowl. "More water, Amity," she calls.

• • •

Later, Sorrow stands before the bathroom, cap on her wet head and wearing her blanket so her stained skirts can dry. She looks like she's been skinned. She's dripping and miserable, sorry to the bone for herself but clean as a stick.

"I hate her," Sorrow says.

"I know."

"I will get even."

"I know that, too."

Dust comes by, holding his hat down and grinning. Sorrow pulls Amity close by the wrist strap. "He's okay," Amity tells her. Sorrow lets the strap slacken.

"What you doing?" he asks them.

"Washing," Amity says. "Mother says we're leaving."

"Yeah? I've seen your car." He slips off his cap and brandishes it at her, daring her to take it. "You two eaten anything?"

Sorrow licks her lips. Amity shakes her head.

"We got food in there," Dust says, pointing at the shop. "Come on."

Amity starts to follow, but Sorrow pulls her back by the strap. "We don't want you to get in trouble," Amity calls and Sorrow yanks the strap again to say that wasn't what she said.

"Nobody comes to buy it now. It's called rotating the stock."

Dust goes in and brings them back the wonders of the world, opening his arms in a tumbling harvest of yellow and orange, foil and plastic, an edible coat of many colors. He names each one as Adam did in Eden: Lay's and Doritos, Sno Balls and Chocodiles, Cheetos and Fritos, Twinkies and pies. Packets pop like seedpods, like touch-me-nots or peas.

Amity takes a thin orange triangle between her fingers and licks the edge of it. Her tongue catches fire in a dance of salt and chemicals. "It's good, Sorrow," she assures her sister, and stuffs it in her mouth. She sticks her fingers in hoops of flour and fat. She pokes her tongue into cream-filled cakes. "You sure can eat!" Dust says as she nibbles at a thing he calls a Ding Dong, taking a bit of chocolate frosting with her teeth and then cramming the whole of the thing in to grin at Dust, chocolate-gummed, until he can't stop laughing.

Sorrow is all reserve, but even she must

eat. She selects only the red spear of a Slim Jim meat stick. She peels open the greasy plastic with delicate fingers and looks away each time she inserts it into her mouth. She chews solemnly, slowly.

Dust says he doesn't want anything, but Amity sees how he looks at the food with hunger. She knows what it looks like now, how it feels. She waits until he's scooping up the wrappers of their gas station feast and throwing away all evidence of it and his hands are full. Then she crams a Twinkie into his mouth, smearing cream into the tiny hairs about his lips, thinking how she wants to lick him clean.

When they go back to Mother they will lick their own lips well. They will bite orange grease from their fingernails and suck sugar from their fingers. When Mother offers them her dirty oats, they will show their hungry faces, even as they taste salt in the pits of their teeth with wandering, searching tongues.

7
Weight of Faith

All great journeys are made in faith. The pilgrim over dark seas, the immigrant to new lands, the pioneer to a salt-baked lake. Faith calls the native to the spirit walk, the vision quest, but Amaranth can only hope, in retrospect, that hers is a great journey.

She has coaxed their car over ruts that would swallow wagons, pointed car and daughters south as doggedly as any pioneer headed west. Her children are born from their father's pioneer stock, his ancestors who trudged toward Zion. It is in their bones to suffer for faith. All pioneers experienced hardships along the way, disasters, even. Think of the Donner party; she should take comfort in the fact that, so far, their car crash had not led them to cannibalism. Though they are hungry.

Six days since she left her husband, nearly one week since she ran, and she cannot help but feel that God Himself has crashed her here. He certainly seems less than keen on showing her a way out, as if He is holding her until her husband can catch up.

She studies the farmer's house and the land around it. The house might have food inside, but it is forbidden to them. Land behind it, a rectangle gray from alkaline water, has been worked and turned, but it hasn't been planted. Potato-sized dirt clods break apart in her hands. His fields show no corn or beans, no trailing vines of squash or peas. She knows he will be growing cash crops, same as they did, food they could not eat until they milled it and ground it, food that wouldn't be ready for weeks or months. She prides herself on her self-sufficiency, but she knows in her bones that her best hope of help remains with the farmer, despite how he dislikes her.

She fills the tin bowl with water and walks

to the edge of his fields. Bowl on her gathered hip, she walks beside the scrub hedge, where crickets click. But at the corner of the field she stops. She must. She thinks of their rules, left behind them now. She lifts a clog and sets it down into the field, water slopping and settling. She waits for the voice that will come to say *Field.* She steps into a furrow between green, hip-high stalks and walks toward the farmer, slowly, steadily. *You will not go in the field!* she hears.

Clog step, clog step, she moves toward him. Marching now.

The field, she thinks. I'm in the field.

He sees her running and runs toward her and then the voice booms in her head and she feels her ears roar and pop. The land swings up before her, to knock her back to the dirt, and the world goes dark.

And then it is cool. A wet hand on her forehead and her cheek. And then she feels a tugging at her cap and fingers at her collars. Her eyes fly open to him and she flings her hands up to ward him off.

"Hey," he says. "You okay?" And it is the farmer before her, not her husband, kneeling over her, blocking the sun.

She starts to her feet and the ground seesaws, left to right. He presses her back down and her hands hit the tin bowl, dropped. “Water,” she says. “Water.”

He reaches for the bowl and holds it below her chin. There are precious few inches she hasn’t managed to spill. He cups the back of her head to help her drink, she pulls away from him, fighting his hands, saying, “No, it’s for you. Water.” She scoots back over the dirt, away from him, farther than he can reach.

He looks at her and he looks at the bowl. Then he tosses his cap down and unbuttons his shirt, leaving it open over his shoulders, and she turns away as he cups the bit of water to splash on his face and his chest, the back of his neck, and beneath his arms, where the hair is dark and damp. When his shirt is on again, she swivels her head back and smiles.

“That what women do where you come from?” he asks her.

“What, faint?”

“No,” he says, and chuckles. “Bring out water to the fields.”

“Fields are forbidden,” she says.

“Are they?” He looks down at her, lying

in a field. "You should stick to the shade, all that fabric you got on." He picks up his cap and knocks the dirt from it against his leg. "I don't know your name, do I?"

She thinks of her names, all the ones she has used and the ones she's been given. She could tell him anything. But she finds herself wanting to tell him the truth. "Amaranth," she says. "It's a plant. A grain."

"I know what it is."

"I was always called Amy."

"Fine name, Amy."

"I don't like it now."

"Well, I'm called Bradley 'cause everyone here on this land is Bradley, like it or not. We've been Bradley here longer'n this has been a state."

"That's nice," she says. "To have that history." She doesn't even know her own.

"Nice like a straitjacket. That what you come racin' out here to tell me?"

"No, I—no."

"Maybe you come out to tell me what you're gonna do? What you gonna do, Amaranth?" He holds a hand out to her, but she doesn't take it. "That what you come out to tell me?"

She stares at his hand, up his arm to

the strong bones of his face. She wants his help up. She wants his help with everything, but she has forgotten how to trust. She has forgotten everything.

"Well," he says, and walks away from her, smacking at the standing rows with his cap.

She watches him go, wondering if she should leave him or chase after him, come leaping out of crops later with her desperate pleas for help. She picks up the bowl and totters after him, calling, "It's just, I don't know what to do. We can't stay—you don't want us to stay. We don't want to stay, but—how will we leave now? How can I get us somewhere safe with the money I have?"

He stops. "How much?"

"Twenty-three dollars."

"Well, that won't get you far. Not even a tank of gas. Bus tickets, maybe, over to Enid? I could drive you somewhere, Oklahoma City, more buses go on from there."

"You couldn't know where we're going."

"I wouldn't follow you. Jesus, you're one paranoid—"

"No," she says. "He would find you, make you tell."

"Your husband?" He puts a hand over his eyes to scan his fields, as if he's searching for brake lights. "No wife's worth it," he says, but when she doesn't laugh he tells her, "You really think that, you need a shelter. You need the police."

"No police!" She clutches the bowl.

"They after you, too?"

She shakes her head. "I don't want you involved. I don't want you to know. We won't stay—we can't stay—but I don't know how to go."

"You all need more money."

"I have nothing to sell. I only have nothing." Even the ring, if she could find it, would be worth one tank of gas, two. It would hardly get her through the next state, even if she could drive her car.

"And you don't reckon you can just go home?"

"There is no home." She looks up at him and the hot white sky behind. She sees a brown hawk stalking, wings wide, to hunt some creature that crouches in the fields. He sees her watching and follows it with his eyes. They are silent as they watch its flight, silent as its wings, holding their breaths together to watch the hawk circle and take aim. And then they hear the screech of it, watch it pull in its wings and plummet to the ground.

8
The Car

Sorrow pulls Amity hard by the strap. She even dares to whisper before the boy, "Don't you leave me." But Amity has to. As soon as Dust came to tell her men were coming for the car, she knew she would have to, for all that is still inside it. She pulls her arm from Sorrow's. She can feel Sorrow's eyes on her, burning her all the way down the red dirt road, after Dust. She hops and skips to keep up with him.

By their car she sees the farmer and two fat men, round-bellied and bearded, adjusting their trousers beside a giant tow truck. She watches them slap one another on the back and hoot about women drivers, until the farmer sees her and ducks his head. The men attach a metal hook to the car's front axle, which is sticking up. When they start a motor, a giant spool tries to wind the car in to it, but the car hangs on to the tree with all its vehicular might. The farmer holds his hand out to keep Dust and Amity back, while the two men grunt, gesture, and swear until the wire is finally stretched tight and singing. The car protests and grinds against the black bark until finally it is made to lurch upright, rise like the dead, and walk on its bumper before crashing back down to the ground, right side up and smashed flat. It shimmies on its shock absorbers.

Amity rushes around to the trunk. The farmer calls out, saying watch the cable, and she presses her thumb into the release button, hard as she can. But the lid is dented, squashed against its frame. It won't open. She hops and points until Dust steps beside her and the man pokes a crowbar into the gap. Then the lid pops open with a puff of flour and feathers.

"Oh, man," says Dust.

"What the . . ." says the man.

All that Mother packed is jumbled and broken. Honey soaks petticoats. Goat cheese has melted to a rancid, oily slick. She plunges her hands into the mess of it.

"There's broken glass," Dust says, but she nods. She knows. She flings out their filthy linens and pillows. She shoves aside the greasy bedding and honeyed envelopes, while the fat men and the farmer argue over money. Finally they shake hands, sealing some deal, and Dust tells her to get out of the trunk, it's time to go.

"Wait," she begs. She leans in, balancing on her belly, feeling far into the edges and corners of the trunk until she finds it, at last. Her fingers curl around it in triumph. She pulls it into her sleeve and hops back down.

When the car is rolled away, the space that was beneath it is rotten with paper and candy wrappers, strewn like gems across the glass and feathers and dirt. The farmer puts his fingers into the weeping wound of the tree bark, then he gives it a pat. "Who wants to follow it to the yard?" he says.

"For sure," Dust says, but Amity can only look up into his face in silence. She cannot answer or speak to the man. It is still a rule.

He smiles at her. “Way you banged through that trunk, thought your mother had a body in it. Maybe your pa.” He laughs. “Y’all are pretty strange creatures, ain’t you?”

She blinks up at him. He doesn’t know the half of it.

Down the road, the truck makes a dust train, fanning out like a smoky veil, as it turns and speeds away. The man goes back for his truck and Amity can only watch it.

“C’mon,” Dust says.

“Is it far?”

“To the scrap yard? Just past town, twenty miles or so. I go to pick parts.”

“We couldn’t walk twenty miles,” she says.

“Why would you want to?”

“Sorrow wants to go home.”

Dust bends down to look at an envelope. He sees the drawing there and looks up at Amity. “Bradley said your ma crashed ’cause she fell asleep.”

“We drove four days.”

“Where did you come from? Do you even know?”

Amity looks at the picture of the temple in his hand and shakes her head.

"Four days, you came pretty far. You can drive all across the country in three, if no one falls asleep. Not that I've done it, but I aim to. I aim to see the whole of the country and the other ones besides. Listen, were you driving into the sun or away from it?"

"Neither," she says. She doesn't know what she's supposed to know or tell. She only knows how the sun pursued them, swinging left to right above their heads, melting their winter to make this spring. "Where are we? What is this place?"

"This is Oklahoma," he says. "Don't you know?"

She sets her hands in her pinafore pocket, feels her secret drop out of her sleeve to hide there.

"I should get you a map," he says.

"That would be nice." She doesn't know what a map is, but anything he gave her would be all right with her.

"Won't help you walk to Canada, though. I don't figure Sorrow would walk even half that far. Wouldn't make it to the end of the road. She'd just sit down in a ditch and expect somebody to come by and pick her up."

She giggles and turns away from him. The car and the truck and the dust cloud are gone.

He puts his boot through a gap in the low hedge by the roadside. "C'mon, there's a shortcut back," he says.

"Through the field?"

"It's fallow. You can't hurt it."

"Fields are forbidden."

"Who says?"

"God. My father."

"Why?"

She looks at him. What can she tell him of all their rules? She doesn't know why herself. "Bad things happen there."

"They don't," he says. "Only place where good things happen. You still here come harvest, you'll see." And with that, he is into the field and gone and she wonders if that is why fields are bad. Because she wants to follow him.

9
Rules

Amaranth circumnavigates the house beneath the noon sun. Her eyes follow the length of boards, apricot now from the red dust; their paint peels and curls like rose petals. She mounts the porch steps and pulls back the screen door. The doorknob burns in her hand and she scuttles back down to the dirt and the tree.

She makes a loop around the house, past the patch of chalky soil and the powder-blue propane tank. She comes around to climb the porch, open the screen, and push the wooden door back. It slams in her face, as if the house itself has rules it wants to keep.

The next attempt she manages a foot inside, where she can smell the dust and must of the shadowed room, feel her feet on its painted boards. His voice in her head shouts: *No man's house! No man's house!* until she has to run back outside, shaking, fists over her ears, telling herself how ridiculous she is, afraid of ghosts and a man's old house. She must get inside while her daughters are gone, while the farmer works and no one can see her.

She climbs the porch and turns the knob. She flings back the screen and shoves the door open, throwing herself into the room to grip the back of the sofa before the voice can even draw breath. Then it gives her all it's got. *Betrayer! Judas! Whore of Babylon!*

She clings to the sofa like a shipwreck and shuts her eyes. One hand grips coarse velvet and horsehair. The other, she realizes, holds a thin cotton shirt, unbuttoned and abandoned. The farmer's, by the dirt of it. She bends to smell the smoke and the skin of him, then her hands fly up, shocked by the intimacy of it. What is she doing? And then she is spinning and the room is spinning and her husband's Revelation is roaring in her head: *You have abandoned the love you had at first! Remember from what you have fallen and repent! If not, I will come to you and remove you from your church!*

She backs her way to a wall, rough paper hung straight over boards. There are dark squares on the paper, where pictures have been removed. A nail digs into the back of her cap like an accusatory finger.

Jezebel! She hears. *Repent of your immorality. Those who commit adultery I will throw into great tribulation. And I will strike your children dead!*

She yanks her cap free. She deserves his prophecies and condemnations. She has heard them all before. *Salome, Delilah, Lilith! Eve. Eve. Eve!*

She pleads to the empty room and his vengeful God, "My children are starving. Your children are starving. Please."

The voice pauses, as if considering. It becomes a tinny tapping. *Tap-tap-tap.* Like a ring onto glass. The pricking of her conscience. The devil's fingernails on her skull.

Tap-tap-tap.

She turns, expecting Bradley, tapping on the window, calling to her, "Get out of my house." But he is not there. There is no one.

She walks silently across the floorboards to look through an open doorway. "Hello?" she calls into a faded, sunny kitchen. She calls up the spindled stairway. "Hello?"

Tap-tap-tap. She hears its rhythm, like words: Let me out.

Her heart pounds back—let me out—and all she wants to do is run.

Tap-tap-tap and the thump of her heart, *tap-tap-tap* and the flash of something, caught in the corner of her eye. She dives behind the sofa, awaiting the devil and his justice, come for her at last.

Tap. Tap. Tap. More insistent now. Let. Me. Out. It is coming from within the room, she realizes, and she peers up, sees the glint of something inside the woodstove, a twitch of movement behind its smoke-smeared glass. Then the tapping. When she bends before it, she can see it is the pointed beak of a baby bird. It blinks its yellow eye.

She flips the stove handle to open the

door and catch it, but the bird darts out, flaps madly in the dark room. It rises, hits the ceiling, and drops. It rises to beat the air again, hits a wall, and lands, dazed and trembling. Its heart thrusts its puffy chest out, hard and fast as her own startled organ. She reaches down to take the bird and it scuttles back from her, frightened as she is, as if she is its monster, its devil.

She opens the door to flood the room with light. The bird studies her, deciding, then gathers the last of its courage. It waddles a step and shoots out the door and she watches the baby flap and lift until it is only a needle point in the flat, white sky and she is alone again in the room with the thump of her heart, the hum of a faraway tractor, and the papery shiver of the old tree's leaves.

And then the tapping comes again. Louder now. A knocking. It makes ash trickle from the open stove. It makes dust drop from the boarded ceiling.

It is coming from upstairs.

She puts a hand on the newel post. There is someone in the house with her.

The knocking draws her feet up the dog-leg stairs, up to a dark landing with three closed doors. *Knock. Knock. Knock.*

It cannot be her husband. It cannot be the devil. And yet she calls, breathless, "Hello?"

She turns the first doorknob, but it is locked. She knocks on the door. "Is some-one there?"

And then she hears a voice from behind the door that sends her hurtling back down the steps, out the door and down the porch, down to the dirt and the old tree and the very edge of the fields, gasping, staring out at the farmer.

"Let me out!"

10
The Spinning

Sorrow swishes her hands through smoke. "I can see the temple," she says.

"No, you can't," Mother says, feeding grass into flames.

Sorrow dances her hands over them. "We should pray," she says.

"We should wash," Mother answers.

Amity had brought floury armfuls of clothes from the trunk and given them to Mother, who praised her and thanked her, and then went through every inch of fabric, every stitch and seam. "Is this all you found, daughter?" she'd asked. "Are you sure?" And Amity'd felt like crying.

"God doesn't want us clean, he wants us faithful," Sorrow insists.

Mother drops another underskirt into a steaming bowl of water, working the oil and honey from it. Already, strung across the length of the porch railing, there are skirts and blouses and stockings, flapping and drying in the sun, waving like old friends.

"If we prayed, we would know what to do," Sorrow says.

"We can't pray without the temple," Mother says.

"But God is everywhere," Sorrow sniffs. "Even here."

Mother lifts her eyebrows at her. "I think you are feeling better now, daughter."

"I am healed," Sorrow says, smug as a cat.

"How are you healed?"

"God the Father heals me."

"Is that so?"

Amity dips her head at this, so Mother won't see her smiling. She heals Sorrow, too, she thinks, with the thing she found in the trunk. When she set it into Sorrow's palm, the bright blue piece of china, Sorrow looked down at it with wonder. "Am I Oracle still?" she asked.

Amity could only gape at her. If Sorrow wasn't Oracle, then there was no order to the world. If the signs and answers weren't in the Oracle bowl, they were nowhere. Sorrow was the holy one and always had been. She was Oracle and firstborn of the Father, the first daughter. She was his helper, beside him at the altar, by his hand in worship. She was the one who watched for God. Even before they all knew of her gift, Mother said Sorrow had been set up on the altar so they could watch her. Mother said it was because she was naughty and putting her on the altar calmed her, all that attention, but Amity is sure it only increased her natural holiness, made her aware of the gift God had given her up in heaven.

The blue Oracle bowl had been Sorrow's tool forever, for at least as long as Amity could remember. The bowl was as old as the church, old as the house and their family, older even than the second mother, whom Amity had never met. The bowl might be as old as God Himself, but now it was broken.

The Oracle bowl was there to show Sorrow the seven seals and all of God's signs. She watched them, in its water, and spoke of what she saw to her father and his church. "Blessed is she who reads aloud the words of the prophecy, and blessed are those who hear, for the time is near," she'd say. Amity hadn't known the bowl could be broken. She didn't know it was possible to break such a thing, any more than it was possible to break a church or a family. "What do you see, Sorrow?" Amity had whispered, but Sorrow had only stared at the blue shard, eyes wide.

Mother dries her hand and strokes a finger down Sorrow's cheek. "What shall I do with you, daughter?"

Sorrow leans into it, so that Mother will cup her face. "Pray with me."

"No, Sorrow," but already Sorrow is taking her mother's two hands and pulling her up. Already she is walking her in a slow circle, around and around before the fire.

Amity itches for them to open their hands and take her into their ring. She wants them to spin her proper, but they will not. They cannot. She is a child still and cannot be spun. Only women and wives can spin in worship. Another rule.

Now Sorrow and Mother speed their circle. Their skirts flare out and their clogs pump the dirt. They spin their circle faster and faster, twirl until they are a blur and the red dust rises to surround them like rusty angels. Amity watches as they fling their heads back, pulling hard against one another's hands, and Sorrow opens her mouth in prayer. Then Mother releases her, so that she spins off toward the tree, toward the house, like a red dust whirlwind.

Mother stops suddenly, panting, as if trying to catch her breath.

"I miss this! Mother, don't you? The temple?" Amity hops to her, to catch hold of her hands and swing them. And then she can see that Mother has stopped because of the man, the man who has come from his fields to stare at them.

"The dust," Mother calls. "Stop, Sorrow! Look at the dust we raise!"

It coats the house boards, the railing of skirts and petticoats. Sorrow swings back around the house, spinning still, shouting her guttural prayer as she winds and wheels, caterwauling. Then she freezes. From above her, there comes a scraping sound, from inside the house. A window yawns open.

"God," says the farmer.

The devil, thinks Amity.

Through the window there comes flying a large brown leather shoe. It drops square at Sorrow's feet.

The man stomps toward his house, then turns back to Mother, pulling something from his pocket and shaking it at her.

"What's this?" Mother asks.

"For your car." He crosses to the porch steps and Mother follows.

"What do you mean for our car? You said you couldn't fix it."

"Sold it for scrap. Got you some money—so you can go. Just go." He opens the screen door with a whine. He pokes the money at Mother and goes inside.

Sorrow picks up the leather shoe and puts her hand into it. She waggles it at Amity. "I have the devil by his shoe. This is the devil's house and he will hobble now, when he comes."

Mother looks at the screen, fists clenched, and then she plunges straight inside it.

"Mother!" Amity calls. "Don't!"

Sorrow drops the shoe and takes Amity by the hand.

• • •

Amaranth is inside his house before she can be frightened of it. And then she is only angry. "Where are you?" she calls. He has kicked his boots off. They lie, fallen, behind the sofa. Dirt from the treads lies like worm casings. "Bradley!" she calls.

He bounds down from upstairs two at a time, in his dirty socks. "What the hell are you doing?"

"I'm sorry, I—"

"You don't just walk into people's houses."

"And you don't just sell people's cars! You—you take this back." She holds out the sweaty ball of money.

"I can't." He walks past her into the kitchen and flicks a buzzing light on.

She follows him in. "I didn't ask you to sell it. I didn't say you could sell it."

"You said you need money, I got you money." He strikes a match and lights a cigarette, throws the rest of the pack at the table.

"That car was all I had," she says.

"Then you didn't have nothin'." He blows smoke out the screen. "You had a wreck. Lucky I didn't get charged to get it towed—off my land."

She nods and leans against a cupboard, adding the money mentally to the money in her skirts. How on earth can they move on with this? "I had things in that car," she says. She sounds petty, but she doesn't care.

"Flour and feathers. Your girl got what she could. Good girl, that Amity."

Her thumb goes to her bare finger. No wedding band and nothing left to sell. Amity wouldn't have known to look for it.

He sits to smoke, stretching his legs beneath a clattering drop-leaf table. "I can't have you all stayin' here."

"No," she says.

"Can't have you dancin' 'round my yard like lunatics, hangin' your scanties like some Chinese laundry on my porch. Come harvest, I won't have time for this. Got my hands full already and no one here to do the work."

"I can help you."

"Fat load of good you done so far." He taps ash onto the tabletop and she moves to him, scoops the ash into her palm, then throws it in the sink. He shakes his head at her.

She wonders how long it is until harvest,

when he might need to take on extra hands. She wonders how she could help him then. She wonders if he has food.

"So that's that, then," he says and scrapes his chair back. He opens the door to a rusting Frigidaire and she glances into it to see what he has: cans of beer and condiments, opened cans of soup and beans. The squat dome of a half package of baloney and a stack of cheese in plastic sleeves. He sees her looking. "You want one?" He snaps a beer can off a six-pack ring and holds it out to her.

She turns her head away and he laughs at her. She imagines opening a beer with him, sitting down across from him, at his table, the spray of the pull top, the fizz of foam on her tongue, and the cold bubbles of alcohol rushing down her throat. She swallows.

What if she confided in him, told him all that had happened to bring her to this moment? Would he understand her? Would he sympathize? Would he tell her what to do, tell her how to push on for Mexico, or help her find a better plan? Would he ask her to stay? Would he tell her she was right to leave her husband after all?

"Well?" He wiggles the can before her.

She sets her two thin piles of money on the table.

"That's yours," he says.

"It's for the use of your porch. We will go."

"I ain't rentin' you my porch. And I don't see you going." He pops the tab on his beer and takes a long slug of it. He reaches in to pull another can out, then he stomps back up the stairs, leaving her money to lie where it is, calling a quiet "'Night" down behind him.

There are coffee grounds speckled over Formica countertops. There are giant tubs of Folgers and Coffee-mate in his cupboard. There are drawers filled with battered cutlery and rusting tools: cheese graters, cherry pitters, paring knives with blades sharpened into crescent moons. Rubber bands, bread bags, foil balls, books of matches from bars: Mac's, Dino's, the Do Drop Inn.

She thinks of the commercial refrigerators back home, scavenged and bartered, crammed full to the brim with the industry of women: curds and creams, sausages and cheeses. What wouldn't she give for chokecherries, huckleberries, sweetgrass honey from their hives? Hand-milled and roasted chicory, fresh and frothy goat's milk?

She counts out the money for her car. Through his window, she sees the dark shapes of her children, playing shadowy hand games before the fire, and she pulls out a ten-dollar bill. She yanks open his fridge and takes the baloney, a squeeze bottle of mustard. From the crisper, two wizened, forgotten apples. She ransacks his cupboards to find cups and plates, two mugs. Leaving the kitchen, she stops to peek behind a kettle-cloth curtain, thinking she will find a sink and toilet and use it, rather than crouch again behind the tree.

She finds, instead, a pantry cupboard, the size of a closet and lined with shelves, covered in sticky paper and fly droppings. It smells of weevils, of flour gone off. But there is food. Food in rusted cans, food cloudy in Mason jars. There are plastic bins on the floor filled with dried beans and grains: kidney and lima beans, split peas and lentils, pearl barley, black-eyed peas. Food. Food enough to feed them all for weeks.

"Thank you, God," she whispers. At last, a sign.

Overhead, she can hear him walking, doors opening and shutting. She hears voices and the hiss of a TV coming on. She plunges a hand into turtle beans, cool and heavy, and drops a fistful in her apron pocket. Then she snatches up her plundered items and goes.

She silences her daughters with her outstretched hands, stopping all questions and complaints with baloney. She soaks beans in water, to boil them come morning, and settles her daughters into a mustardy tangle to sleep. Tomorrow, she tells herself, she will go back into his house. No voice or daughter or man or devil will stop her. He has food and she will take it.

BEFORE: *The Fiftieth Wife*

The first of the patrol cars came while Zachariah was still away, at the golden end of summer, when little fingers worked to strip the last of the berries, overripe, nearly fermented, from the rows and vines before the house. The leaves were turning ruby at their tips.

It was Amity who came for her, lips stained and swollen, berry-red. “Mother, a car!” she said. “Is it Justice? Is it Adam? Are they come back?”

Is it Hope, Amaranth thought, heart leaping. She brushed the buckwheat flour from her hands and hurried out. Hope,

Dawn, and the two boys had been gone since late spring. She missed them, particularly her oldest friend, her confidante, mentor, and midwife.

At the end of the gravel path she met the black-and-white car. She told Amity to run back to the house and to keep everyone in. She approached the driver and leaned into the open window. "You got a warrant?"

"You think I need one?" A tubby policeman swung the door out toward her and squeezed his gut past his steering wheel.

"If you want to come on this land, you need a warrant."

"Just want to ask you a few questions," he told her. "You got some ID?"

"No."

"Maybe I could come inside. We could have a chat. Hot day and all."

"Get a warrant," she said. She turned to go.

He nodded and pulled a small pad from a top pocket, scratching his chin against its spiral binding. "You know a woman called Hope?"

She glanced back at the house, checking for wives and children. "Maybe."

"She came in and told us some things. Said she knew you and that there were problems with a child here."

"We're doing nothing wrong here," she told him. "There's no law against what we're doing."

He raised dark brows. "I think there is."

A curly-haired boy led a goat between them, pulling it by a striped tie. He was the child of Wife Thirty-Eight, she thought. Or maybe Forty. "Look at me, I'm a goat shepherd, Mama," he said. She shooed him away, goat bleating. The policeman watched him walking away in the skirts all the boys wore.

"This is a consensual community," she told him. "We are adults here and there are no laws about cohabitating or having children out of wedlock. None."

"Well, and that's a pity," he said. "It's why the whole of the country's going to pot, but I'm not here about that. I'm here about the child."

"What child?" She thought of Adam and Justice, remembering the day they were sent away, banished by her husband.

"Let me see here, it's a funny name." He

riffled through his pages. “Sorrow? You got a girl here called Sorrow?”

She looked the policeman in the eye. “No.”

She waited until he inserted himself back behind the steering wheel and took his slow, methodical time in turning the car, reversing and forwarding around on the gravel. She watched until he rolled away. And she told no one. But the cars continued to come.

The summer had been fraught and frictional from all that had happened in spring. Women squabbled and fell out over petty matters, moving unattended pans off burners so that jam wouldn’t set, or neglecting to change or nurse a child who wasn’t strictly their own. Children watched, sucking their fingers, as mothers sniped and snapped.

With Zachariah gone, there was nothing to tether them to each other but hard work. They didn’t have the inclination to pray, to spin, or to worship. There was simply too much work in the summer, some wives might have said, too much preparation for the hard winter to come. But the truth was that the women needed him for spinning.

With no axis in place, they might have spun off in every direction and never come back.

Other wives worried, every year, that he might never come back, and then what would they do? Every summer seemed to last longer than the one before; some years he didn't return until almost fall. It was Amaranth's role as first wife to hold them together, this collection of abandoned women, these hippies and spinsters, reformed junkies and winos, embittered divorcées and single mothers. They had nothing in common but their husband and a longing for utopia. She realized she had lost track of them, of what they wanted, since Hope had left.

After a supper that was filled with shouting, upset pitchers of goat's milk, and spoiled squash, Amaranth called the women at last to the temple. It surprised the newer wives, who had never seen her do it and who wondered aloud to each other whether she could, while it reminded older wives of the last time she did it and the state of their community at the time. They had worked to heal much since then.

Amaranth drew them into a circle and

told them to close the door. When she told them that the police and then a social worker had come, the women hissed and clicked their tongues. None of them had any love for the police. All had suffered at their hands in some way—from their whims, their laws, their searches, or their discriminations—even Amaranth. "They've heard things about us," she announced to them. "They're looking for someone who will talk."

Sorrow listened from the altar, chewing her fingernails into ragged stumps. She stared at the closed temple door.

"We don't know what they know or what they've been told. They'll be fishing for information on our backgrounds and our practices. Do not tell them anything unless you're prepared to follow through."

"Through with what?" a wife called.

"Our marriages are eternal," Amaranth proclaimed. She felt herself spread her arms as her husband did. "Our bonds are indissoluble. And yet wives have left us. It can be done. You've seen it done."

Women buzzed and chattered. What was she suggesting?

"If you're thinking of leaving, be careful,"

she called above the noise. “That’s all I’m saying. You can try to go, but you will be watched, do you understand? Do you want to leave? Because now is the time to do it. Does any of you want to leave?”

The temple door flung open and Zachariah entered, white hair pulled back and his traveling suit rumpled. He looked tired and worn, but he clapped his hands to silence the women. “Who calls you to pray?”

The wives of the room pointed at Amaranth. She turned to Sorrow. He greeted his wives and kissed them all, then sent them away. He bent to Sorrow, so that she might whisper into his ear. Amaranth watched her, stony-faced, until her husband sent her away, too, and they were alone.

“You talked to the police?” he hissed.

Amaranth backed toward the altar, hands out. “Better me than a young wife. Better me than one who might tell them something. I dealt with them.”

“Dealt with them? We don’t ‘deal’ with the police. Know that you are watched, wife.”

“We are all watched, by you and God.” And by Sorrow and by other wives, she thought.

“Know that you are first and will be last.”

He stood before her, ramming her into the altar, and she could see, through the window, how the sun set on the clump of wives around his van, welcoming, no doubt, some new young woman, another reason for his delayed return.

"First, I am. Not last."

"No one replaces you." He put his hands about her waist and leaned into her, so she could feel him. He pulled her apron strings open and she caught the garment, setting it aside lest she lose what she kept in its pocket, what Hope left her.

"It was a long summer, husband," she told him.

He felt up the front of her, her bodice, her breasts. He felt her belly and cupped her crotch. "Not so long," he said. "You are much the same."

She nodded. She took care not to become pregnant after Hope left. Not all wives were as careful, but who would pull their babies free now? Amaranth knew the work would fall to her and she did not feel prepared for it, did not feel sufficiently trained. She never thought that Hope would leave them—Hope, a name none of them dared utter now.

His hands worked their way up into her skirts. They pulled at her shift, worming their way between her legs, and her body welcomed him home—Jezebel—as it always did, betraying her year after year.

The girl he brought back, a shy and pockmarked girl, would become his fiftieth wife once the vines were lacy with hoarfrost. She would be the last to wear a veil over the black roots of her bleached hair, last to slip the ring onto her finger, last to watch it slip up and down the finger of every wife before her. As with every wife before her, she married them one and all; each took her salty kiss.

Across the temple, he called, "The end of time will come with the marriage of the Lamb!"

Sorrow called back, "Worthy is the Lamb who is slain for power and wealth and wisdom and might and honor and glory and blessing!"

"The end of the world will come with fire!"

"Hallelujah!" wives called and spun. They spun about the room and took the fiftieth wife. Each wife took her as her own.

They spun her hand to hand, and then he spun her into bindings. He spun her around the temple, clothing her as he would any wife, as wives wrapped her, embraced her. Then he spun her back to remove the bindings, making her nude as Eve. Amaranth watched her husband take the pink plums of her breasts into his hands, watched him nuzzle the woman, consecrating and anointing her skin with his mouth and his words. Wives spun, unmindful, unheeding. She remembered when his wives could have fit in one bed, then one room, then one house. Now women stretched across the temple.

He held his hand out last for Amaranth, calling her to the fiftieth wife. But she was watching Sorrow; Sorrow, who sulked and stroked her china bowl, stroked her belly.

Her eyes met her daughter's across the winding sweep of women and the new bride, her new mother, and there was something in her face that she couldn't define. Something like regret tinged with hope, or anger mixed with triumph. Something like love and betrayal. It was a look she had never seen on her child, after all that happened, and she wondered what her own face showed, what Sorrow could see were she looking.

Could she see that it was still hard to watch it, though she had had years to get used to her husband's hands on other women?

But then, she thought, so had Sorrow.

11

The Gas Station Oracle

Two sisters stand, strapped together on either side of a bathroom door.

Sorrow stands inside the dark room, the strap stretching through the doorknob hole to Amity at its other end, outside and sweating in the sun. She watches the orange ball spin and listens to Sorrow do her work. The sink fills and splashes, then drains away with a sucking sound and Sorrow's groan. She hears china ping off the sink and chip off the wall tiles, as if it has been thrown, but that could not be. It is far too precious to Sorrow.

The strap goes lax and the door crashes

open. The strap comes flying through the hole. Sorrow barges out, the front of her chest soaked and her eyes red. “I can’t see anything.”

“But you are the Oracle.”

“It doesn’t take this long at home.”

“We’re not at home.”

“Don’t you think I know that? Dolt.”

Amity knows her sister wants the temple, where she sits at the altar and searches the water, where she tells Father in secret prayer all she sees. It is silent, holy work, and Amity knows that Sorrow probably doesn’t think it should happen where people go to the bathroom. And then she thinks that maybe Sorrow can’t do her work without Father. And if that is so, how can the bowl show her where Father is?

“Maybe you need a new bowl,” Amity says.

“Idiot. This is my bowl.” Sorrow shakes the shard at her.

“The bowl isn’t the Oracle. You are the Oracle.”

“Idiot,” Sorrow says again. Then she begins to smile.

• • •

Sorrow twirls water in the plastic bucket, spinning the piece of china within it. She hunkers down on her knees and elbows, pulling Amity flat, strapped again. She peers at the water across the top of it, with a frog's-eye view, then she swoops up to stare down with a high bird's eye, pulling Amity onto clog tip and her strapped arm saluting. She floats her hand on the surface, like the feet of Jesus. She stares at the water to trouble it, tries to fairly bubble it with her glare. She rocks the bucket from side to side, then plunges her head into it, only to rise up, choking and spitting. She dangles her fingers in the bucket of water, stroking the shard, wishing for God.

Amity prays to the spinning ball, which is whirling, as mothers do. "Please help Sorrow" is all she can think of to say. God answers back with the spinning of the ball, bright as a sweet in the lace of His clouds, and the pensive whir of its motor. The sound builds with her praying, grinds with His passion, and she is sure the motor will burn and the ball burst into flames and come crashing down like the heavens falling at the end of time.

“Can you hear that?” Sorrow asks her, head cocked.

“Is it a sign?”

“Yes, it’s a sign—it’s a car, you dope.”

“A car?” And then the sound is unmistakable. It is a car’s engine, growing louder, coming toward them. “Thank you, God,” she tells the ball.

Sorrow shouts and runs from the gas station, waving her arms at the dirt road.

“Car!” Amity shrieks. They jump for joy as a car emerges, dirt rising and steam pouring from the hood. They call the car in, toward the gas station, guiding it to a pump in the canopy’s shade. The car slows, hissing and ticking.

“Thank goodness you all are here,” a woman says, bright-lipped, a blond thatch of hair ricked high on her head. She fans the back of her neck with a magazine, eyeballs and elbows on every page. “We didn’t think anybody was down here, did we, but I said a body’s got to have faith.”

“Oh, we have faith,” Amity chirps.

“You all work here?” A jowly man scans the forecourt. He looks the girls up and down, their long skirts and caps, and he looks about the station and its little shop.

"You don't even look open. This your family's place?"

"Yes, sir," Amity says, leaning in toward his window. "We all pitch in and work it. We all do our share." Sorrow shoots her a satisfied grin. In the backseat Amity sees a car seat and a baby in it, jiggling the fat rolls of its legs and arms. She wiggles her fingers at it.

"All righty," he says. "What else can I do? You all pump or are you self-serve?"

"I'll pump you," Amity says, and she leaps to unscrew his gas cap.

"I'll need some coolant, too," he calls back to her, drumming his fingers on the wheel.

"Yes, sir," she says to him. "Right away, sir."

The hood release pops and smoke billows over the car, sweet as syrup. Amity fiddles to unhook the gas pump as Sorrow, on the passenger side, spots the baby. Amity squeezes the trigger, but no gas comes. She doesn't know how to work it. She turns to the pump and she hears the man holler, which makes her drop the pump, fling her hands up, and scream. Then she turns back to see that he is hollering at Sorrow, who is reaching in through the car's rear window, trying to unhook the baby. She fumbles with the car seat's webbing, some complicated kind of strap, while he turns his bulk around in his seat and the woman reaches over the back of hers, slapping at Sorrow's hands.

Amity takes hold of the driver's window frame. "Will you take us with you? Will you take us home?"

"Get the hell out of my car!" The man starts his engine as Sorrow tries to get a better grip on the baby. The woman crawls over the back of her seat, cursing at Sorrow, and the car begins to roll forward, hood up, traveling blind. Sorrow jogs to keep up with it, arms in the window, pulling at the baby. The car speeds up, Sorrow trotting beside, and she makes one last desperate snatch. She misses. She drops back from the car, arms reaching, and it drives off, smoking and steaming, swerving and weaving, the man yelling, the woman howling, and, finally, the baby giving its own confused mewl.

Amity waves her arms from the station. "Stop—stop!" But they will not.

Sorrow stares, her eyes as small and sharp as pins. "I had him."

"They would have taken us. Isn't that what you wanted? To go home?"

"I had him," she whispers. "Lamb of God."

12

Home Preserves

Amaranth stands in the cool of the curtained pantry, itemizing. Old cans of candied yams, creamed corn, and succotash, labels crisp and flaking. Rust-topped Mason jars of home preserves, okra, wax beans, beets, applesauce, and spiced peaches in cloudy syrup. She counts and sorts the beans and grains, pulling what can be eaten from what is spoiled.

There is food enough to feed her family. Not as much as her community had saved for Armageddon, but then they were nearly a hundred mouths. Who was meant to eat all this food? It is a sin to let it go to waste—surely that is one rule worth keeping. It is her duty—her right—to use this food before it rots. And before it is gone, she is certain that a sign will come for her and she will know what to do.

She has her hands in barley pearls when she hears Bradley stomp onto the porch, the squeal of his door, the thud of his boots dropping, one, two. She freezes like a looter, fists full of grain. He hums his way into the kitchen with a tune she can almost remember, from long ago, something about love and dancing. He sings words here and there, taps out a beat on his table. She hears the rustle of a paper bag and a cap unscrewing from a bottle, his long, deep drink. She holds her breath but she knows it's only a matter of time before she shifts something, makes some noise, and when she does he flings aside the pantry curtain, broom held in his hand like a sword.

"Thought I had rats," he says.

"Bird," she says.

"In there?" He sets the broom down and goes back to the table, jamming the bottle into the bag and folding his arms. "What are you doin'?"

“It was in your fire. You should cap off your chimney.”

“I’ll add it to the list.” He looks at her, all the lids off the bean and the grain bins. “Somethin’ cookin’?”

“Well, you have food here,” she blurts. “Did you know? Grains, some flours. Beans?”

“Gone off now. Old.”

“Not all of it. I can sift out what’s good. I—I can pay you for it.”

Bradley hitches a leg up to sit on his table, its joints creaking. “I asked what you were doin’ here, Amaranth.”

“We need food and I can’t—all ours was in the car and that’s gone now and I . . . of course, I could feed you, too, feed you and your boy. I could work for you—I’m a good cook, I’m a hard worker and there’s food enough. I mean, what are you eating?” She looks at him, the bone and sinew of him, and she realizes he isn’t eating. Not really. His sustenance comes from cans and bottles. Her shoulders droop. “I’m waiting, for a sign.”

“A sign.”

“To tell me what to do.”

“Signs take long where you come from?”

"They can take years," she says. "Oh, but we won't be here for years. God crashed us here, and we'll have to wait until He tells us where to go next."

"You think God crashed you? You crashed you. It was you." Bradley reaches around for the bottle and slides it from the paper bag. He unscrews it and takes another drink, watching her all the time. Then he wipes his mouth with his wrist, fingers curled over his face. "I'm tryin' to be nice here, but I'm nobody's fool."

"You're a good man." She winds her hands into the pantry curtain.

He laughs. "I wouldn't kick women out on the streets, but honest to God, I ain't runnin' a flophouse. This ain't a charity; I got a farm to run here."

"We want to help you."

"I don't want your help."

"You'll need us in the harvest."

"You any idea when my harvest is? You even know what I'm growin' out there?"

She shakes her head. She can't even imagine how she will get her children in the forbidden fields. "We're used to hard work. This—isn't like us, how we are here."

He hops off the table and sets the bottle

down, roots through his drawers for a book of matches. He folds the cover back to light one, then lights his cigarette. “When you left,” he asks her, drawing smoke in, “why’d you leave with so little?”

“It was all I could grab,” she says. “I got the girls, that’s all that matters. I know you think I should have stayed.”

“No, I was thinkin’ that when my wife went, she took the lot. Must’ve planned it for some time, what she was gonna take and when she’d go. You just grabbed what you could and ran.”

The pantry curtain is around her arm like a tourniquet. She nods, unwinding it, wiggling blood into her fingers. “But she left you food here. Before she left. Didn’t she?”

He looks into his pantry again. “I suppose.”

“We had a room like this,” she tells him. “Well, bigger, but there were more of us.” She thinks of all the food stored in the room below their temple, food made in those last frantic months, women jostling over stove tops, scooping food into boiled jars to preserve it. What they hadn’t thought to keep, and what his wife must have kept, were seeds. Because Hope was gone.

At the back of the pantry she'd found jars of seeds, stacked and unlabeled. She held them up to the light to see them, their myriad shapes: hard brown balls, pale disks and cylinders, yellow crescents thin as fingernail parings. A jar of tiny black specks could be anything—onion or nigella or poppy. She unscrewed a few to sniff them, to see if she might cook with them, but she knew better than to experiment with seeds she didn't know. "How late can you plant here?" she asks him.

"Depends what you're puttin' in. We plant September, earliest, put in winter wheat and the rape. Too dry to plant anythin' now, this drouth. Grain sorghum's gone in and it was too dry when we did it. The playa and the wallows are dry, too. If we had pump or pivot irrigation you could do what you wanted when you liked."

"I could water them."

"My fields?" He coughs and picks tobacco from his tongue with dirty fingers.

"No, your seeds."

"What seeds?"

"The ones in here. You've a good patch of soil behind the house."

“I know it’s good. Been workin’ it since I was a boy. It was my ma’s kitchen garden.”

“I don’t know what these are. No labels.”

“Leave ’em be. Don’t need you adding to my work here.”

“But they’re good—it’s a waste—”

“Leave ’em!” He stubs his cigarette in the sink. “I got acres of rape out there and I don’t know what I’m doin’. We was always wheat here but the price drops and someone says they want rapeseed for oil, so you buy it and you plant it and then they call in a loan. You plant soybean, then sorghum, and you keep settin’ your share, diggin’ deep, diggin’ broad, puttin’ in things you never grew before ’cause they say someone’ll buy ’em. And everythin’ you grow you sell and put back into seeds, ’cause they won’t let you save seeds anymore. And then you have to spray and you have to buy their spray. And then out of the blue, folks want organic, but your seeds and spray ain’t green and if you don’t spray you’ll only harvest cheatgrass and shattercane. And then they tell you to plant corn for ethanol when that’s what all the rape was for.” He turns to the window, hands flat on the tabletop. “When all of this was dust once. And before that it was buffalo grass and they made it worse, men like my pa, settin' their shares too deep. Wantin' too much. Turning everythin' over 'til nothin' would grow." He turns back and sees her watching. "Hell, anything growin' here is a miracle."

"All growing is a miracle."

"No. It's what seeds do. What they're made for."

"Then that's the miracle," she says quietly. "Knowing what you're made for. Knowing what to do."

Bradley stares down at his hands, scarred and stained. "Well, I was made to work this land. Look what I got to show for it."

She watches his reflection in the window glass and her own, capped and skirted, tiny behind him. "I thought I knew what I was made for."

"And then you left it." He takes the bottle, pushes past her, throwing back, "Don't put seeds in you can't tend."

Once he's gone, she hears the knocking come from above her, as if it has waited for him to go and her to answer. She does not. She goes back into the pantry, to count and sort, to plan and wait.

13

The Map of the Panhandle

Sorrow works harder to be the Oracle now. The bucket is filled and dumped. The blue china shard is splashed and spun. The baby and the car are ineluctable proof of God's signs, Sorrow says, even if they were too slow to catch them. Or too greedy, Amity thinks.

Sorrow drags Amity from door to spigot, spigot to door. Finally, late in the hot afternoon, when both of them are damp and cross, caps dripping, blouses sticking, Sorrow raises her arms in the air and makes a great pronouncement. "God the Father sends a sign!"

"Hallelujah," Amity grumps.

"He will send us a car."

"He did send us a car."

"A car of our own."

"We had a car."

"Crashed, it was. By the Jezebel. The devil crashed our car. The Great Red Dragon!"

Amity sighs. "If God sent a car, how would we drive it? He'd have to send a driver, too."

"I can drive."

Amity sneaks a look at Sorrow. Sorrow does not know how to drive and, with her head hung down for most of the four days that her mother was driving, she couldn't have learned it. And even if she saw the arm part of driving, she never saw the foot part that Mother did, under skirts, where no one could see. "How can you drive?"

"I've been in a car before you, you know. I've been places you haven't."

In any contest with Sorrow she is bound to lose. Amity shrugs. "How will He bring us a car?"

"A truck."

"What truck?" Amity has a bad feeling about this sign.

"A red truck. A faded truck."

"The man's truck? You can't just take his truck."

"God put it here for us."

"God gave the truck to the farmer. He won't just give it to us."

Sorrow reels Amity in by the end of the wrist strap. "God says the boy will take it for us, just as he took the food. God will make him."

Dust unfolds a giant paper before them, in the wide shade of the gas station canopy. He pulls it open and it looks like a folded flower, pink and yellow and green, veined with ribbons, red and blue, unspooling, meandering across it. "This is a map," he says.

The girls touch the paper together. "It's beautiful," Amity breathes. Sorrow nods.

"Said I'd get you one. So here you go."

"What does it do?"

"What do you mean, what's it do? It's a map." He spreads it flat on the cement. "It shows you where you are and where you want to go. Look, this map's Oklahoma, see? We're here on the Panhandle, like a handle on a pan, and the pan is the rest of

Oklahoma. Down here's Texas, and up there's Kansas, Colorado. This purple bit here on the handle is us. No man's land."

"It's your land."

"Bradley's land. Not mine. It's just a small farm, not even big enough to put on a map. Over here is New Mexico and the Santa Fe Trail, which ran right at the end of the road there. You can still see the wagon ruts if you know where to look. I could show you sometime. And past that is Black Mesa, holy land, where the dinosaurs are."

Sorrow raises her pale eyebrows at this, but whether it's to exclaim, "Holy land in Oklahoma!" or to scoff at the concept of dinosaurs is hard to say.

"Other way, over here, is the road to town, Boise City, and the scrap yard, the hog farms, and you'd have known about them if you came in that way, 'cause you'd have smelled them. So I'm thinking you came in this way, down from Utah. You all from Utah?"

Amity can only shake her head with wonder. "Is the world so very big, Dust?"

"Dang," he says. "You sure are stupid."

Sorrow elbows Amity. She knows what Sorrow wants her to ask, but she knows what he will make of it. She knows what he will think of them. “We want to go home,” she tells him.

“I know it.” Dust nods. “But you have to know where it is.”

Sorrow tugs the strap again. “We need someone to take us. We thought—maybe you could help us.”

“Help you how?”

“Maybe take us home in the man’s truck?”

Dust pushes his cap back. “You got money for gas?”

“Mother has some.”

“Then she can take you.”

“She doesn’t want to go home. She brought us here. Sorrow can drive some.”

“Oh, that’s a doozy,” Dust hoots. “Sorrow can drive but she can’t read a map? She can’t even talk! Look, I can get you more maps, so you can stick ’em together, figure out where you come from, but I won’t take his truck for you, I can promise you that. And I’ll be watching you like a hawk now. See if I don’t.” He stands and brushes the dirt off his jeans. Amity pushes the map back to him.

“You keep it. They’re free. They just give

them away. Dang. But fold it up at least. Don't you people know anything?" He walks away from them, backward, pointing back and forth from his eyes to theirs to say, I've got my eyes on you.

Amity takes her end of the strap off. It drops onto Oklahoma. "That's that, then."

"That's not that, then. God will make him take the truck. I've seen it."

"He won't."

"You think you know better than the Oracle?"

"I know him better than you. He hates us now. He won't help us."

"He doesn't hate me." Sorrow narrows her eyes at Amity.

"Why would anybody help us, Sorrow? We don't even know where home is—we couldn't find it on a hundred maps!"

"I'm only telling you what the Oracle sees."

"Well, the Oracle can fold the map, then."

Sorrow stares at it doubtfully, its squares of creases. "We will go home."

14
Paper

Amaranth carries a bowl of plain cooked grains up the stairs. She does not know what she will find behind the locked door. She can almost picture Bradley's wife there, imprisoned for threatening to leave, now deranged and knocking, wasting away. Or perhaps it is some twisted, demented child there, the son he won't acknowledge, the son he fears. Gothic plots unspool in her head from her brittle paper childhood, all the dog-eared paperbacks of Victoria Holt, Mary Stewart, Phyllis A. Whitney, in great stacks from the library. She filled her head with fairy tales and romances, female spies, and damsels in distress who expected rescue. When she met her husband, she emptied her head to make room for his revelations. Now she has nothing and she wishes she had stocked up on survival manuals to stuff herself full of ways to cope.

She tests the door; it is locked still. She tells herself the room may be empty. The knocking is a loose shingle, a wayward branch. But she remembers the flying shoe and the voices.

A brass key hangs from a bent nail on the door frame. She thinks of Bluebeard's wife and the blood that sang out from her husband's key, to tell on her. She thinks of the wife's hands, filled with blood, and Sorrow.

She knocks, heart thumping, and a voice comes, frail and scratchy. "That you?"

She takes the key and turns the lock, then drops the key in her apron pocket. Once in, she is hit with the familiar tang of bleach and piss. She sees an old man, thin and still in a single brass bed, a parade of bones beneath a sheet. She smiles at him. "I've brought you up some soup."

"Who are you?" He pulls his sheet up to his chin.

She sets the soup on a small bedside table and tugs up his window for air. She looks down onto the shingled roof of the porch, sees the burned patch on the dirt where she builds her fires, and then her clog kicks a plastic bucket, half filled with bleach, beside a single worn brown leather shoe.

The old man screws his face up at the sunlight and lifts a twisted hand over his eyes, the skin mottled with liver spots. She pulls the curtains closed again. "Sorry. Will you have some soup?"

"I don't know you."

She leans down and speaks loudly, into his face. "Will I feed you?"

"Go away." He rolls away from her and the bedding hitches up over his buttocks; she scans him for bedsores.

"My name is Amaranth," she tells him. "I'd like to thank you for letting us stay."

He doesn't turn back to her, his voice muffled in cloth. "We don't want you here."

She stands, trembling. She knows it's true. She hurries back out and locks the door. She fumbles the key back onto the nail head, then stumbles back down the stairs, hearing his words, how no one wants her. She heads for the kitchen to count and sort, but a glimpse of paper stops her, stacked on a crate that serves as a coffee table. Old magazines, bordered yellow, *National Geographic,* window to the world and the only reading matter in her grandmother's house aside from the Harlequin romances. It has been so long since she has held or handled paper, turned a paper page.

She wipes ash and fluff from a cover and a bright green fish darts up from beneath her finger. She could pet it. Inside there are photos of the Great Wall of China, the Serengeti plains, the holey moon, all the paper wonders of the world and heavens, from when she was a little girl, alone and reading, and she wants nothing more than to turn herself into a paper doll and climb inside.

I caught you.

His voice comes, so close she can feel the heat of him. Husband. *I caught you.*

She jumps to her feet and cracks her knee on the table. Magazines slide from her lap in a paper avalanche.

But it is Bradley who stands there, Bradley who laughs at her.

"I only sat for a moment," she babbles. "I don't—I wouldn't—has something boiled over? Is it the girls? What time is it?" She starts, parched and woozy, for the kitchen.

"Calm yourself down, woman," he says, pulling his cap off and flinging himself on the sofa. His forehead is white above the red dirt of his face and his hair wet with sweat. "Ain't you hot with that thing on your head? You're makin' me hot."

She leans on the threshold. "It's for Saint Paul."

"Patron saint of hats?"

"Paul said, Cover your head, lest you snare angels." She checks the rim of her cap and pushes a stray hair in at her neck.

"Well, Saint Paul never came to Oklahoma in the spring. Hotter 'n hell this year and twice as dry. Y'all must have a lot of time on your hands, nothin' more to worry about than if your hair'll catch angels. Whole lotta crap in the Bible."

"Probably." She takes a breath, her binding tight. "Do you have one?"

"A Bible? Don't you?"

"No. We don't use them."

"God won't think mucha that." He pads up the stairs in his dirt-ringed socks. She hears him unlock the door and she bends to tidy the magazines, scoop them back into a stack. He returns with an old Bible and an empty soup bowl. "You feedin' my pa?"

"I heard him knocking. I'm sorry, I—why do you keep his door locked?"

"Why do you tie up your girls?" He tosses the Bible onto the sofa before her and walks the bowl to the kitchen.

Chunks of brittle leather drop and flake off its cover. She runs a finger over the embossed writing, eases open the cover to see if there are names written inside, birth dates and death dates as she read that families keep, and sees a long line of Bradleys there, just as he said, in pencil and ink. All the Bradleys and the women they married. At the very bottom, she sees this last Bradley and the woman he married. Below their names, linked with an *m*, are three small red dots.

She hears the sink running. When he comes back, she tells him, "Sorrow runs. First time I stopped for gas, she jumped out of the car and ran right into the street, like she didn't know what cars were. I strapped her to Amity, to keep her in the car. I didn't want to lose her."

He sits on the back of the sofa. "Pa used to sneak to the fields, rip out what I'd planted, pulling up anything that wasn't wheat. When my wife left, I—well, I couldn't keep an eye on him anymore. Found him in a fence once, like he was tryin' to escape."

She holds his holy book in her hands. She stills her mind and asks God to send her a sign. Then she opens the book and spears a passage with her finger. She reads aloud, "I will judge thee, as women that break wedlock and shed blood are judged; and I will give thee blood in fury and jealousy . . . and burn thine houses with fire . . ."

Bradley leans over to shut the Bible on her hands, holding her hands within it. "Find a nice bit. 'The Lord is my shepherd.'"

"I shall not want."

He pulls the Bible from her and sets it on the sofa back. He shifts, so she can feel the heat of his thigh along her shoulder. She can feel him over her skin.

"The Bible is an oracle," she says calmly. "It can be used for divination, to give you guidance. To tell you what to do." Her hands make hot fists in her lap.

"So you thought you'd ask it. What do you want?"

"We can't have what we want."

She feels his breath on the back of her neck. He reaches a calloused finger down to her fists and she opens them, shows him her palms, involuntarily, as if her fingers are petals waking for the sun. He traces her hand's life line, hovering above her skin in the air. "Gypsies read your fortune and tell you your whole life is down there, written out. No difference."

Her palm tingles, itches below his. She can feel his finger before he has even touched her and when he does it makes a blue spark jump between them, snapping in dry air. She leaps up and they crack heads.

"Jesus!" he says.

She rushes to the door, out to his porch, and down to his hard earth. She looks up at God's hot sky and asks Him, again, what it is that she should do as, inside the house, a crash and shatter comes, as if he has overturned the table, sent the magazines' mountains and great seas flying. She closes her eyes and asks God if their escape was meant to be a test or a sign. Did He crash them to make them stop here, to be here? Or did He crash them to stop them, so that they could be caught? Was it God on this land, in this house, or the devil? For it is surely the devil, in the house, in her body, that makes her listen out for Bradley. That makes her want to touch him and him her.

She waits for him to come rushing out and shake her, slap her. It is what men do. But she only hears him breathing behind the screen door. "I was raised on the Bible," he tells her when she turns. "The hard love of God. We all were, so I know what's in there. Says we have free will, but it don't feel like it. Feels like everything's mapped out already and you only gotta follow it."

She thinks of how she left her husband as she walks up the porch steps. "Did you never want to leave?"

"Only 'bout a few hundred times a day. Who'd want to stay here?" He opens the screen, but she pushes back on it, to keep him inside and contain him. Her hands press flat on its weave. He pushes his hands onto the screen then, against hers, and she can feel him through the wire. "We're all waitin' for signs." He flexes his hands against hers, as if he wants to reach through the screen. She can hear the weave of the wire stretching, snapping.

She hears footsteps behind her and she steps back, turns, even as Bradley, still pressed against the screen, is released and tumbles out onto the porch.

Amity sees the two of them, their hands held out and open before them, and she spins on her clog and darts away.

"Daughter!" Amaranth calls, but she won't stop. "Amity!"

She looks down at her hands and at his hands and sees their palms look quilted, covered with squares from the screen that stands between them, marked with the same sets of lines.

BEFORE: *The Banishing*

Easter time and Hope had ground seeds to make the colored dyes that children patted onto small, blond goats to turn them red, black, and blue. They were roped and grouped, bleating, outside the temple, where children clapped their pudgy hands when their father came to see. “The four lambs of the ’Pocalypse!” they said, and giggled.

A marvelous addition to their pageant, their father pronounced it, though he stopped short of letting the goats into the temple. Amaranth could only beam at him. Easter was the best of times, with the baby

Jesus returned to them, reinstated on His cross, and her husband still at home. It was spring at last, after a hard, long winter, and he had healed from the sicknesses that had plagued him and their community. The whole community had healed. They had lost some children, born too early, and they had lost a wife to icy cold, but now all of them were together and celebrating renewal. The bad times felt far away.

In the temple, children rehearsed. For the first time ever, Sorrow tried to opt out. "I'm too old for pageants," she said, and tried to hand her Woman of the Apocalypse costume down to Amity. Her two elder brothers, Adam and Justice, said they would sit out, too, until their father shouted them all down. "I'll tell you when someone is too old!"

Sorrow pouted but let herself be dressed, putting on her bedsheet drapery, boiled in goldenrod, to be clothed with the sun, like the woman in her father's Revelation. She placed the crown of twelve cardboard stars over her cap and took her place aboard a rickety cardboard moon. Her hands clutched a huge goose-down belly and she cried out, so realistically aping the pangs of birth—which rang often throughout the houses—that mothers tittered.

Adam roared up behind her in red zip-up coveralls. “Behold, the Great Red Dragon!” He had six cloth heads stitched beside his own head, and each wore a tiny crown. Justice, in another red suit, played his tailed other half, the younger’s lot. The tail swished down all the stars of heaven, knocking toddlers across the temple floor as though they were bowling pins. The two halves of the Red Dragon pursued Sorrow. Around and around the temple they ran, Sorrow squealing, until at last she ran to the altar to be caught up by her father, his arms like the two wings that God gave the woman for escape. Zachariah caught her under her arms and tried to swing her up and Amaranth could see that he could hardly lift her now. She was too tall, too heavy, and he was older, suddenly. He seemed an old man. He tried again, then plopped her down.

Sorrow scowled. “I did say.”

That night, Sorrow was full of complaints. “I’m too old to play like this. I’m a woman now.”

"You may be a woman, but you're still a daughter and you'll do as you're told," Amaranth told her. Sorrow wore the skirts and cap of a woman, first of the children to begin her bleeding, but her heart and her head were young still. She would be a child, Amaranth supposed, until she was a wife.

"I'm not a child," she said. "I'll show you."

Sorrow was sullen through the performance. She spoke her lines but exhibited no fear when chased by the Red Dragon, nor did she tremble at the thought of it eating up her holy child. Amity was dressed in a bedsheet, oldest of the seven angels carrying the seven plagues. "Go and pour out the wrath of God upon the earth!" she intoned.

Her sister Gratitude tipped the first bowl, the sores on men, and the Red Dragon writhed with relish. Truth tipped the second and great red cloths were opened out, waiting wives turning the temple floor to blood. Joy and Harmony tipped bowls of berry juice into Grace's gold bowl to blot the sun. Zachariah lit a candle at the altar beside the blue china bowl and Sorrow, still standing on her cardboard moon, crossed her arms above her counterfeit belly. “This is real,” Amaranth heard her say. “I don’t see why we’re playing at it.”

Zachariah, not one to be shown up, had his own part to play. He flung off his white robe to reveal the purple and scarlet he wore beneath, adorned by the strands of pearls and paste jewels that women had brought with them over the years. From beneath his white curls there dangled hooped golden earrings. “It is I, Babylon the Great,” he called out. “Mother of harlots and abominations of the earth.” Women about the room clapped and cheered. One dared a wolf whistle and he gave a mocking curtsy, as if to display his absent cleavage.

“The war in heaven is begun,” Sorrow called out from the altar table. “This is no play!”

Her husband snapped at her, reminding her it was his line, but at seeing her, intent on her bowl, he was suddenly serious. “Tell me what you see.”

She raised one arm in the air, while the

other rested on her pillowed front. "One of us carries the Lamb as God's seed." Wives exclaimed and cried out.

"Sorrow!" Amaranth hissed. "Stop making a show of yourself."

Zachariah put his hands on his child. "When will it come?"

"The Lamb will see that the scroll is opened," she said. "The Lamb will break the seals."

"Who is it that will bear the Lamb?" he asked his wives.

Sorrow looked from wife to wife.

Amaranth watched Sorrow in worship, watched her spin among the women. All were watching for blood now and each was praying it wouldn't come. She studied Sorrow's flat bodice, the fullness of her skirts, the smugness of her face. She saw how their uniforms concealed their bodies. The binding made them all of a kind, which was its purpose, but it and the skirts could hide pregnancies for months.

Amaranth asked Hope for her herbal bag and Hope made up a pouch of wild yam and chasteberry. She put a small indigo bottle into Amaranth's hand and told her it was pennyroyal, said it should be used topically, as it was toxic, but it was effective.

Sorrow wouldn't take the herbs or let her mother run a bath with the tincture or rub it on her belly. "I'm too big to be bathed," she said. "Leave me alone."

As for Amaranth, her own cramps had led to bleeding, thick, black-red clots and strings. She counted her days back and counted too many. Then she stuffed herself with rags and cramp bark, knowing in her bones that something was leaving her. She was surprised at the rush of her own grief after so many losses, as if she, too, had wished to bear the Lamb.

Hope bartered eggs for a chemical pregnancy kit, but Sorrow wouldn't use it. She claimed she had no urine every time her mother caught her in the outhouse. "Stop following me!" she'd shout. Finally, when Zachariah was deep in prayer in the room below, she snatched Sorrow and Hope drove them into town. Sorrow was nauseated, sick in the car. She squeezed her eyes shut as they left their land, whimpering the whole way.

"What if they find something?" Amaranth whispered.

"It had better be divine," was all that Hope would say. She turned the car radio up and a man reported that seven people had been blown up by the side of the road in a faraway land that Sorrow had never heard of, in a war none of them understood or were aware had started.

In town, Sorrow didn't understand why her mother wanted her to show her naked loins to a strange man. She cried out when her feet were placed into stirrups. She screamed at her mother as the greased speculum was inserted and squeezed open like scissors. "Mother, make him stop!"

Amaranth thought of their children, how they were growing up. She remembered when the first boys realized that there were two sexes, and that boys were in the minority. "When do we get us some wives?" Adam had asked, hands on the hips of his skirts.

"What would you do with wives, little man?" Amaranth had swatted him, wondering what his mother had told him would happen to him once his voice had broken, once he sprouted hair. Every woman there would be his sister or his mother. How would he get wives?

"When I get me some wives," Adam said, edging his rump away from more swats, "I'm gonna tell 'em all what to do, 'cause that's what the man does."

When the boys were older still, she would hear them roughhousing in the room below. Once, she heard the sound of cloth ripping and whipped open the hatch, thinking someone was stuck in a hinge. She was ready to discipline them, tell them it was no place to play, when she heard a boy's voice say, "You're just a girl—you can't make Jesus."

"I can too make Jesus. Just watch me!" The other voice was Sorrow's.

When they returned from town, Amaranth called her family into the temple. It was her first time and there was no precedent for it. If the wives wondered why she should initiate worship, they knew better than to voice it; she was the first wife. The women and children were assembled before Zachariah heard them and lifted the hatch and rose through the floor to them, surprised but pleased. He remarked that going into town must have shocked her into action as it did him, each trip, every summer. If only they were as aware of the dire conditions of the outside world as he was. If only they knew how near the end they were.

Amaranth stood at the center of the room. She spun slowly, to look each wife and child in the face. “Someone has been at my daughter.”

“Wife,” he cautioned. “Amy.”

She pointed to him. “She has been broken into. She is no virgin.”

“Who tells you this?”

“I tell you! Look what comes from a faith such as ours—look at us!”

Zachariah took hold of Sorrow’s chin. “What have you done, girl?”

Sorrow whimpered, “Father.”

Then he roared from the altar. “This is holy work we do! This is my holy child! Who’s been at my holy daughter?” He left Sorrow to circle his family, master of them all, pushing Amaranth from its center. She moved to the altar, to take Sorrow’s hand, and Sorrow let her. He looked each member of his church up and down until he came to a stop before his sixth wife and his seventh, each the mother of a growing boy. How tall they were, suddenly, beside him. Young men. Not children. He looked each boy in the eye. "Which of you has been at my daughter? Your sister?"

"There were harvester crews up," Wife Six, Dawn, said quickly.

"And junkies, looking to buy—it could have been anyone!" Wife Seven said.

Each stepped before her son, her child, and Amaranth could remember the triumph each woman had showed when her child was pulled from within her, the tiny button that marked them out as first son, second son. What man didn't want a son?

Zachariah hauled both boys to the altar, mothers clutching and trailing, and bent them over the table. He ripped down Adam's cotton britches—they were too old to wear skirts now—and then he pulled down Justice's beside him. He shoved the tunics out of the way. Then he took hold of the cross and he whacked their buttocks, one after the other, until their mothers pulled at him, calling, "Hit me instead!" and lifting their arms up to catch his cross.

"I will hit you!" he said, and he raised the cross above their heads.

"Please, Father," Sorrow cried, clutching her mother.

Zachariah stopped, breathing hard but gripping the cross. "You will tell me the truth," he said to both of the boys.

Adam turned his head to him. "Really?"

Zachariah hefted the cross higher and Sorrow went to catch his arm.

Adam rose to his full height, taller now than Zachariah. Braver. "The truth is she is my sister and you are a dirty old man."

"Get out of my temple!" Zachariah swung the cross as women and children leaped out of his way. Sorrow staggered back from him. "Get out of my church!"

Adam would not look at Sorrow or his mother. He gave Zachariah a small nod, reached back for Justice, and the two of them strode out the temple door, mothers following, each howling and accusing the other.

"Husband," Amaranth cautioned. "They are your sons."

"Who needs sons?" He spoke childishly, rashly. "The first was never my son. Adam was a rotting seed in her when she came."

She remembered the girl then, young Dawn, black-eyed and enormous with her first child, product of her stepfather. "You said blood didn't matter. You said families were made from love, and so they are. Look at us."

"You asked if I could see what came of a faith such as ours."

Amaranth looked at Sorrow, saw how desperately she searched the windows for Adam. "I meant a faith with too many women." And boys who grow up, she thought.

"Was she with child?" he asked her.

Amaranth looked at her daughter. "No," she said.

If your right hand offends you, cut it off. They had all heard him say it.

The boys were driven into town, left, and banished. Their mothers clung to fence posts, forcing themselves to stay without their children. It was only a matter of time until they packed their meager possessions in the night and snuck off to follow them, to freedom, the sixth and seventh wives.

Amaranth found Sorrow in the temple, searching her bowl for the sense in it. "I'm sorry I had to take you," she told her. "You didn't know what you were doing. We have made your world too small and that is our fault."

Sorrow gripped the bowl. "It's what these places are made for."

"What?"

Sorrow placed a hand on her chest, then another on her crotch, pressing her skirt in. "It is what these places are made for." When Amaranth spoke, saying no, Sorrow, you're wrong, Sorrow silenced her. "I have eyes, don't I? Don't I see how it works?"

"Not with a brother. It's not your fault but—it's wrong, Sorrow. I didn't know we had to teach you that."

"My brothers," she spat, "were trying to keep me safe."

"From what?"

"From what will happen. You can't see it."

Amaranth reached for Sorrow's hand, but Sorrow put them both around her bowl. Her daughter wasn't pregnant, but the gynecologist had confirmed that she had been sexually active. For some time, he had pointed out, just as he was asking Sorrow to tell him her age. She wondered what would happen to the file he wrote in, about her.

Hope came to them in the temple. She carried a fat bundle, wrapped in a quilt. "I'm going, Amy," she said.

"You can't go. I need you too much."

Hope smiled her crooked-mouth, freckle-face smile, the lines in her face long and deep now. They had been friends for more than twenty years.

"He won't let you go," Amaranth said and instantly regretted it, wanting to pull the words back into her mouth. She loved Hope far too much to threaten her.

"I don't care. I'm in love, Amy. Foolishly."

"My God," she said. "Not with him."

"No." Hope laughed. She, out of all of them, had never loved Zachariah, not as any wife would. "It's Dawn," she said. Wife Six. "I can't live here without her. I can't live here. It's all breaking apart. You don't see it." Hope lowered her voice, looking at Sorrow.

"It's getting better. He's getting better."

"It's changed, Amy. We've lost something here. We've forgotten what we were trying to be."

But Amaranth shook her head, bitter to

the core. “Get out, then.” When she turned her back on her, she felt Hope’s hand drop something into her pocket. She stood as still and sullen as she could, for as long as she could manage it, and then she went racing from the temple to chase her car, waving it down the path and the trail, away from the world she had helped them build. Hope skidded to a stop. “Will you come?” she gasped. “It’s not right this, with Sorrow. Someone should stop it.”

“I know,” Amaranth said and she started to cry. But she didn’t know. And she didn’t dare to think it. She watched her oldest friend in the world drive away.

Back in the temple, it was dark and empty. She stood at the altar, head down, praying to be told the truth. For God to come and tell her, whatever it was.

But it was Amity who came creeping in, to place her two hands on her mother’s heart as if she could stop its two halves from breaking. “I saw, Mother,” she whispered. “I was watching.”

“What were you watching?” She pushed her child back to look at her. “Who told you to watch?”

“Sorrow. He says if the daughter of a

priest profanes herself, she should be burned with fire. I don't want Sorrow burned."

"What did you see, daughter?"

"I saw the Father. I saw them make Jesus. I saw him tell Sorrow he is God."

Amaranth looked at her daughter and the altar. She could feel them all on the edge of some precipice, as if the floor were cleaving open before them, to show them the very foundations of their church. With every act of her husband's, every change in the church, she had moved her own line of what was acceptable further and further away, for love.

Who was her husband, who claimed to be God? Who was her child to believe him? Who was she to have sanctioned this when it all started so long ago, back when their faith was made of charity and compassion, a dream of creating a family for women who had no one? How had love led them here?

"Tell no one," she told Amity. "It's Sorrow's secret." Her arms did not go around her youngest daughter, to comfort her or explain to her. Her hands did not move to her child's own heart. They went, instead, inside her pocket to find what Hope had given her.

A key.

15
The Key

Amity runs from her mother and the man and the house. She runs from the devil and the half-dead tree, past the fields and Dust in them. She shouts for Sorrow, but Sorrow is gone. Not standing at the bathroom door, not shaking the strap. She isn't in the bathroom, isn't splashing at the sink. "Sorrow!"

She runs past the pumps to the red dirt road, but there is no Sorrow, no dust cloud of her running. She thinks that God has swooped her up, like the Great Red Dragon, for their mother's wanton wickedness. She thinks Sorrow will be glad of it, to be taken up so that God might rescue her, and that Amity, too, will be free of her.

Then she sees that the door to the man's little shop is open. It shouldn't be.

Inside is Sorrow, touching his things. Her fingers are everywhere. She opens his glass-fronted refrigerators, where bottles glow blue and orange. The room grows cold from them and the bottles bead and drip. Sorrow runs her fingers through the mist, making smeary lines and swirls, but Amity can only think of the man and his fingers on her mother.

Sorrow moves to the wooden countertop to touch pouches and packets, stacked in boxes, swinging from metal arms. She picks at everything, pinches and pokes.

"What are you doing, Sorrow?"

"Looking for the key, dolt. Where did you look?"

Amity swallows. Sorrow told her to look, but she didn't see any key. What she did see she saw plenty of.

Sorrow pulls open drawers to rifle through them, ruffling papers and receipts, then scattering them. She tosses everything that isn't a key onto the counter, onto the floor. "Aha!" she says at last, and holds her hand up. But there is no key. She holds a box of wooden matches and gives it a little seedpod shake.

"What do you want those for?"

"Never you mind." Sorrow drops the box into her apron and turns back to her searching.

Amity's mouth is dry and she aches to take an orange bottle, to open it and see what's waiting inside. She knows that it is theft and there must be a rule about it, but she also knows that she comes from a place where everything is shared. If her mother let a man touch her, did that mean that the man belonged to all of them now? Would he touch her next and would she let him? And then she wonders if that is the devil talking, snaking in her reasoning out of want for a drink? Her fingers curl around the neck of an ice-cold bottle. She watches its contents dancing, fizzing like a storm. She pulls at its metal cap, but she cannot turn it or pry it off. It hurts her mouth when she tries to bite it.

Sorrow rattles tiny boxes of candy and flexes bendy sticks of gum. She pulls on a locked drawer and then pulls it hard. She can't get it open. Amity slides the bottle back onto its shelf, defeated, and shuts the refrigerator doors, one by one, to keep herself from any further temptation.

Sorrow bangs her fist down. "The key isn't here. We'll have to check the truck and if it isn't there, you'll have to go inside the house and check the man's pockets."

Amity gapes at her. "Go into the house? Touch his pants?"

"It's for God."

Amity follows Sorrow from the shop to where the truck is parked, where the red dirt road starts. God has left its windows rolled down and the doors unlocked. Sorrow slaps dust from the seat and slides behind the steering wheel. She tests the gear stick and the pedals, doubtfully, commanding Amity to open the glove compartment. She finds more bits of colored papers, matches and work gloves and an empty cigarette packet. No key.

"I was certain we would find it," Sorrow says. "I saw it."

"You didn't see where it was?"

"You don't know anything about being an Oracle." Sorrow sets her head on the steering wheel. "I have been good. I have been so good and I don't know how to do it."

"Do what?"

"Make God come."

God says the end of the world will come with fire. But God says a lot of things.

Sorrow sits in the man's front seat and prays a key into the ignition. She prays the knowledge of gears and pedals, prays the tank full of gas. She prays while the sun beats down on the two of them, blistering the glass and cooking all they ask for. When she can stand it no longer, she tries to make God come, with fire.

No one sees her light the match to flame it. No one sees how Amity screams. No one sees Sorrow set fire to the truck.

No one sees Amity and Sorrow at all, not Dust, who said he would watch them, not Mother or the man, who only watch one another, showing each other their hands.

No one is watching the sisters at all now, except God the Father, of course.

BEFORE: *The Daughter of Waco*

Fire broke out in the metal barns across the fields, barns where the fourth and fifth wives had worked and slept since the house filled up with wives. The fire might have spread, might have burned the land down around it flat, or skipped and jumped across the ripening fields to the campers and tents where the families slept, or sparked the hodgepodge house and the temple. But it did not. For Amity was watching and Amity screamed.

Amaranth reached across her bed for her husband, but he was gone, she was alone, and Amity was shouting Fire! Fire!

Amaranth leaped from her room as women and children tumbled from bedrooms, hastily doing up buttons and ties. Fire! they heard.

Outside, across the fields, they could see an orange glow from the east, as if the sun were rising early. Amaranth counted the heads of wives while wives counted children. Missing were Wives Four and Five, Wives Nine, Ten, and Twenty, and their husband. All children were counted and cuddled.

"What do we do?" she asked Hope.

"Come on," Hope said, hoisting her skirts and legging it toward the fields. Running behind her were Amaranth and Dawn, Wife Six, but all three stopped at the edge of the forbidden fields. This was no time for rules, Amaranth knew it, yet she felt she couldn't enter. She clutched her robe and she wrung her hands. She wondered what would happen to their family, their community, if their husband were suddenly gone.

"For fuck's sake," Dawn clucked. "It's a stupid rule," and she lit out for the barns. Still, Amaranth stood, unable to disobey. She stood and watched until ash began to blow at her, stinging her eyes, forcing her back to the rest of her family.

When Hope and Dawn returned, faces streaked with black, they spoke their news. Five wives were found, but no husband. The fourth and fifth wives were taken to the VA clinic in the city and left with no forms of identification but as much money as the wives could muster in a hurry. The ninth and tenth wives stood and watched while the flames died down, stomping out any sparks that flew, while Wife Twenty-One would only say that the fire was nothing to do with her. She'd been with the goats.

A thorough search was made of the tents and cars, the temporary buildings, and any structure that had not been burned. No one could find Zachariah and no wife would claim to have been with him. Heads turned to thoughts of Rapture; surely he had been taken in the night. Other heads turned to gossip, whispering if it was Amaranth's night with her husband, why didn't she know where he was?

It was Sorrow who said that they should clear the altar and check the room below. And there he was, in a deep, deep sleep.

It took multiple wives to shake him until he came to, roaring and sore-headed, red-eyed and shouting, "I am trying to open the scroll!" They all looked at Amaranth, their eyes asking why he would choose to sleep alone on a night that should be hers.

Amaranth dragged up piles of linen from the room below, to wash and bleach them. They reeked of urine, chemicals, ammonia. The white sheet with their stitched names had been soiled. There was a transistor radio, its batteries drained, and bits of biblical text she didn't recognize scrawled onto the walls. Something snapped beneath her clog and she bent to collect it. A thin glass tube wrapped in cloth.

She showed it to Hope, who had combed the cooling metal barns. Hope told her that she had seen chemicals in trash barrels, set alight: iodine and ammonia, paint thinner, drain cleaner. Discarded batteries, heaps of them, far more than their community could need for its jumble of portable radios. Coffeepots and filters, when none of them drank caffeine.

"What were they cooking?" Amaranth asked her.

Hope was too angry to guess. "There

was cold medication there, fancy decongestants, things we never had here—when we've had to make do with willow and eucalyptus, mustard plasters. Selfish bastards," she said.

The ninth and tenth wives stood before the altar. Their faces were gaunt and their work clothes black with smoke. Their teeth were as stained as the teeth of the fourth and fifth wives. Amaranth held the glass tube out, while Zachariah watched passively, his head bobbing on the slender stalk of his neck. She noticed how much weight he had lost. Had no one seen he wasn't eating? She looked about at the wives, but no one spoke. No one knew what to say.

Amaranth squared up to them. "We know what you're doing," she said. "We know what you're making in those barns."

The two wives looked at one another. One coughed wetly into her hand and looked down into it.

"You're making him sick, do you know that? You're feeding his fantasies and his fears. You're—you're making bombs, aren't you, like the ones in the East?"

Wives about the temple began to stir.

"We have to protect ourselves," called the thirty-ninth wife, the daughter of Waco. She had come to them years after the firestorm started by the government during the standoff with her prophet, David Koresh. "We have to be ready, for when they come."

"No one's coming here," Amaranth said.

"They'll come to see about the fire now," the daughter of Waco said. "They'll search our land and our houses. They'll take our children. It is our right to bear arms and we must."

Wives began to whisper.

The daughter of Waco had told them what the siege was like, how they were told that people were coming for them. They were told to put on gas masks. They heard helicopters circling over the compound, then shots and windows smashing, felt the choke of tear gas. She said the news reported that the Branch Davidians shot first. "But we didn't," she said. "I will next time." She told them the government drove tanks over the graves of her people and ran their flag up their church flagpole.

Wives began to speak. "You said we would be safe here!"

"You are safe. Look, you're safe," Amaranth called. She looked to her husband, for the words he would say to calm them all. She could see the doubt in their faces. So many had arrived after the towers had fallen. Their ranks had swollen as city women came, their compact cars filled with canned food and handguns, fearful and desperate to live off the land but having no idea how to begin. She could only imagine what had happened from the women's descriptions, the towers of finance falling and the people jumping, the clouds billowing below as the towers shrunk in place, as if consumed. Her husband had said it was a sign of God's displeasure, a testimony that their community was on the right path.

"Husband," Amaranth pleaded with him now, holding the glass tube out. "Were you trying to kill us? Were you trying to *bring* the end of the world?"

His eyes were cloudy, unfocused.

Finally, Wife Nine spoke out. "Not bombs," she said.

"What, then? Poison? Would you poison our well and kill us? Make something for us and ask us to drink it?" She thought of the Kool-Aid administered in Jonestown by the cult leader who was building Eden in Guyana. She could still see the bodies of the dead, lying flat and embracing one another. She had seen it on TV as a child, the camera flying over them.

"Not poison," said Wife Ten.

"Meth," said Wife Nine.

"Crystal meth?" asked Hope.

"Why would you be making that?" Amaranth asked.

Zachariah gave a dopey, smoky laugh.

Hope and Dawn cleaned out the one barn that could be salvaged and pulled down the one that couldn't. They itemized what had been burned and Amaranth realized, with a start, that the fields had been forbidden to them not out of her husband's fear of his wives running away or leaving or out of a desire to keep them safe, but to protect the barns and what they brewed.

"They're junkies," Hope said of the two in the hospital. "They were junkies when I met them and I guess they're junkies still. They were clean for a long time. Well, I thought they were clean."

"They've been running a lab, right under our noses," Dawn said.

"I suppose this is why they're always driving into town," Hope said. "Bringing supplies back. Dealing."

"We've probably all been living off their meth making for years. We're the meth church."

"Stop it," Amaranth said. It was true that they were the only wives who regularly drove to other cities and towns. She remembered when they had driven to Mexico. But she could only think of their kindnesses to her when she needed them most. She reminded Hope and Dawn that they were family, come what may. It was the vow they had made, each to the other. It took the fourth and fifth wives a long time to heal and when they did, their hands had been singed into keloid claws, lest they should forget the work they did. God would not allow them to use those hands again.

No one reported the fire, so no one knew to come. No one came to investigate, for nothing was insured and no claims were made. Still, the daughter of Waco was convinced that the government would start Armageddon at any time.

Amaranth thought it was only the newest wave of eschatology to hit them. The world was filled with sects who waited for the end. Here, wives were afraid that outsiders would overrun them, townie addicts who would hear of the drugs they produced and come to buy. Wives grew ever more insular. No one volunteered to drive into town, to run the errands that the fourth and fifth wives had run for so long. No more errands were needed now, and no one wanted to leave.

Wives in the kitchen began their process of stockpiling, preserving more than they could ever hope to use before the next year's harvest. Amaranth knew that they only needed something productive to do with their fear and that preparing for disaster would keep them focused and comforted. They lined the walls of the room below, her husband's secret place for prayer, devotion, quiet contemplation, and clandestine drug taking, with shelving. It would become the storehouse of the wives' labors, packed with the food and supplies that they would need. And then it was all they talked about. All they wanted and hoped for. It kept them busy while Amaranth and Hope worked to clean out their husband, holding him while he sweated and shivered and yelled the drugs out, cursing them to hell and begging to be killed.

She didn't know he could make home feel like hell.

She didn't know that preparing for the end of the world would make it that much more likely to come.

Part II

JUNE

16

The Devil in the House

Amity runs from the fire and the smoke. She runs from her sister and her sister's matches.

She runs from the truck that is flaming now, pouring smoke through the door she kicked open to run, because she is not ready for heaven.

"I will make God come," Sorrow said.

Dust is dark in the fields and the man is a faraway stain. Amity tries to shout to them, but the smoke has choked her. She can do no more than bleat and cough. Mother is in the devil's house and she won't come out for Amity's clapping. She makes herself reach the devil's screen door, pull it back on its hinges, and slap the door with her clog. "It's Sorrow," is all she can crack out. And then the man is running toward them, in from the fields with his long spider legs. "Is that smoke?"

"Where is she?" Mother asks her, grabbing her hard by the arm. And then she's running after the man, faster than Amity can catch up, toward the rising plume of smoke that spins behind the gas station, turning the orange ball black.

She doesn't want to follow. She has betrayed her own sister. She drops to the porch and folds her hands over her cap. She wonders what her sister will do to her.

They bring back Sorrow and set her onto the porch, but no one swaddles Sorrow now, no one says "sorry" or coos. The man sets her down as though he is stacking logs for the winter and Mother sweeps into the house behind him, Sorrow all but forgotten.

"You okay?" Amity whispers.

Sorrow's face is black with smoke. She pulls the blankets around her knees. "I'm cold," she says.

Amity shuffles to her, to tuck her in. She

knows people get cold when they are afraid. It has happened to her, too, though it isn't cold here and she can't imagine it will ever be anything but bone-dry inferno, night or day. From inside the house she hears chairs scraping and drawers slamming, the voice of the man, upraised, shouting, and her mother, wheedling, pleading, like the mothers back home. When she pokes the blankets in around Sorrow, Sorrow snatches Amity's wrist. "Tattletale."

"I'm sorry."

"The devil will fork your tongue and fry you."

"You wanted a key," Amity says. "You didn't need to set it on fire."

Sorrow squeezes her wrist, tighter than any wrist strap. "You don't know what I need."

"I do, Sorrow. You need home. You will get there."

"How will I?"

"I know that when you want something, you get it. That's what I know."

Sorrow smiles at that, her teeth white as stars in her night-dark face. She snuggles down into the blankets, pulling Amity's arm in with her. “The Father will come now,” she says. “I’ve called to him.”

Mother flies through the door and the screen. Amity hears the man, shouting behind her, “Coulda set the whole damn thing on fire! What if the pumps had caught? It’s a gas station, for Christ’s sake!” He slams the door.

Mother worries her hands. “Cars are machines—they’re full of gas and electrics. You didn’t know what you were doing, did you? You didn’t know that they could catch fire?”

Come morning, the man smacks the door beside them. He stomps his boots hard on the porch’s boards, not caring if he wakes them. He cuts the words of Mother’s calling with the back of a slap-giving hand, cuffing the air.

Mother turns to them, hands on hips. “This is not home,” she pronounces.

Sorrow rolls her eyes at Amity, as if this is any kind of revelation.

“But there are chores. You work at home. You would never lay about like this there.”

“What work would you have us do?”

Sorrow asks. "We cannot pray. We cannot worship. What would you have us do, sweep dirt and pump gas?" She dares a laugh.

"I've had enough of your lip," Mother says. "You don't speak to me like this at home."

"This is not home, you said."

Mother stands over her. "You will respect me as if it were. You will respect me as you would any one of your mothers. You will do your work with glad hearts, just as at home. You will earn your keep here."

"Keep," Sorrow says. "Who would keep this?"

Mother stamps her clog and hurries into the house. In a heartbeat, Sorrow is up and out of her blankets, still filthy from the fire, and when she hears the front door open again, she lights out for the path to the gas station. Amity has never seen her move so fast, as if the devil has her in his sights, but it is only Mother behind her, crashing out of the house with a broom. She sighs when there is no Sorrow to give it to. Amity holds her hands out for it.

"You tell me what happened. Did Sorrow start that fire? Would she?"

Amity can only whimper, "Mother, please."

"We could stay here, don't you see? There's food here."

"Sorrow would never allow it."

"Sorrow!" Mother hisses. "I'm tired of what Sorrow wants." And then she is grabbing Amity to pull her inside.

Amity clings to the door frame. "No man's house! It's a rule!"

"There are no rules." And Mother slams them both inside.

All rules must be broken, it would seem, and Mother will break them. Mother will make her break them, too. Mother hauls her across a shadowed room and yanks her up stairs even as Amity hangs on to the handrail, catching hold of each baluster with her clog.

"Let go," Mother grunts, dragging her. "We made the rules up, every one." Mother pushes her up toward a door, mercifully locked, but then she whips a key from a nail there and opens the very door to the devil.

Amity screws up her eyes, but she cannot help but see. She looks inside the devil's bedroom. She sees his bed and chifforobe and the devil's two horned feet, looks up the devil's legs to his white raisin face, his bald head like a speckled hen's egg, with wispy bits of hair in a feather fluff atop.

"This is my daughter." Mother gives her a little shove forward, into his evil lair.

The devil opens his mouth and licks his pleated lips. "What do you want me to do about it?"

"She can keep you company. She's looking for ways to be helpful."

"Is she, now?" The devil gives her a crooked smile and pats his bed. "Come on and get a proper eyeful."

Amity doesn't want to sit on the devil's bed. She doesn't want to get any closer to him at all. She knows how he puts his number on the skin of the saints, how he writes his name on sinners' souls. She looks away at his devil playthings—his black plastic box with its metal ears, his shotgun.

"You gonna just stand there and gawp at me?" The devil looks a bit sorry for himself, clever devil.

"Say hello, Amity," Mother says, and gives her another little shove. Amity's mouth pops open. Now the devil knows her name! But Mother is out the door and behind it before Amity can protest.

"You're gonna catch flies," the devil tells her.

She snaps her mouth shut, afraid she'll catch worse than that.

"Did you set my boy's truck on fire?" the devil asks her.

She shakes her head.

"Who did, then?"

She gives him a look that says, Why don't you know? He's the devil so he must know everything. That's most certainly a rule.

"You think I'm so old I don't know what's what? I hear you down there, missy. I know what you all want."

Amity backs away until she bumps the door. She turns around and bangs on it.

"Oh, come here," the devil says. "I'm not gonna bite you. Got sumpin' to show you." The devil flips over in his bed to scrabble his claws around on the floor.

Amity awaits the unleashing of the Great Red Dragon or the Beast from the Sea. She waits for him to open the hatch to hell beneath his bed, but all he does is pull up a bound square of paper. "What is it?" she asks him then pulls her lips in. Another rule smashes.

"Open it," he says. "But be careful, you can see it's old."

"You're old," Amity says.

The devil snorts. "Older'n you, so you can bet your britches I know more than you. Go on."

Amity looks at it in his hands. "Is that your Bible?"

The devil laughs at that, a full-throttled ha-ha. He closes his eyes and tells her, "'To the red country and part of the gray country of Oklahoma, the last rains came gently, and they did not cut the scarred earth.' What do you make of that?"

Amity is amazed. Wait until she tells Sorrow that the devil reads through his hands.

"You ever heard of a Mr. John Steinbeck?" the devil says.

"No, sir."

"Dumb and ignorant to boot. This ain't no Bible. This here book is *The Grapes of Wrath.* You heard of that?"

"Not exactly."

"Either you has or you hasn't."

"God the Father says that anyone worshipping the beast will receive a mark on her forehead and drink the wine of God's wrath and that must be pressed from His grapes of wrath, sir."

"Well," says the devil. "Maybe you ain't entirely dumb. Just mostly. You all are dumb for God, ain't you?"

Amity nods. She supposes they must be. She could hardly hope to keep a thing like that from the devil.

He grins with his brown horse teeth, just the size for chewing souls. "You know he keeps me locked in here?"

Amity smiles at that, the devil playing her for sympathy. "It's for your own good. We wear a strap. It's to keep us safe." She holds the strap up and then it's his turn to stare.

"Tell me, girl, what age are you and you wearin' a leash?"

"Twelve, sir."

"Twelve. Someday you'll be an old bag of coat hangers like me. You're old enough to know your own mind, not let people drag you around by a string. Why, your age, I was out battling dust."

"Dust?" she cries. "My Dust?"

"My dust," he says. "My whole land, turned to dust. That's what this book's about," he says, poking it with a pointed nail. The devil rotates his head to glance at his window, as if he can still see the people of his land drying up and blowing away.

"I like stories," she tells him. "Father tells us stories all the time."

"These ain't stories, girl. This actually happened. Where is your father, then?"

"God only knows."

"That right?" He pushes the book toward her. "You go on and read me some, if you're lookin' for occupation."

She will not open it and she will not read it, not the devil's Bible, not even if she could. "I can tell you a story, if you like."

"What about?"

"The end of the world." She leans back against his door.

When Mother comes to let her out, Amity is surprised to find the door wasn't even locked. She could have escaped at any time. She tells the devil good-bye and runs out into the sun and her soul's freedom. She never sees how wide the devil's eyes go at the stories of Father's she told him, or hears his words to Mother: “That child is crazy, nuts and crackers. Some cockamamie story ’bout God having sex with a planet full of wives to make more gods, so they’s can each have a planet. Little girls shouldn’t be thinking about the end of things so much. Why you fillin’ ’em full of the end?” She never sees how her mother hangs her head or how, when she goes, she forgets to lock his door up.

17

The Switch

Amaranth holds a paring knife, bone-handled and sharp from a kitchen drawer. She fits her fingers into the handle's grooves and fancies, for a moment, that it belongs to her, something from her history, handed down over generations. An odd thought, really, for nothing belongs to anyone at home.

She boils beans and grains, but Bradley does not come for them. She brews coffee for him and lets it go cold. She whittles a stick from the old tree when she knows that it isn't whipping Sorrow needs, but schooling. But it is only whipping that she knows. Back at their community, children were taught only what they would need when they were wives and mothers: canning, preserving, baking, butchery. To skin an animal, to fire a gun. They were given skills for Armageddon and taught to want nothing but the end of the world.

They could stuff sausages at four years of age but they couldn't write their names down, so the devil couldn't trick them into signing his book. They didn't know their address, so they couldn't tell it to the police, who would want nothing more than to come onto their land and snatch them away. Isn't that what they had been taught? She allowed it, even knowing that, should she ever lose her blissful, ignorant children, they would not know how to get back to her. They wouldn't know where home was. They would stand by the roadside, waiting for a sign from their silent God. Knowledge was power, but ignorance was holy. It kept them humble and pliable, docile and safe as milk cows. She whittles and, when the stick is smooth, pictures it swishing and cracking across the pale flesh of the backs of her daughter's legs. She calls for Amity to bring Sorrow to the house.

Sorrow is haughty until she sees the switch. Then, two pin spots of blood rise on her cheeks. She lowers her shoulders and lifts her chin. Amity twists herself around Sorrow's arm with the strap.

"Sorrow, I am going to hit you," Amaranth says.

"Mother, no!" Amity begins to cry. She tugs on the strap, to get Sorrow to run with her.

"Do you know why I'm going to hit you?"

"Because the devil is inside you."

She bends her daughter over the porch railing and pulls the strap from between her daughters, throwing it down. "Do you know why I'm going to hit you?"

Sorrow folds her hands behind her back, over the knot of her apron, as she had seen wives and brothers do at home. "Because I will not forget my God."

Amaranth lifts the bottoms of Sorrow's skirts and folds them over her hands, to pin her down. Her underclothes are soiled and filthy, as are her legs, her arms. Her children are living like savages. Amity slides atop Sorrow, crying, "Hit me—it's my fault!"

"Out of the way, Amity, or I'll hit you both—now move!"

Amity sobs as she's shoved off Sorrow. She rears back, flailing, and Amaranth raises the switch to her. Only then does Amity slide down the porch steps to watch and snivel from the dirt.

Sorrow lies across the railing, still but alert. Amaranth brings the switch down on the backs of Sorrow's legs, hears the swish and crack. Sorrow chokes back a sob and Amaranth wants to throw the switch down and cradle her, hold her like the child she was and never was, but Sorrow turns her head then, daring her, and she raises the switch again. She cracks it down. Two white stripes rise on the backs of her legs, white ridges in red furrows. She lowers the switch.

She thinks of the women and children hit, the belts and ties, the occasional cross. She remembers the feel on her own legs, the skin snapping, lifting, rising in welts as thick as snakes, for questioning a rule that said they should be kept from the fields, when for years she had walked wherever she liked. They all had, before the temple was built. They had the woods and a path along the rock mountain. She remembers when it had been a kind of paradise: fecund soil, abundant water, azure skies, and open land.

"Father can see you," Sorrow says.

She hoists the switch and cracks it down a third time, hard as she can, raising a third stripe across the other two. "Good," she says. "Let him watch."

She takes up the switch and rushes for the fields. Her clogs totter over furrows between bristle-topped grasses, yellowing, crisp, and whispery on her skirts as she brushes past. The earth opens in great ruts between the crop rows, great crevices that speak of thirst and bare roots, burning below the unforgiving sun.

She sees him, arms outstretched, palms down to stroke the tops of crops. His eyes are dark beneath his cap's brim.

"I hit her!" she calls to him, fields away. She works her way over dry rows to reach him. "I hit her." She gestures with the stick. "I've taught her. I've done it."

A dark row of spikes stands between them. "That what you people do?"

"She is willful. She has to learn."

He nods. "My pa used to beat the crap out of me. Didn't teach me nothin', 'cept he was a bully. Big man, hittin' a kid."

She squeezes the stick. "I don't know how else to reach her."

"Nothin' to do with me," he says, and he slides his finger down a stem.

"She burned your truck. I know she did. She is selfish, but I've never known her to be so—willfully destructive."

"She play with matches back home?"

"She doesn't play." She drops the stick, ashamed of it. "I want to tell you something."

"Don't need your confession. She needs to say sorry."

"Well, I raised her. We taught her that the end of the world will come with fire. So . . ."

"I love my truck, but it ain't the end of the world."

"My husband set our temple on fire. He tried to kill us."

He looks at her and his eyes are dark, tired, and lined. She is wearing him down just by being here. "So you can't go back. I got it."

"He wouldn't let us go. Not Sorrow. Not me. He let some go, but—not us."

"Some?"

She takes a deep breath and another. She looks up at him. "I am the first of his fifty wives."

"Fifty? Fifty wives?"

"So if you're picturing him alone somewhere, missing us, abandoned, I—I know he's not alone. He deserves no sympathy."

"Fifty wives! That's why you won't go to the police. What you're doin' is illegal."

"It isn't illegal. It's immoral to some. This isn't bigamy, it's polygamy. It's consensual. There are no laws against living with people or bearing their children."

"How 'bout settin' 'em on fire? You're damn right your daughter set my truck on fire. She's learned from the master. Jesus."

"I wish you wouldn't do that."

"What?"

"Use His name like that."

"I can't see your religion doin' much for you here. Can you?"

She shuts her eyes. She wonders how to help him see what it was, not how it ended. How it began, who she was before it started, and who she became because of it. How each wife was brought back to life and given hope, the God-shaped want in them filled in a spinning circle, by the family she chose. "I have known such rare love," she tells him, cautiously. "An ecstasy in worship I did not think I had the right to feel. I don't want you to think it was dirty. Or shameful." He bends to one of his plants and she knows she's shamed him then. "I don't want you to think that's how I am, somehow frivolous or changeable. I loved him and I loved hard and I made some hard choices out of that love, because I thought we were building something. A new faith. Jerusalem. Utopia." She looks up at him. "Standing here, it sounds foolish."

"'Cause it wasn't. Ain't no utopia. Don't I know it?" He checks the underside of a floppy leaf and sighs. "It okay with you?"

"What?" she asks.

"Being one of fifty?"

A lump clogs her throat. No one has ever asked her. Not even her husband, really. She tells him what her husband told her. "It is a good practice, in theory. It means that labor is shared. There's never a shortage of child care or companionship. Historically, it meant that there would be a home for surplus women, on the prairies and whatnot, that everyone would be able to be a part of a family, not just the ones who were lucky or pretty or wealthy. There are so many women with no one."

He nods. "And it's okay with you?"

She shakes her head at that. It's not okay. None of it is okay and it hasn't been for a long, long time. She thought she had run to save her children. She now wonders if, perhaps, she has run to save herself from the husband who, long ago, had saved her. "I don't know."

"Fifty wives," he clucks, shuffling down the row to bob leaves along his hands. "Fifty wives and I couldn't keep one."

She watches him go. She looks down at the stick at her feet and the hard cracks in the ground, running beneath her.

BEFORE: *The Wife Who Wasn't*

When the wife who wasn't to be a wife came, Amaranth thought she knew her husband's history from his pioneering, polygamous ancestors who stitched their names across a sheet. But she didn't know how many polygamous generations there had been since then, or that he had family, living among them still.

They were a family with twenty wives when Rebekah came, arriving on foot up their gravel path, carrying a cardboard suitcase tied with rope. It was midsummer and the wives were amazed. No new wife had ever arrived before autumn, before their husband did. He would still be months away, preaching.

She wore a pale pink gingham dress, full-skirted and puffy-sleeved, embellished with lace and rickrack trim. She looked like a frilly sweet pea against the dark shrubs of wives, their utilitarian work clothes all denim and black so as not to show dirt. More extraordinary was her hair—elaborately braided down her back; swooped, sprayed, and sculpted into arching wings around her face. Wives had taken to wearing bandannas and head scarves, as it was hard to make enough hot water to keep twenty heads of hair clean.

The girl said she had been sent up from Mexico to live with them, for she was Zachariah's niece. She told Amaranth, over chicory and oatmeal squares, that she had come up the length of the country by bus then hitched to their road, told to look for their gravel path and mountain. She had been shown pictures of them, she said.

"Pictures?" Amaranth asked. "Like the tithing envelope?"

"No," she said. "A photograph." And she pulled one out of her gingham pocket. There it was, their mountain and their woods, but from a long time ago, back before the temple was built or any of the outbuildings, back before the trees had been thinned. The only car in the photo was her husband's van and none of the raised beds were there, not to mention the wives or their numerous cars. She wondered how old the picture was and how it had traveled to Mexico.

Amaranth found Rebekah a bed among the children in the attic, but she was alarmed. None of the girl's story rang true. How had her husband come by a niece, when she knew he had no family?

Rebekah fit into their family immediately. She shared in the chores with a glad heart and taught the children to sing, "Come, come ye saints, no toil or labor fear." When women complimented her dress, Rebekah told them it was how they all dressed back home, and she ran circle skirts up from bedsheets on the sewing machine to show them how easily they were made. Amaranth drew out stories of her community over foaming mugs of goat's milk, learning how each wife had her own house built for her and how a husband would never take more wives than he could care for himself.

When Zachariah returned in the fall, he was introduced to Rebekah. He was hot and rumpled from the journey, impatient, and Amaranth could see he did not recognize the girl. Her name and costume meant nothing to him. But when Rebekah told him her father's name was Lehi, something shifted in his face, as if a thing long buried was being unearthed. "We'll see you home, girl," was all he would say. He stomped into his house, past wives and children who proffered lips of welcome.

Amaranth followed, pestering him. "Who is she? Who is Lehi? Where are her people? Why is she here?"

"Leave me be!" he said.

Outside, Rebekah was surprised to see that two young women had arrived with her uncle, dressed in skintight T-shirts with short, short skirts. They studied each other with wonder and judgment as wives crowded around to watch.

After prayer and over dinner, Zachariah pronounced that the girl would be sent home. The fourth and fifth wives stood immediately, said they would take her all the way to Mexico if they had to.

Rebekah began to cry, "Don't take me

back. They'll marry me to the prophet. He's about a hundred years old." She laid her head on the table and sobbed like a child. "I'm supposed to stay and marry you. You can't send me back!" But she was bundled into his car and driven away, the two girls, not yet wives, watching in stunned silence.

In Amaranth's bed, he got no peace until he told her what he knew. "You said we would have no secrets, husband," she reminded him. In the dark of her room, he told her about the Short Creek raid when he was a child, when the government burst into their chapel during worship to arrest four hundred fundamentalists, pulling babies and children from parents' arms to put them into foster care. "They took me and they took Lehi," he whispered. "And by the time they sent us back, I didn't recognize my own family. They could've been anybody."

"But they were your family?" she pressed. "You did have family?"

"They were changed and I was changed. I left before they could send me away."

"Why would they send you away? What had you done?"

"Me?" he said. He sat up and the bed jostled. "They let the government take us—they just handed us over, like we meant nothing to them. Like I meant nothing."

"That can't be so," she told him. She couldn't picture it. She couldn't imagine the government wanting to separate families unless there was serious cause for it. "Why would they do that?"

"We were polygamous. It was illegal and the government thought it was abuse—that we were being abused by it. You can't make laws about how people live or love—no government should—and you can't let them take your children, no matter what."

She shook her head. She didn't understand any of it. Here, she thought they had been making their own rules for their community, out of faith, charity, and love. Now she felt they were following some blueprint she didn't know existed and it hurt her. "Why did you tell me you had no family? Was it because you knew I didn't?"

"No," he vowed. "You are my family. This is my family. I left Short Creek and I left that faith and I never looked back. It's Lehi looking back, trying to be some kind of family to me, but I want nothing to do with them, not how they are. I've made a new faith here. A new family. We're nothing like them and we never will be."

"We're polygamous," she spat.

He lay back again on her bed with a sigh. "I'm tired." His hand reached for her and she took it, thinking of the girl and her strange hair and dress, the black-and-white photo she had clutched in her hand. She tried to put the girl out of her mind, but her influence remained.

Wives were caught fussing their hair into her shapes when they thought no one was looking. They sewed skirts in circles and piled them up, to wear in layers, full as hers, then fuller. With their abundance of skirts, wives took to spinning on the hard, smooth temple floor, in prayer.

Amaranth watched him watch them during worship, the wide skirts of women spinning before him, and wondered if it felt like a memory to him, this family the women felt they were creating, inventing for themselves out of raw materials and sheer hard work. Was this a new world for him, as it was for them, or did it only remind him of something older, something he swore he had forgotten? Something he swore he didn't want?

18

The Sacrifice

Amity and Sorrow kneel, wrist to wrist, by the bathroom door. The bucket is empty. The china shard sits, dry, in its bottom. It cannot show Sorrow what she wants to see. It cannot take her home.

They crouch until their knees are numb. They stare at the bathroom door and each other until Dust comes, holding up a screw-driver.

"Outta the way," he tells them.

But Sorrow won't move, and Amity has to tug her away by the strap.

Dust opens the bathroom door and looks inside. "Jeez," he says. "What are you two getting up to in here? Do you gotta make a mess of everything?"

Amity leans in to Sorrow. "What have you done?"

Sorrow slowly closes her eyes.

"Is it critters making mess in here? Because it better not be you. And I'm not cleaning it up, either, I can tell you that."

Sorrow won't look at him and Amity can only look down, in Sorrow's shame.

Dust screws a metal eye to the door frame and a swinging hook to the door. "We'll keep this locked, to keep the critters out, whatever they are. Prairie dogs. Or rats." He pulls the door shut and hooks the eye.

"We're sorry," Amity tells him. "I'm sorry."

But Dust only flicks the screwdriver around in his hand then jams it in his pocket. As Sorrow is investigating the hook and the door, he goes, not looking back.

Once he's gone, Sorrow yanks Amity inside. And she kicks the door shut.

And then it is dark and cool and close. She can feel Sorrow spool her in, in the silence. "I'm sorry for what I did," she says. "I'm sorry Mother hit you. I'm sorry I ran and I'm sorry I told, only I thought you were in trouble. I thought you needed help."

"Who are you to help the Oracle?"

"You can't just set everything on fire."

"Can't I?"

Sorrow lights a match that flames her face. She holds the match at the tip of Amity's nose. Amity pants and the flame flickers. "We must make the Father see us," Sorrow says. "We must catch His eye and ear."

"How?" Amity huffs, hoping to blow the match out.

"A sacrifice." Sorrow drops the match on the tiles and stomps it. And it is dark again. "Put your hand out," she says.

Amity sees spots before her eyes, bright from the match's flame. She stretches her strapped hand for Sorrow and it bumps into something hard.

Sorrow lights another match. "Hold still."

Amity's hand shakes, palm upward and strapped. She watches as Sorrow pulls from her apron pocket a bone-handled paring knife. She raises it and holds the point over Amity's palm. Then Sorrow drops the match and as it falls she lowers the knife, to slit the star of Amity's hand.

Amity cries out and Sorrow pulls her by the strap. She puts Amity's cut straight onto the tiles and smears it across them, side to side, up and down. She lights another match then and shows Amity the red cross she has made, there on the tiles like some holy sign. Amity can see other dirty marks and signs around it, made by Sorrow, red and brown.

"I'm sorry!" Amity says.

Sorrow takes her end of the strap off and lets it drop. She opens the bathroom door and holds the match up to the sun as light pours in. Amity's eyes flame and flood as she moves toward it. And then Sorrow is slamming the door on Amity, plunging her back into darkness. "Don't leave me in here!"

She hears the hook scrape into the metal eye and catch. She bangs on the door and calls to Sorrow. She thrusts herself into the door, but it is firm on its hook. She lurches, crashes into the sink she cannot see. She follows a pipe across the wall and into a corner, finds the cistern, one solid, cold thing she can wrap herself around. She crouches beside it and puts her cut hand to her mouth. She tastes dirt,

Sorrow, and her own hot blood. She tries to rock herself calm.

It is as dark as the room below the temple. She feels as if she is back inside it, back beneath it, hiding in the dark. But even that room had its spiracles, three breathing holes that let down three pinhole shafts of light, like the fingers of God. In the room below she hid herself in the far corner, between the metal shelves of food that no one could eat. There was so much food down there that when the world ended, it would feel like a party. There would be second and third helpings and everyone would smile as they used to. That's what she thought then.

Here, in this darkness, Amity can hear things. Mice nails or bird claws, the sound of some hook-faced roach, jaws snapping. She can feel things reaching out for her. Dark hulking shapes that rub themselves against her, rats or kittens, crawling babes, nudging and nestling as if they want something from her, as if they wait to be born. As she could in the room below the temple, she can hear and feel the soil shifting beneath her, something scratching up through the dirt, like plants growing too fast and things reaching upward, pale asparagus or finger bones or the dead all rising up from their dirty holes at Rapture, all winding sheets and skeletons.

She hid herself in the room below because Sorrow told her to. Sorrow told her to watch and to wait.

She heard the altar table slide, wooden legs on the wooden floor, and saw the hatch door open, pouring light down onto the pile of quilts. Two stocking legs dropped down with the squish and plop of skirts. Sorrow. And then there were more legs, white linen, long and lean. Adam, she thought, and she waited for Justice. But Justice never came and the hatch was pulled shut, and then it was dark again. Three slivers of light from the spiracles fell onto Sorrow.

Amity saw someone put his arms around her and pull her down. Adam, she thought. Someone pulled Sorrow onto the blankets and did not let her up, did not let her go. They weren't supposed to play down there, any of them anymore, but rules had made their land small and the children only got bigger.

Sorrow was flat on the ground and her

skirts rose, up to her waist, her legs in the air. Amity didn't know this game. She could hear Sorrow, and it didn't sound like her playing, but what could Amity do? She was told to watch and wait. She wasn't told to spring out and announce herself or ask questions when she was meant to hide. And besides, everyone there was family. Family couldn't hurt you, no matter what they did.

Amity saw a white ponytail and it made her hold her breath. She pressed herself back, into the corner. She dared not tell Father she was watching and waiting. She was Sorrow's secret and Sorrow's work with Father was a secret prayer, secret as the sounds he made, secret as their movements.

When Father left the room and pulled himself back up through the floor, he left the hatch open and the altar pushed away. Sorrow lay in a pool of gold, light and pale on the blankets. Amity called to her. She waited for Sorrow to rise and shake her skirts down, chatter away as she always did. But Sorrow stayed flat on her back, flat as the stitches, flat as the sheet.

"Didn't you hear me?" Sorrow said quietly.

"You wanted me to hear," Amity told her. "You told me."

"Why didn't you come?"

"You told me to watch and wait."

"Oh, what use are you?"

Amity crept to her sister. "I did what you told me. What did I do wrong?"

"Nothing." Sorrow sighed.

"Is that how you pray with Father? Is that your prayer?"

Sorrow turned her head away from her then and Amity could see the light pour into her sister's tiny ear. "Sure, that's how we pray. He turns into God—didn't you see him? Just like he did when he made the Virgin pregnant, when he made her have Jesus. Didn't you see?"

"I did see him," Amity said. "I didn't see God."

"Maybe you can't see God because you're too stupid."

Amity wanted to lie beside her, to feel what she felt, to look up into the light and pray. "Are you the Virgin Mary now?"

Sorrow pulled herself up into a ball, tidy as a knot.

And now Amity is here, in the darkness, wondering which of the sounds she hears are here and which are only holy ghosts.

For there are ghosts here. Anyone could tell.

19
Seedbed

Amaranth turns the soil in the old kitchen garden. It is too dry for ants or pill bugs, but below the crust there are the slender chambers of earthworms. The soil is good and rich, few stones. She pulls up clots of dirt to throw down, smash apart. She carries bucket after bucket of water from the house to dampen it. She carves rows with the end of the broom handle.

She carries the jars of seeds from the pantry, sets one at the end of each row, and pulls a handful from each, sowing the tiny balls and specks in straight rows. She doesn't know what they are, but hopes for lettuce greens or medicinal herbs. She wishes for the big hard balls of sweet peas, or broad beans, but she knows they aren't. There isn't a one she can recognize. Whatever they grow, she waters them in hope.

In his house she sweats steam, boiling old beans. Soft thumps land on his rooftop and she thinks it is the old man knocking for her, but he tells her it isn't and to go away. She looks out from his window and sees the old tree above them is dropping its buds, throwing them down in the relentless heat. The sky is heavy and white.

But the old man scowls. "This ain't drouth, I tell you; drouth is a million times drier than this. Why, back in my day, drouth'd suck all the moisture from a man, leave him standing there, nothin' left but a rind a skin, a peel of man. A human scarecrow. Where's your daughter?"

"I don't know," she says. She leans out his window but all she can see are fields. She won't be there. "Off playing, I suppose." She has no idea.

"Tell her I wanna see her."

"You're kind to her."

"I ain't. I'm bored."

"Will I turn on your TV? Will I read to you?"

"Quit your fussin'."

"Men like fussing," she says.

"That what you doin' here? Fussin' so we'll like you, let you stay?"

"I'm not doing anything," she says. She picks up his piss bucket to dump it and swill more bleach around. She brings it back from the bathroom and sets it beside him. She pushes at his pillows until he tells her off then she tugs his window open, in the hope of a breeze. When was there last rain on this land? "You should get up," she tells him.

"You don't know much about old people."

"Actually, I do. I cared for several, for my grandmother, right up to the end. I know if you stop using things, they leave you."

"That so?"

She smiles. "Your legs will drop right off you."

He sits up and takes a rattled breath. "Fat lot you know. You think you got it made here, don't you? Down in the kitchen, bangin' our pans? You think you'll win my boy that way, through his stomach? You seen his stomach? No, I don't guess you would have."

"I'll leave you be," she tells him.

"Women think my boy is a soft touch, 'cause he don't hardly yell," he tells her. She stops at the door. "'Cause he don't throw his weight around and he could do. I taught him to fight and he took in that half-breed boy. I taught him to plant and he ripped out my wheat. I taught him all a man could know and look at the women he drags home."

She closes the door between them.

Sorrow lies on the porch, limp and languid. Amaranth looks for Amity, then is glad to have Sorrow alone for a moment. "Are you sore, daughter? Will I salve you?"

Sorrow gives an almost imperceptible shake of her capped head. But at least it is not a toss. She has been humbled.

Amaranth kneels. "What you did was wrong, Sorrow. You know it."

Sorrow turns her head away.

"I know what you want. You want to go home. I know you do."

"Then why are we still here?"

“He hurt you, Sorrow.”

“It didn’t hurt,” she whines.

She reaches a hand for her daughter, sets it on the rail of her back, and she feels Sorrow shudder through the cloth. “I know how you miss him. I know what you lost. I know you don’t know any better, but—my God, what he did was wrong, Sorrow. What we all did. It was—all—all of it, wrong.”

“I don’t understand,” Sorrow whispers.

“I know you don’t. We never said—I didn’t think we had to say it. I would have thought your father . . .” She lies behind Sorrow, fits herself into the crooks behind her hips and knees, and Sorrow allows it. She thinks of how close their family was, how physically close, how few boundaries there were between bodies or beds. Children slept in half-clad clumps, baths were shared to save on water. Lonely wives shared beds and blankets, dark comforts that no one spoke of after. Sorrow had seen all of it, but there were laws and rules that were older than their community’s, laws and rules about fathers and daughters. “He took advantage. Of your faith.”

“He didn’t.”

“You think he didn’t. You couldn’t have

stopped him." Maybe no one could, she thinks, or she took too long to try.

"I didn't want to stop him."

"Oh, Sorrow." Sorrow stiffens in her arms, like a bundle of sticks.

"I will go home," Sorrow tells her.

The air is close and clammy. It presses down like hands.

Amaranth lets her child go, and it is silent. Deadly silent, as if the earth is taking a breath. And a sweetness comes from the dirt, from the air, with a snap-crack of thunder. Sorrow flips the blanket over her head. Drops begin to fall, making pits in the red earth.

Rain. Come at last.

"Come, Sorrow," she calls. She moves to the hard dirt to feel the water on her skin. The drops are soft, few and far between. They dot her long sleeves and smack her in the eye when she looks up and laughs at them. The drops come harder, fuller, coin-sized. They dampen her arms and cool her neck where she pulls her collars open. They roll up from her wrists, where she unbuttons her cuffs. She turns her face up to open her mouth, let it drop on her tongue, and then Bradley is running in from his fields, hat off and waving. "Rain!" he hollers. "Rain!"

She turns to him, hands open to feel it. He opens his own to catch it, to cup it.

She pulls the tie to her cap and undoes the bow. She loosens the gathers that hold the cap in place and she pulls. And then it is raining on her head and scalp, raining in her hair as she unpins her braids, fat as snakes, and lets them drop onto her arms. She looks at him and lets him see her, and she shuts her eyes.

She walks a slow, wet circle on the dirt. No wives, no daughters, spin with her. This is no spin of worship. It is, instead, the spin of a woman being watered after a long and lonely drought, and he steps beside her. His scalp is soaked through his cap. Points of hair make needles with raindrop tips. She can feel her skin, calling to him, and his wet hands on her wet arms. Water runs from his face to hers.

The rain comes harder still, sharp as knifepoints. Splashes join to form lakes. He puts an arm up, to shield her, but it is raining too hard.

Sorrow sits up to shout, "It's the end of

the world!" And Amaranth laughs. "It's only rain!" And then, the heavens open.

They run to the porch to stare out at the water. "Where is Amity?" she calls. They'll need an ark. Rain pours through the porch roof onto Sorrow, who is shrieking. Rain creeps between rotting shingles to dampen joists and soak the old paper on the boards. Bradley hurries into the house and holds the door open. "Come in, both of y'all," he calls, as Amaranth watches a wall of water. Where is her other child?

Sorrow burrows back beneath the blanket as rain savages the tree and the low scrub, flushing creatures out in torrents, stripping branches of dying leaves. Rain runs red dirt over fields. Rain strips the stalks of browning rapeseed. Rain flattens the wheat fields, flattens the sorghum. It washes the seeds and the jars and the freshly planted soil of the garden away.

"Where is your sister?" she yells to Sorrow. And she thinks of the whipping, the switch she threw down, and she thinks of the bone-handled paring knife that she hasn't seen since and she hasn't missed. And she wonders, again, if she even knows her child Sorrow.

20

The Scar

Amity does not wear the wrist strap. It lies on the tiled floor of the bathroom, where Sorrow threw it. It lies in the room that Dust hoses out now, the room filled with water and waste and red dirt painted in signs and symbols up and down. He takes great care to remove her stain of a red blood cross.

She waited and listened so long to the ghosts in the room that she thought it was days until Dust came, opening the door and letting in all the light.

"Is she there?" Amity asked him, her voice cracked and broken.

Dust ran some water from the sink and cupped it in his hand for her. He tried to pull her up. “She locked you in here, didn’t she? The hook was on.”

Amity tried to stand, but her legs were stuck. Her hand was throbbing. “I hurt her,” she said. When she came out of the dark room, she was amazed to see that the world had changed, entirely. What was pale red was brick red, bloodred. What was dry dripped. The world was fresh and made clean, as if it were she who had made it so with her sacrifice.

Dust brings the hose out and shuts the door. “I shouldn’t have put that lock on,” he says.

“My wrist strap,” she says. “Will you get it?”

“No. Why’s it your job to look after her?”

“I don’t know, but it is.”

Dust sucks his teeth, but he goes to get it, snapping it between his hands. Amity rips a strip from her underskirt to bind her cut and takes the strap onto her other hand, her wrong hand, her good hand now. Dust shuts the door and hooks the eye again.

"Who's gonna be the one who tells Sorrow no?" he asks her.

Amity can only shake her head. Not her. Not ever.

The devil sleeps like a dead man, cheeks sunken and jaw unhinged. Amity looks close, to see if fallen angels slip out with every snore, and when he awakens he finds Amity staring into his mouth. "What do you want?"

"You told me to come back."

"I didn't tell you to come sneakin' up on me."

Amity doesn't know how to mind people anymore. "I'll go."

"Seein' as you gone and woke me up, you may as well stay. What you got on your hand there?"

She pops her bound hand behind her back. "Nothing."

"Keep yer damn secrets. I don't care. Got secrets of my own, you know."

She smiles at him. She already knows his biggest secret, that he is the devil himself, and then the devil pulls a fast one. The devil hands her a Bible. She doesn't know it is a Bible, of course, but she knows it when the devil opens it up and reads it, passages she knows in her blood, about the beginning of the world and God's face over the dark of the waters.

"Let there be light," the devil tells her. "Let there be firmament and land and vegetation, let there be lights and birds and fishes. Should've stopped right there, old God, but He kept it going, makin' animals, makin' man, and then, by gum, goin' and makin' up woman."

She waits for him to burst into flames of damnation, but he does not. If the devil can hold a Bible and read from it, then all bets and rules are well and truly off. "I think you're just an old man," she says.

"As opposed to what—a horse's ass?"

"Only I've never seen a man so old. You're God-old. Older than my father."

"That so?"

"I've seen old women. I've seen lots and lots of old women, older than you."

"They live longer, 'cause they don't do any work."

"Well, women work harder than Father. All he does is pray and the other thing. Old women die. Are you going to die?"

The old man nods. “Eventually. I’m waitin’ for it.”

“Where will they plant you?”

“Plant me?” He squints at her. “Bury, you mean. ’Neath that tree, if I’m lucky. Put in when I was a boy. Used to be millions of ’em, windbreaks from the government, to slow down that fearsome wind. Came all the way from Siberia, them elms did. You’ve never been to Siberia.”

“I’ve never been anywhere. I don’t like the government.”

“Well, I never been to Siberia, but I was out in the Far East. Did my time and I can tell you I love this country. I don’t care two squats about the government, but I love my flag.” He puts his hand onto his heart and Amity wonders if it’s stopped. He shoves the Bible toward Amity and she dares to sit on the very edge of his bed to be near it. “Now, you go on and read me some. You’re a freeloader in this relationship.”

She looks down at the leather cover. Even if the devil could touch it for himself, she knows better than to try. She can hear something buzzing in the room, like God’s disapproval, as she tells him, “We don’t read the Bible.”

"Why not?"

"Father speaks it. He tells us what it says."

"Girl, I'm gonna tell you sumpin' about fathers. Sometimes they want too much and it makes 'em go strange. That man Icarus flew too close to the sun 'cause his daddy wanted them to fly, and most men'll set themselves on fire outta all they want. A man on fire is liable to tell his children anything."

"God is a father," she tells him.

"Well, sometimes God wants too much, too. Think about His son, eh? Think of all the people He killed in the Bible, sweepin' 'em out like ants."

She looks at his Bible, but she will not open it. She looks at her white cotton hand and sees a fly land on it, rubbing its legs together with glee.

"You can't read, can you?" the old man asks her.

"I don't need to read. I only need to cook and spin."

"Shoot," he says. "Who gone and done that to a pretty little girl like you?"

She smiles at him. "I'm not pretty, and that's a vanity besides, but I'm trying to be good. I'm trying ever so hard." She shifts her hand to get the fly off and pain grabs her palm. She can't help but cry out.

"What's with your hand, girl?"

"Nothing." She puts it back behind her.

"All right," he says. "Let's get them Joads on the road," and he reaches for his *Grapes of Wrath*. The next day, when he asks her about her hand, she tells him nothing and the Joads pack their jalopy, but by the third day, when he asks her she says, "I don't know what's wrong. I'm too afraid to look." The Joads grind to a halt.

The old man stares down the gristle of his nose at her. "Girl, you better find somebody to tell what's goin' on with you. I don't care if it's me or no, but I reckon I'm as good as any. You can't shock me. Many has tried."

She bites the knot and unwraps the bit of skirt from the wound. When it is off she can see her hand is white and puffed up, Sorrow's cut as red and gaped as a mouth.

"There's some whiff off your paw, girl," he says. And as he reads about the Joads, she can feel herself flying clean out the window and away from the house, up from Oklahoma to a world that steams, somewhere lush and green, like their California. Her hand thumps like a heart and the ground shimmies. It buckles beneath her, rises and falls. She circles the house and rises over the fields, where the soil is rich and ripe below her. She stretches her clogs out, long and low below her skirts, but she will not land—she cannot land—not in the field. Birdsong calls her from the white cloth clouds that twist above her, like bedding, and she rises, bodyless, mindless, Godless.

"Amity!" she hears and she crashes down flat. She expects the old man, but she sees it is Dust there and he is slapping her, hard. She feels the weave of a scratchy blanket beneath her good hand.

"You were real brave," he tells her. "You took it like a man."

"Did I?" She tries to sit up to look about. "What did you do to me?" She wonders if they broke a rule.

"Put this on it," he says. He gestures at a brown plastic bottle. "You got an infection, worse than when my ear went septic. Tried to pierce it with a pin, but it closed up." He tugs his earlobe. "Why didn't you tell me?"

She looks at the dark boards that make the room's walls, lined with tools and ropes and chains. She sees what looks like a row of stalls and wide barn doors, open on a slant of late sun. She sees an old motorcycle, buffed to a shine, propped on its kickstand.

"Where is this?" she asks him.

"Barn, where I sleep. I found you in the field."

"The field?"

"You were lying there with your hand up in the air, like you had a question."

"I was in the field?" Another rule, gone. She hardly had any left to mind now. "Will I live?" she asks him. She looks into her bad hand, but it's pink now and the cut subdued, like a mouth pursed.

"Let's wrap it." He searches the room for a bandage or cotton, something clean, and finally he unbuttons his own shirt and rips the sleeve off it. She lets him wind it around her wound and knot it down. She wiggles her fingers above the bandage and nods.

He rips off the other sleeve, to make them match, and she looks at his bare brown chest. He sees her looking and turns away to put his shirt back on, and that's when she sees it, a long pink scar running around the back of his arm and across his shoulder blade, across his back, like a wing removed. It is upraised, a fat channel of tissue, like a worm burrowed in it. There are stitch marks running off the scar, as though the doctor had only just tried his hand at sewing.

"That's a fine scar," she tells him.

"It's gross."

"Can I touch it?"

He looks back at her for a moment then gives a nod, the shirt loose in his hands. She wouldn't ordinarily ask to touch something. She would wait to be told or just do it, out of need, but it is a big scar and she thinks she can help it. She hopes she can. She reaches out the fingers of her good hand and puts them square on a twist of skin, a hot knot. The scar is soft and fragile, like something not yet ready: a chicken embryo, a rareripe baby. She doesn't know if she can heal anything with just one hand.

"Thresher," he says.

Her fingers slip along the length of his scar.

"You can feel where they sewed my arm

back on. It's like I couldn't grow enough skin. It still goes hot in the sun."

She feels each tiny stitch of it, trying to smooth them flat.

"You ever see a thing move that you couldn't understand?"

She thinks of the women spinning in the temple and all she'd seen in the room below. "I have," she says.

"We were cutting the field," he says. "Must have been a big crop, 'cause Bradley hasn't brought a crew in since. My *papi* was working and he let me come out with him, to stand behind the straw walker when the chaff dropped. I'd never seen anything so big, so fast, never been so close to something so magic. I must have stuck my arm in. I can't remember anything, only next thing I'm in the hospital and some nurse is saying my pa is waiting. Only it isn't my pa. It was Bradley. Anyways." He pulls the sleeveless shirt back up over his shoulders.

"I hope I get a scar as good as yours," she says.

"You're weird." He helps her up and walks her farther into the barn, hay crunching, away from the open doors to a stall.

He kneels in the straw and waves her over and she wonders what will happen, what he'll do next. But he only points down at a cardboard box, writhing with kittens, striped and plain and tortoiseshell, wriggling around a gray mother, nursing.

"Oh," she breathes and reaches in with her good hand until the mother cat screams at her.

"She's fierce," he tells her. "I'm gonna raise them to be mousers. If I stay that long. Might not, you know. You could have one, if you stay."

"Could I?" She points at a white one, its eyes as small and pink as a rat's. She would have that one and it would be her very own. She wouldn't have to share it with anyone.

"You reckon you'll stay?"

Amity looks at the kittens, wriggling like grubs, hungry as babies, and thinks that, if the time came and God came for her, she'd like to have a litter like that, five little babies, tiny and furry, clustering around her to feed. How fierce she would be then.

21
Ghosts

The fields are red mud, wet dough. Rain has filled the playa, turning flat grass beneath cottonwoods to a lake bed where stilt-legged waterbirds have magically appeared to bend and strut. Bradley assesses the damage in the rapeseed, where rain has stripped the pods of their flowers. Yellow petals crush and smear beneath their feet as Amaranth totters after him, clogs sliding, beneath a borage sky.

He presses thumbnails into browning pods, checking their moisture, waiting for them to dry. "Too wet," he says. "I swath these now, they'll mold in the ricks. Seed'll be no good then. If I wait too long they'll shatter, drop their seed." He strides on. "Shoulda stuck to wheat. I knew where I was with wheat. I don't know."

"You'll know," she tells him. She skids behind him on her wooden soles, then slips sideways from them into a rut and onto her skirts, hard on the mud.

He holds a hand down to help her up and she holds up a hand gloved in red soil. He laughs at it and she begins to laugh, and then they're laughing together and at each other, dirty in the fields. She wipes her hands in her skirts and takes his calloused hand in her stained one, coming back to her feet. She does not let his hand go.

"You keep doing that," he says.

"Falling over?" Her skirts are streaked and sodden. Mud climbs her arms.

"You need boots."

"I need hosing down."

"Go on and get a bath in the house, then," he says. "Then come on into town with me."

She drops his hand and turns away from him as a bird lands, stabbing its beak at a seedpod beside her. Bradley flaps his arms at it, stomping and frightening her and the bird to flight. She starts back for the house. "I don't think so."

"You can't hide here forever," he calls, and that stops her. Her hands grab her skirts.

"Thought I'd head in," he says. "Ask around who's cuttin' now, hire a draper header."

She turns toward him. "Am I hiding?"

"Looks it. Maybe he ain't comin' for you after all."

"You don't know him."

"A man can change his mind."

She shakes her head at him. He doesn't know what her husband has done, what he is capable of. She has hardly told him anything of what has happened and she has no idea how she will tell it to him, how to start telling. She cannot afford to become complacent or comfortable. He is coming for them; she knows it. He is only waiting for her to relax and stop watching.

"Stay, then," he says, and he marches past her, toward the house.

"You stay," she says, chasing after him

to catch him, grabbing hold of the damp back of his shirt.

"I ain't hidin'," he says, twisting out of her grasp. "Your husband don't want me. 'Less he wants himself a husband."

"Funny."

"Thought I'd get a paper, too," he calls back, over his shoulder, his thumbs jabbing seedpods reflexively, left and right. "See if there's any news of a church on fire."

"Don't!" She hops and slips behind him, pulling her skirts up from the muddy ruts. "Don't!"

He stops. "What you so afraid of?"

"Everything!" she gasps out. "He won't let us go! He won't let us live without him. We are family eternal—beyond the grave."

"That's a vow you make. Don't mean it's true."

"He'll kill us if he finds us here."

"Thought I'd kill my own wife when she left. I was that angry. But you can't keep carryin' it. It just—goes."

"Does it?" Her hand reaches for his shoulder. He turns his head for the house, so she can study the sinew of his neck, the bone and string of him, the dark hairs of his jaw on the turn to white. She puts a hand on his other shoulder to turn him to her and his arms come around her. “Don’t go,” she says, and she presses herself to him until she can feel the buttons of his jeans at her waist. She presses her hip bones to his thighs.

He looks down at her, opens his mouth to say something, maybe tell her to stop it, maybe to leave him alone, and she brings her mouth up to his, to taste his sweat and salt. Grit slides from his tongue onto hers. His hands move up her back, feeling the bodice and binding she wears. She is bound within them. There is no easy way in to her. Her breath pushes her ribs against her bindings and the circle of his hands. Her collars bite at her neck. She jerks the buttons of his jeans open.

“Hey,” he says, and she bends on the mud to him, to take him into her mouth, but he pulls her up, pulls her back up to him, then comes onto her skirts, saying, “Christ, Christ, Jesus.” He looks down at the stain of him, spreading on her stains.

She bunches her skirts in her hands to hide it. “It’s nothing,” she says.

“Nothing.” He pushes himself back into

his trousers and does up the buttons, turns his back on her.

"I mean, it's fine—I don't need—" She comes around the side of him, looking up at him. "I'm no girl, I just . . ."

He scratches his head and finds his hat gone. He scoops it up from the field and knocks it clean against his leg.

"It's only, I'm grateful to you," she starts, "and I wanted—"

"Grateful?" He jams his cap on and stomps down the row to get away from her.

"Wait!"

"I been waiting!" He stops. "Four years, my wife's gone. Four years and I ain't even looked at a woman. I've loved nothin' but fields. How long you been gone, and you're here on your knees to me?"

"I've been faithful."

"One of fifty, faithful."

"There are thousands of polygamists. Tens of thousands. It isn't only me."

"So that makes it okay?"

"It makes it hard, but we're not freaks."

He takes a step toward her. "How's it work, then? You all got a rota? You got fifty beds or do you share him?" He looks at her filthy skirts, her bodice, her cap, and he shakes his head at her. "This what you do in your church when you're grateful?"

She puts her hands over her face. It is.

A crow flaps up behind them, startling her. Its caws come like laughter as it beats the air with jagged wings. She sees its tiny feet tuck, safe under its body, how it rises and leaves them both to their standing, their silence, and another faraway crow caws its laugh.

The seedbed is flooded, more lake than garden now. The seeds she planted have drifted on water, like tiny rafts, and the furrows she made have flattened. She can't tell if any seeds remain or if they'll grow. The jars she left there have filled with rain and flushed out their seeds. She has ruined it, all of it, but she scoops the mud back into the bed, waiting for Bradley to come back.

She tucks her daughters in, lights kerosene lanterns for him in the dark. Still he doesn't come, and she begins to worry that he never will. She feels the fear her husband had when he feared they would lose their land. If Bradley were gone, they would have to leave. What right would they have to stay? And the fear comes, of leaving and of staying. She has to do something, make some kind of plan.

She takes a lantern by its handle and walks from the house, the flame throwing shadows of her over the towers of the castoffs, the car parts. Rusted metal catches the light. The gas station is lit up and she looks around the shop for the light switch or keys. If he never returned, who would care for the place? Who would care for his father?

Behind the station she sees his truck and she runs for it, lamp bobbing, to find him in the burned-out front seat, head flung back and snoring. There is a bottle half poking from a brown bag beside him, and a stack of newspaper. She doesn't look at it. She watches him sleeping, the lines of his face soft and shadowed, his eyes darting back and forth beneath his lids.

Before dawn he wakes and his steps come shaky on the ground. He follows the light of the kerosene lamp from the pile of junk around the house, where she cannot sleep. He follows her light where she moves his soil, his legs bent like a spider's, to kick a plastic bucket. He steps into its handle with his boot and it trips him, knocks him over as he tries to shake it off, while she's saying sorry, sorry. The newspaper flutters down from beneath his arm and he lands on his backside, rocks his hips to rescue the brown-bagged bottle from his back pocket. He pulls it out and feels it, checking to see if he's broken it. Finding he hasn't, he unscrews the cap and tips it back to his mouth, paper rustling. He takes a thoughtful swallow and extends it to her. "Is it late or early?" he asks her.

She looks at him and the bottle. "Did you eat in town?" she asks.

"Sure," he says. He stretches his frame along the grass. He smells strong, of alcohol and cigarettes, gasoline. She wants to kiss his mouth.

"I been drinking," he slurs. "Old Mullaley's dead. Cuttin' in the storm and fork lightning struck a grain bin. Old as my pa and still up farming, not stuck in bed hopin' to die." He sees the newspaper then, soaking up water, and he crawls over the mud path to retrieve it, shaking his knees up each time they find water. He curses, shakes the wet outside of the paper loose so she can just see, in the low light, all the pictures inside it, oversized faces, explosions, and men in camouflage, all the miseries of the world come back from town with him. "They're swathin' outside Dalhart. Reckon I'll hire a draper header, make a start." He looks down at the newspaper again, as if trying to remember how it came to be in his hands.

"Are we there?" she whispers.

He thrusts the paper at her and she flips through the pages, leaning it into a lamplight. She sees fires and the flames, but when she looks at them they are not her fire. There are fires all over the world in the paper. Perhaps no one even knows about their fire.

He takes another slug of his bottle and sets it on the dirt. "You ever seen a ghost?"

She thinks of the voice of her husband, the lights behind her in the car, pursuing her. “Yes,” she says. Maybe that is all he is.

“Thought I seen her tonight. Thought I seen her, walkin’ ahead of me, and I followed her to a bar. I was waitin’ for her to turn ’round and see how fine I was, how I was doin’ fine, and I wanted her to see it. So I followed her in, only when I got to the bar and made her look at me, she weren’t nothin’ like my wife. I’d forgotten what my own wife looked like. Don’t know who it was. And it made me drink more.”

“Sure,” she says. “I know.”

“You don’t drink,” he tells her.

“You don’t know me,” she says. “I did. I used to do a lot of things.”

“Before you got God.”

She puts her hand around the neck of his bottle. “They say God is knocking on your heart, all the time, and you only have to open it for him. I never heard it. And all of a sudden, here I am, fifty wives down.” She unscrews the top of the bottle and looks at the newspaper, fanning its wars and disasters, and she knows that someone will have reported them. Someone will have seen and told, reporters and authorities. They must be news in other papers. There is no escape. Unless—unless there is no one to tell of it, no one who will talk, or no one who survived.

The paper drops to the dirt, to flap its pages. When she shuts her eyes, she can still see fire. She hands him the bottle to take a sip. He comes to her and takes a long pull on it. She smells the liquor on him and she moves toward him, to burn herself on the liquor of his tongue. He lets her. She could drink him down. She could drink the world all of a sudden.

She pulls her cap off and pulls at her braids. They swing down and he grabs at them, like a baby beneath a mobile. She tips the liquor into him then brings the bottle to her own mouth. She kisses its familiar fire back into him. His hands pull uselessly at her bodice and lacing. There is no way in to her. Only she can pull at his buttons again. Only she can hitch her skirts and jerk her shift aside, to take hold of him and guide him into her, press him in. She fits herself over him. She tastes his tobacco, his sweat, and his liquor. She tastes something bitter on his tongue like aspirin, like regret, and she pushes herself onto him. She feels the place she kept for her husband all these years break within her, there on the wet ground, below the wide, dark sky and the bed she has planted.

Let the end of the world come, at last.

BEFORE: *The Raising of the Temple*

There were times of abundance, years when Hope's raised beds yielded miracles and bumper crops and fields burst with grain and straw. Harvester crews reaped bushels for profit and cutting crews felled ancient trees, planted when the land was young. Money flowed in from farmer's markets and arrived with the wives who would come.

There were five wives and then there were seven: Dawn, the sixth wife, who would arrive pregnant and give birth to Adam, and the seventh wife, a free spirit raised in a commune, who gave birth to

Zachariah's first son, Justice. Amaranth weaned Sorrow to suckle both boys. If she had to share her bed, she would share their babies. All would be shared. Sorrow danced and spun about them, pinching infants, making mischief with her ever-flying hands, as Zachariah blessed them, bouncing his babies, stroking the milk-full breasts of three wives.

There were eight wives, then nine, women who arrived after summers of preaching, drawn by his stories of the end times and the community that was waiting for them, all of them. The twelfth wife brought unwanted heirlooms that could be sold and deeds to land she had been living on alone, happy to give it to a family, the cost of belonging.

With twelve wives, they outgrew the house. Amaranth thought them family enough, but then there were fifteen wives, twenty wives, parcels of land and silver and cars, and the ring was passed hand to hand around the circle.

Through it all, her husband was as good as his promise. There were no secrets. Her bed was his first and she was a part of every ceremony, every ritual taking of every bride. And it became familiar to lie beside him, to watch and listen to the ragged breaths of her husband and another woman. It became easier to watch them swell and ripen from him, for they all were family, young or old, buxom or bony. No one was lonesome; no one wanted for more. She could watch him swing any babe into his arms and believe it was her child. She could watch him kiss any wife there and believe it was her wife, too. It was.

Amaranth cultivated her sister wives, learning their ways, teaching them her own and the community's. She harnessed herself to the work of the family and delighted in its growth and its bounty. She kept accounts of the riches that the family could draw upon, money the women brought. Soon they had outgrown the outbuildings and yurts. Wives and children filled and spilled from every room.

"Husband," she told him, as he returned from another summer away, two older women, future wives, struggling stiffly from his van. "Husband, we need to build something here."

"Yes," he said, and smiled. "A temple."

"No, a bigger house." Weeks later he

was scuffing his shoe heel into soil, making a line where cement would be poured. She wasn't the only wife to remember what it was that he was tracing his line around.

Builders came in from town to lay a foundation. Zachariah watched them watch his wives, all the ages and states and sizes of them, their odd mix of coats and shawls. He watched them work as if he were their foreman, hands on hips and legs spread apart, his long white hair beside the workmen's yellow hard hats, his pale linen suit beside their ripped jeans and dirty padded jackets. He did not engage in their banter or sidelong comments. He was old enough to be their father. Perhaps their grandfather.

Young wives looked for reasons to walk beside them, to make a great show of not looking at the builders, the bulk of their muscled frames. He began to urge them to hurry. Amaranth caught him examining himself in a mirror, the lines around his eyes, still pale and bright, and the sagging along his shaved jaw. She wondered if he wanted them to hurry before he got older or before they could lure away a wife. She never told him what she saw, but she was glad he could have a small taste of jealousy, a scoop of the dish his wives swallowed every day and never mentioned.

He rushed the builders, even as they said it was too cold to pour cement. The pad wouldn't harden, they said, should an early frost come. He told them to stop shirking and start building. Even so, the builders didn't finish. Nearly Christmastime, with Sorrow and Amity and his many children beside themselves with excitement, and the temple consisted of a concrete pad and a cinder-block foundation. The builders packed up their tools and wanted paying; they had their own families at home. Zachariah sent them away and told them not to return in the new year, out of spite.

That night there was an unseasonable snow and the fresh concrete cracked and chipped. He cursed the builders, having the kind of tantrum she would have expected from Sorrow. "Husband, calm," she said, putting a hand on his forehead.

He shook it off. "The world is ending, woman. There is no calm."

Amaranth could only hope his rush and

worry had nothing to do with what lay below the foundation. Her husband had marked the rectangle with his heel and said, "Upon this rock, we will build our church." And he built it upon her, the old, old woman who had owned the land. His second wife. Her body would be bone now, nothing but teeth and spiraled nails and flat land to hold a church up.

On the last night of the year and the decade and the century and the millennium, he gathered his family around where the temple would be. Women wrapped themselves in layers, every piece of clothing they had. They swaddled sleepy babies in blankets. They huddled in a circle to watch their patriarch raise his hands to the frosty sky.

He started grumpily, piteously, deriding the builders and their lack of a work ethic, the lack of a shelter on such a night. But then, as if remembering the occasion and the company, he began to preach as he always had done when he had met his wives in some town, some city, some field, or parking lot. "All the world prepares for the end of time. You can feel it, like a sickness. I feel it in my haste. Machines conspire against us. Our enemies lie in wait.

The world is coming apart at the seams and the great clock wound by God is out of time. Do you feel it?"

The two newest women, not yet wives, nodded and sobbed, clinging to one another. To Amaranth, it felt like a news report from the moon. Over the last years he had spoken names to them, examples of the wickedness of the world, but they meant nothing to her: Hale-Bopp and Heaven's Gate, sarin gas in a Tokyo subway, the Order of the Solar Temple, Waco.

He told them to make their reparations and say their good-byes. They all must be ready to meet their God, temple or no. The newest wives began to cry out; they begged to go into town, to call their loved ones. Amaranth clutched her daughters to her—Sorrow complaining, Amity compliant—knowing she had no one to contact. Here was all she loved.

Sorrow squirmed away to stand with her father, to raise her hands as he did.

"Here is your family," he called to them. "Here is the family that chooses you! Fear God and give Him glory!"

"Fear God and give Him glory!" they called back.

“For two thousand years ago a baby was born who changed the world. A baby was born, like any baby, born like every child born here. Let us remember that every child can change the world. Every baby can be a new Messiah!”

Wives with rounded bellies patted them. Wives with babies rocked them. Older women’s eyes glistened, hopeful and dreamy. Each could remember a world of solitude, of hostile and silent cities, lonely nights that stretched into lonely years. Each spoke of what her family meant, how it saved her when the world itself had failed.

The newest wives spoke first of their terror and the lifeline that was thrown to them when they heard him speak in the parking lot where they had gone looking to steal or buy anything but redemption or hope. An old wife called out, her voice low and scratchy, “I had no one and nothing. Here, I have a family.”

“I have found people who do not judge me,” said Dawn, the sixth wife. “I have found a place to heal,” said the fourth and fifth wives together. “I have found a sisterhood,” Hope said, and she gave Amaranth’s elbow a squeeze.

All eyes fixed on Amaranth, and as she opened her mouth to speak, a new wife spoke out, “It’s almost midnight!” Eyes fixed on battered wristwatches and babies’ faces; eyes fixed on husband and the sky.

Sorrow began her counting down, proudly. “Ten. Nine.”

Adam joined the counting. “Eight.”

“God,” a woman breathed out while another gave a nervous giggle.

“Seven.”

“Praise the Lord!” called a dark-skinned wife, her face wide in smile.

“Six.”

Amaranth felt a surge of love radiating from the circle. She had only ever wanted to feel a part of a family, to feel a part of something bigger and older and deeper than herself.

“Five.”

“I love you,” a wife called across the circle, to no one in particular.

“Four.”

“I love you,” another called back.

“Three.”

Amaranth called out to her husband, to everyone. “I love you.”

“Two.”

Then all of them called it, "I love you, I love you," in a tangled chorus until—

"One." And Zachariah reached his arms out in either direction, as if to say goodbye.

Sorrow cried out, "I want to see God!" They waited for him to be taken up. They waited to follow, to see the very face of God together.

When the sun was pink in the far horizon and children had fallen asleep where they stood, he turned and walked away from them. Mothers huddled their children into their shelters and cars and beds, unwrapping their layers with frozen fingers, too cold and tired to give thanks anymore. The world had not ended and no one minded. In the spring, they would start to build their temple again.

22
The Field

Machines cut the fields down, toppling stalks, chopping them off, and flinging them into piles. Amity watches from the old man's window.

Mother asked for help in the harvest, but Sorrow said no and told Amity she'd better not, either, though Mother said they were needed in the fields.

"Fields," Sorrow snapped. "Fields, Mother!"

"There is nothing in these fields," Mother said, and another rule burst into flame before them. "We made up the rule to keep you out of them."

"What was in them?" Amity asked, pestering, but Mother ignored her.

"Rules are all we have," Sorrow said.

"People are all we have."

Sorrow scoffed. "We don't need people."

"We don't need rules. They're like a story," Mother said. "Like a fairy story you read. Well, you wouldn't. But you know what a story is?"

Sorrow shook her head and Amity thought of the Joads, still trying to get to California. She didn't think they'd ever find Eden at the rate the old man was reading to her.

"Next you'll tell us Father's stories are made up," Sorrow said. "Or that the Bible is made up." She'd grinned at Amity.

"Well, the stories of the Bible are written by men, so they are stories, yes."

"But not made up! It is God speaking, every word, and I should know it!" Sorrow marched across the porch. "You speak with the devil's mouth. You shake the devil's body!"

"Stop it, Sorrow."

Sorrow pointed her strapped hand, making Amity point. "I see how you look at that man. I hear you in his kitchen. He is shamed for the way he looks at us."

"He's not looking at us."

"I see him look."

"He's not looking at you. Not all men look at you."

"Can't we pray?" Amity said, and both her mother and sister glared at her. "If we pray we'll know what to do."

But when the farmer caught Mother trying to pry Sorrow's hands from the newel post and drag her to the field, he hauled Mother into the kitchen, where they could hear him yelling at her through the screen. "She's afraid of it, ain't she? What's the point of scaring her more? I don't want her out there, working near equipment, if it scares her. It's too dangerous. She's a hazard."

"She's spoiled," Mother said.

"I won't argue with that," he said. "But it's too late."

Sorrow's face was tight as binding. She pulled Amity close. "You will not go in that field," she said. And at that very moment she knew it. She understood why fields were forbidden. Fields could make you want more for yourself than God and Sorrow wanted you to have.

"C'mon back to this story," the old man says.

Amity jams the wet towel into the gap around his window, as Mother told her to, to keep the dust of harvest from the house. The old man says all of Oklahoma used to feel like that when he was a boy, like the very air was made of dirt. It was all you could do to breathe it in.

"It's too hot," she tells him, fingers on the glass to look out at the harvest and all she's missing.

"This ain't hot," he tells her, coughing. "When I was a boy you could cook an egg on your own head, it was that hot. You could put your cow out in the sun and have steak for lunch; just take a bite off her rump."

He opens his old book at the front again. "Listen here," he said. " 'In the roads where the teams moved, where the wheels milled the ground and the hooves of the horses beat the ground, the dirt crust broke and the dust formed. Every moving thing lifted the dust into the air.' "

"Wait—are you starting over from the beginning?" she asks.

"So what if I am? I'll tell you, girl, for a man born in California, your man Steinbeck knows his apples from his onions, even if all we grow is wheat. Well, I grew wheat. Don't know what he's growin' out there, damn fool boy."

"Why do you grow things when the land wants to be dust?" she asks him.

"Land can't think, girl. It ain't got no opinions. Land just does what you make it do."

"It turned to dust on the Joads. It didn't want to grow wheat for them."

"We made it grow. We weren't no Joads. We didn't go nowhere." He puffs his chest out and takes to coughing, giving such savage hacks that she finally has to bang on his chest to get him to stop. "My ma did that," he tells her, and he lies back again, comforted. "We were the ones that stayed, even when dust put the sun out."

"Just like the end of time," she whispers.

"You cut me open, you'll find me stuffed full of it, like a vacuum bag. It'll kill me one of these days. You wait and see if it don't."

Amity looks at him. "I've seen people die."

"Well, I have, too, but I don't go 'round braggin' 'bout it."

"I hope you don't die," she tells him.

"Well," he says. "Well."

• • •

The field is calling to her, calling from the old man's window, calling from the house. It calls from the dirt-strewn threshold, where Sorrow kneels to rock, and Amity would do anything to get away from her. The field calls her like Dust calls. She runs to its edge to call back, "Don't you have any rules, Dust?"

"No!" He broadcasts seed in low, wide arcs, reseeding sorghum. Every time he finishes a row he walks toward her. "I don't need rules. I have sense and guts."

She looks at him doubtfully. "Guts?"

"What your body knows. When something strikes you as right or wrong, right there." He gives her stomach a poke. It flips beneath her pinafore at his touch.

She puts her hands on top of it. She knew he was right. Everything about him was right. Where his fingers poked did a leap every time she thought of him.

He snaps a grass stalk and twirls it between his fingers to make a whirligig. "You'll miss the harvest," he tells her.

"I know," she says, miserable. "We missed it at home, too."

"God makes fields grow. God makes

the harvest and the seed and the rain. They should have taught you God is a field."

"He isn't," she whispers. "God is God, God is the Father." It's all she knows for sure.

"I don't believe in God. Not your God."

"What if you go to hell?" she asks him, eyes wide.

"Your God is hell." He shows her his hands, filled with seeds. They wiggle on his hand from sweat, from static, but they wiggle like they're alive. They wiggle like they want to grow, right now, right into his skin.

She looks at the field and the cut crops, the flying dust. She looks at the boy and her stomach barrel-rolls. And it feels good.

If God made the land and God made the field and God was earth, then how could it be forbidden? If her body wanted the field and the dirt, to run in it and laugh inside it, then how was it wrong? And if God showed her Dust, then he was of God. It made her wish she'd thought to ask at home, when someone might have answered her. Why did she never ask why?

23
Harvest

When the seed in the ricks is dry enough, Dust drives the faded harvester and Bradley stops him often, shouting to check the sieve, check the chaffer and the fans. Dust does as he's told, never arguing, never sulking, as Bradley nods up at the boy, shouting praise and correction in equal measure. They both keep their eyes on the path of the sun and the chain they drag behind them, grounding the static lest they start a fire in the stubble, where black birds squat in the shade of the swaths and rise up, complaining, at the noise of the engines or at Amaranth's approach, the swing of her skirts. They flap and drop back behind the machine to pick at whatever is left in its wake, seed or grubs, as the big-wheeled harvester floats down the rows like some paddleboat on a sea of grass.

In the heat of day, Bradley calls a break and the boy runs the harvest to bins in tar-black barns in the middle of the field while he oils and adjusts the old machine, shirtless, turning brown and hard as seed. She brings them out jars of water and food in napkins, watches them eat, wanting to linger in the easy companionship of the man and boy while her own daughters scowl at her from the house. How has she come to raise two such lazy creatures?

There is work in the harvest, hard work. She cooks dense food that will keep them going, patties and salads of beans and grains, flavored with shoots from the land, the rain: chickweed, wild garlic. She butchers a store-bought chicken he brings her from town, fries it in flour and Crisco. She flits about his kitchen, playing house, emptying the bins of food, while her children avoid her. Only in moments between the hard work of harvest, the carrying and hauling, the walking and baling, does she think of the two of them and wonder what they see of her, there in the fields.

When they get back to work, she wants to fling herself down before him and his machinery, to be cut fast and eased down into stubble, cut hard and made into something good and real.

By night, she stalks bugs in the seedbed with the kerosene lamp. She fingers the fragile shoots, brushing away aphids to crush in her hands. She does not know what she is growing, what the green dusting of the dirt will become. By sundown he is behind her, exhausted, happy, hopeful. She touches his cheek and down the strings of his neck, unsnapping his shirt to kiss the hollow at the base of his throat, the bridge of his clavicles. She unties her apron and lets it drop. She rolls down her thick stockings, tucks them safe inside her clogs. She pulls the tie of her bodice as he leans his forehead onto hers, saying, “Come on in the house.”

She wants to, but she could stop this still. It would only have been liquor the first time. It could be forgotten. The dark tree above them strains across his house. New leaves stand, bright as mint. Could the ghost of her husband reach her there? Was wanting this man in his bed, in his house, any different from wanting him in the dirt? When he takes her hand and tugs her, she collects her things and follows.

"Mother?" Amity calls. "Mother?" Sorrow calls. They watch her on the porch, at the door. "Shh," she says, and pulls it between them.

He leads her up the stairs. This is wrong. Sin, her head says, and she knows it is. She follows him across the landing, past the old man calling, "That you, son? That you?"

He opens the door to his bedroom, musty, old dust and skin. When he switches the light on, she sees a double bed, an old bureau, a spindly telescope before an open window, letting in all the dust of his harvest to coat every surface, the stacks of receipts and newspapers, the crushed cans and cigarette packets on the floor. He flings back his dirty covers and dust puffs up, balls of socks fly, so they laugh and sneeze. He steps out of his clothes and hops under the covers, shy.

She sets her clogs and her apron down to unlace her bodice, eye by eye. She unties the neck lacing of the overblouse and contemplates the layers still to go as she sees the window, open, over her daughters and switches his light off. In the gloom, she pulls off the tight underblouse and then begins to roll the binding that flattens them, unwinding the strip from around her and winding it again to make a ball that she can toss at him. He catches it, rolls it in his hands, and watches her, unbound, the heavy, swinging shape of her in her last layer of linen. How many layers they have. She unhooks the overskirt, the skirt, and the underskirt and shuffles out of the bloomers until she stands in the white cotton shift all wives wear, sewn over the shoulders and split between the legs.

She touches his chest, the bone and skin, the rack of ribs. His nipples harden beneath her hands. She runs her tongue across them and his taste is different from her husband's: dark, metallic, a rock in the mouth. She thinks she should stop comparing them, but doesn't know how.

His fingers find her nipples through her cloth and press them, like testing grain, and she knows these will be different for him; she's suckled children and his own wife and bed were childless. His wife before her will have had breasts that were small, maybe, tight and high as a girl's, thin, flat hips like a boy's. She doesn't care. She is used to these comparisons in her own bed. Whose empty breasts sagged like sleeves before or after her, back home? Whose taut breasts needed no binding to sit flat beneath her husband's hands?

"Where have you gone?" he asks her.

She can feel his sex crawl on her leg. She cannot tell him she is flat on her back in a room filled with women. She cannot tell him her head is filled with women's bodies, wives and a husband, his soft, clean hands.

She pulls herself back to him, this salty scent and their two lonely bodies, this dirt, these rocks. She takes hold of the front of the sewn shift and pulls it hard. She wonders if her daughters below can hear it tearing. When he asks she tells him they are sewn in, all of them, and he takes hold of the fabric himself, rips it wide down the front of her, opening breast and belly and crotch to his eyes and breath and fingers like a slaughter. He reaches his hand between her legs and takes a breast in his mouth.

She looks up at the dark of the ceiling. She tells herself she is not home. This is not a marriage bed and she will not come for him. She should not. She does not expect to, with this dirt and his skin so strange to her touch. She does not deserve to, with her daughters below and the ghosts of her family so close, here in the bed with her, claiming her still. This is not the purpose of this sex, she tells herself. She wants only to bind herself to him, same as any ritual. But with his mouth and fingers and strangeness she can feel herself bucking, tipping and rocking, becoming truly unfaithful in body and in spirit.

Come morning, she hauls up his sheets to boil them. There is a dark stain on the mattress ticking, not her stain. It is an old stain, old blood and a lot of it, and she thinks of the Bible's three red dots. She sets her hand upon it, then lays fresh sheets across, to make it disappear again.

Does he feel the ghost of his wife in this bed still? Or has she banished it with her own skin and its claim on him? Can he feel how she traces her name in finger-nailed loops on him, as if she can stitch herself down to him, like a sheet?

That night, in the dark of his room, she lies hot and sharp beside him, breathing in the stench of their working. He sleeps, still as the dead. She pulls him to her, his skin humming from the thresher, and he rolls over, laughing. “Woman, leave me be,” he says, but she will not until she bursts into flower beside him, heavy with seed. She holds him in the darkness and he holds her back, no bodies but theirs, and she thinks then that redemption is possible. Even for her. Even in this moment of skin and scent is an affirmation that this is enough, and if God or any of His jealous angels were to look down now, surely they would not begrudge her this wild joy.

24

The Living and the Dead

When Sorrow isn't watching and the old man falls asleep, Amity sneaks down the stairs to her mother in the kitchen. There she is, scooping out handfuls of her constant beans. She looks tired and sticky when she asks Amity, as she daily does, to take water to the fields, and then surprised when Amity says she will. "Good girl," she calls her.

Amity spies for Sorrow, creeping toward the fields with the jars of water held in the crook of her arm, heavy as babies. She steps into the weedy strip along the fields and waits for him.

Dust hoots at her, calling for water.

"Look at me in the fields!" she calls back. She lifts her skirt and wafts it over the edge of the field. She lifts a clog and holds it in the air. She holds her breath. She waits and prays for God to tell her it's fine or to stop her, until she must step down and breathe or risk falling over. Then she pulls the field into her lungs and sets her foot onto the dirt. Then she is running for Dust, running for the field, cradling his water, sloshing and crowing, "I'm in the field—I'm in the field!"

He takes her jars and takes her hands. The jars drop and roll, but do not break. He swings her, fairly swings her in the field. Around and around he swings her, very nearly like a spin, but he wouldn't know it, like a brand-new form of prayer. And then he stops her, breathless. "What do you hear?"

She pants, her heart pounding. She poises for thunder, heaven opening to pour down venom from every angel's bowl of wrath. "Birds," she says with wonder. "Crickets. Bees."

"What do you see?"

She shuts her eyes. “Dirt. Rocks. Sky.” You.

He bends to take a handful of chaff. He throws it high, so it falls like straw snow over her, her cheeks, her cap. When she opens her eyes he is looking at her, truly seeing her, and then they are throwing and spinning and cartwheeling in the cut field like the kid she is and the kid he wants to be, there in the fields, before God and all He wants for them. And the world refused to end.

Sorrow is waiting when she leaves it; she is watching for her from its very edge. There is red dirt around Sorrow’s mouth and down the front of her, as if she has been rubbing it into herself and eating it. Perhaps she has.

“You coming in?” Dust calls, smiling.

Amity can feel the straw poking from her skirt and cap as Sorrow’s hands worry themselves around the strap. Her eyes accuse her.

“It isn’t evil,” Amity says. “It isn’t anything. The fields are just dirt, like Mother said.”

Sorrow rushes at Amity and slaps her

dirty hands over her mouth, strap swinging around her neck.

"Sorrow!" Dust shouts.

Amity peels back her sister's fingers, turning her head from her. "Nothing happened," she says. "We didn't do anything."

Sorrow narrows her eyes at both of them, from the dirt of their shoes to their sunburned cheeks.

Dust lets loose a laugh then. "You don't scare me, Sorrow."

"Don't," Amity whispers. "She's proud."

"Scared of a field. You don't scare anybody."

Sorrow looks at Amity and her face is white around her red dirt mouth. She rips off the wrist strap and throws it at Amity's feet. Then she turns on her clog and goes.

"She's nothing but a bully," Dust says.

"I know." Amity watches the shape of her sister, how her long shadow reaches into the fields even if her body won't.

They see then, even as Sorrow is looking back at them, that the barn doors are open. Dust goes to check each metal bin and pull each padlock. "She wasn't in here," he says. In the barn where he sleeps, his motorcycle has fallen over, the kickstand tucked in. "Big deal," he says, tenderly righting it, shaking his head.

Then they hear a horrible howling.

Dust rushes back to the stable walls, back where the kittens are, and she sees him pulling the tumbling bits of fur apart to count them, "One, two, three, four . . ." he counts, again and again as the mother cat screams. "Where's the white one?"

"Was Sorrow here?" is all that Amity can say.

Sorrow is not on the porch, not at her bathroom door. But she has been there. There is fresh dirt heaped before the door and sticky red dirt handprints up its face. There are all of her signs and symbols, her swirls and fingerprints. Set before it is a broad, flat rock and on it are more of Sorrow's symbols, her dots and spirals, telling God and the holy world of Amity's betrayal. She has seen them up and down every wall of the room.

She doesn't have to lift the rock. She can see the small white flattened paw sticking out.

She curls her good and her bad hand in. She knows she cannot heal this. There is no point in rubbing them together to heat them, to press them onto its flesh. Only God can raise the dead and she knows better than to try. She searches for a prayer in her head for the kitten, but all she can think of is, "Make Sorrow stop." In the corner of a field she buries the kitten, the rock planted over it where Sorrow would never see it. If Sorrow notices that they are gone, she never says.

She doesn't tell Dust or the old man. She doesn't tell Mother. She tucks the murder away with all her other secrets, the ones she keeps for Sorrow that she will not, will not tell.

BEFORE: *Eve and Sorrow*

When her daughter was born, Amaranth could only think of Eve. “I will greatly multiply thy sorrow,” the Bible said. “Thy desire shall be to thy husband and he shall rule over thee.” Giving birth, her husband away and Hope panting over her, breathing for her, she knew what she would name her second child, should she live.

Eve had been a thin and placid child. She asked little of Amaranth. Too little. She wouldn’t latch on, wouldn’t try to suck. She might take a little bit of something, honey or whey offered on a fingertip, but then her head would simply drop to the side.

Amaranth was worn from carrying her and worrying for her, exhausted from birthing her and trying to keep her. She had walked for months with eggshell steps, filling like a great balloon of blood and willing her to stay, because she had lost so many. All the beginnings of babies they made slinked inkily into the bowl, season after season, making her body a desert. Perhaps Eve was only as worn out as she.

Hope did what she could with her poultices and tinctures, treating Amaranth's tear wounds and trying to strengthen Eve. But it was the other women, the two who kept to themselves, who finally came to say that they would drive her.

"Where?" said Amaranth, huddled over the limp little body.

"Hospital," they said.

No one knew of the birth or Eve's existence. Born at home, she was unregistered. There would be forms to fill in, people to tell, things to explain, and Amaranth feared that Eve would be taken from her when they saw she couldn't care for her. She would lose the only child that she had kept. But soon, even drawing breath seemed too much of an effort for Eve. The women took the baby to the car and she followed, like a dog after meat. She prayed their way down the gravel path, wishing for her husband and miracles, but Eve was pale and blue by the time they reached the local hospital, staggering into the fluorescence, while nurses hissed behind them, "Hicks and junkies."

Her breasts and her eyes leaked and emptied, useless. They said they would have to keep the baby, to examine it before they sent it to the mortuary. There, she could pick out a coffin and choose her burial or cremation. She knew her husband would not want a record of the death, no paperwork, no government. Hope patted her knee, relentlessly, but she could hardly feel it. Her arms were empty, her body a husk.

Lights of the town flickered over her face. Potholes made her head bounce into the window, until she wanted to shatter her own head. Colors danced across her, a bright neon martini glass and the green bulb of an olive, flicking off and on. A giant, lit-up beer mug endlessly filled up and drained away, reminding her that there was a way she could forget.

"Stop," she said. Voices drew her toward a padded door.

The two women waited in the car, mouths set and radio news on, talking about a famine, but Hope followed her in and up to a bar lined with glowing bottles: emerald, sapphire, topaz. The air was blue with smoke and she breathed it in. "What'll you have, ladies?" a man asked, wiping chunky glasses.

"Bourbon," she said. "No, wine. No, brandy."

Hope smiled and slid a twenty toward him. "Bottle of Gallo, two glasses, two fingers of Ten High neat." She led Amaranth away from the bar stools to set her, dazed, into a booth. Someone dumped coins into a jukebox and some honky-tonk came on. A waitress in a denim skirt plopped the bottle, all the glasses, and a pile of cocktail napkins onto their wood-veneer table. She felt suddenly, sweetly at home.

Drops rolled off the bottle as Hope filled a glass for Amaranth, put an inch in her own glass, and wiped the ring off the table. Amaranth held the wineglass to her nose. It smelled of grass and rubber. She tipped half the liquid back, cold and slightly effervescent on her tongue, grainy in her throat. She grabbed the other glass and slung the bourbon back, shuddering. She hadn't had a drink in years.

"I don't know what I'm doing," she told Hope, feeling the liquor loosen her.

"I know," Hope said.

She tipped the rest of the wine down her throat and set the glass down. She watched Hope reach a hand across the table, as if to refill the glass. But instead she reached for Amaranth's hand, took it in her own. She wondered what a room full of pool-playing rednecks would make of it. "It's my fault," Amaranth said.

"It isn't."

"I lose everything." She looked down at the shapeless tunic she was wearing. She thought of carrying Eve beneath her dress, beneath her skin. "There's something wrong with me. Everybody leaves."

"They don't, Amy."

"Don't you tell me it's God's will, so help me."

"I'd never." Hope raised her glass. "Look at me. I haven't had a drink in over twelve years now. God knows I made some mistakes."

Amaranth looked at her hand in Hope's hand, saw their nails were dirty, both hers and Hope's, dark from digging or trying to save Eve. "You never lost a baby."

"Yeah? I was so high I couldn't remember it. I nearly drank it out of me, gave birth to a body. Was that God's will?" She sank her Ten High and swallowed. "I didn't want it. God doesn't kill people or save them. People do." She shrugged. "Zachariah told me I could clean up and start again and he made me want to try. Simple as that. And as hard."

Amaranth looked into her glass. "You don't know how dark it is in me."

"I can guess. We've all been given a second chance here."

A man in a camouflage cap sidled up to the table, bumping his groin against its edge. "Buy you girls a drink?"

Amaranth looked at Hope, who just smiled sweetly at the man. She looked out the window at her husband's car to see the dark shapes of the two women inside it, waiting for her as her husband was not. She thought, this is my family, these women here.

She turned back to him. "We don't like men."

"Amy!" Hope laughed as the man reared back from the table, saying, "People like you make me sick."

She grabbed her glass and pushed it to Hope for a refill. She had only ever wanted a family, to love and belong to, and she thought of the time when she first arrived, when she saw the women there, women she didn't know and hadn't expected, and thought she was better than them because he'd married her. She thought with a start that she should have married them, not her husband. It was these women who stayed when her husband did not. It was these women who cared for her and loved her in her failing. Her husband didn't even know that she had had Eve and already she'd lost her. Her thumb picked at the oversized ring she wore, hers alone.

She and Hope drained the bottle and ordered more and drank together until the room spun and the music got sadder and her eyes cried wine and all she could say was Eve. She held Hope's hands and kissed her. She sang with her and tried to dance until she'd knocked a table over and the camouflage man called them lesbians. "Lesbians!" she'd slurred. "We only live together!" They drank until the barman cut them off and the two women came in at last to help them to the car, heads lolling, floor tilting, men hooting, and Patsy Cline singing them out and falling to pieces.

"I love you all," Amaranth slurred from the backseat. "I would marry you all, every one of you."

Come autumn, they were married. Zachariah to Hope and the two women, all of them to Amaranth, by the grave of the second wife. Amaranth passed her ring to the three sets of fingers. The two women kissed each other and Zachariah and Amaranth kissed Hope, again and again. At last, she felt, she had a sister.

At the ceremony's end, he took Amaranth to bed, only Amaranth, and they grieved and cried for Eve. It was nothing like after the ceremony with the second wife. He held her alone and was tender with her. He promised he wouldn't leave her, but she knew he would, come spring, come summer. He would always leave—she knew that now—but she was sure he would come back for her. That was his promise. She was first and last. He would come for her and she would wait, after all the running she had done.

She stitched the women's names to the sheet, all the women she loved who loved her, around the name of the second wife. Then she stitched Eve down under her own name, grayed and fraying. She told herself that she would have another child and when she did she would hold it over Eve's name to tell it that once there was a sister. Eve would always be that sister, even as every wife who died would still be a wife. Family would be family forever. It was their best hope.

When her daughter came, the name she stitched was Sorrow.

Part III

JULY

25

The Grain Elevator

Amity and Dust are flying in the pickup bed, speeding down the highway in the sun. They are pelted with pellets, escapees from the haulage truck laden with the season's rapeseed. It snaps on their faces, pings off the truck. Clothes flapping, hanging onto hat and cap, they watch the land turn small green fields to broad brown fields where sun on silver silos and metal hog barns makes them squint. They hold their noses from the muck of pigs.

When they reach the grain elevator, Amity stands to shake the harvest from her skirts. Bradley lopes into the office and

Dust hitches a leg over the truck bed to watch him, explaining how it works, how they'll weigh the truck full then weigh the truck empty. "The difference in weight is the seed we're selling."

Mother and Sorrow sit, locked inside the burned-out cab, holding the wrist strap. The farmer walks back to them with slow, serious steps. His head is down and his shoulders hunched. "Test weight's low," says Dust. "Too dry or too wet. Damn." But then the farmer gives a sudden haroop, boots a little sideways crab dance toward the truck. He takes off his hat and flaps it, like he's too hot for his own good and he knows it. Dust leaps down so they can slap one another on their backs and Mother laughs and claps her hands in the cab, and all feels right with the world. Only Sorrow is silent. Amity hops up and down in the back of the truck, clogs rolling over seed, glad to be unstrapped from her.

"Test weight sixty-two and moisture ten," Bradley calls out. "Not epic by any stretch, but okay. Best yield I ever cut. Okay, first yield I ever cut, still it means that maybe I won't lose my damn farm—maybe it means you girls only went and brung me some goddamn luck after all." He bangs on the cab's roof and gives a rooster crow. He runs around to Mother's side of the truck and hauls her out to swing her. But he's forgotten she's strapped, so Sorrow swings out, stunned and straining, swinging around the two of them before she can free herself.

Once they're off the highway, fields give way to parking lots and rows of buildings on either side. The road narrows as they turn toward town, and Amity watches for Mother's signal to duck down and hide, but it never comes. So she watches as the street does a circle dance around a red-brick building, grand with four cream columns standing upright as apostles. "Is that your temple?" Amity shouts above the roar of cars.

"It's the courthouse!" Dust hollers.

Bradley drives them down a main street lined with windowed shops, bright colors and striped awnings, flags flapping and piles of goods: shoes and ladders, lawn mowers, fruit. He pulls them into a busy parking lot and finds a space beside an expanse of yellow grass, where he points at a dark bar and tells them that's where he'll be if they have any catastrophes, but Amity's off, racing toward a metal gang of animals, dashing from the truck and across the grass to mount the back of a giant squirrel. It grinds on a rusty spring. Mother shouts behind her, "Watch where you're going—watch for cars; stay with Dust—do as he tells you!" She doesn't see Mother telling Dust what it is he may and may not tell her to do.

Dust calls her from the squirrel and walks her through the town, the fluttering, glorious wonder of it, all the people walking and driving, all the people staring. She smiles back at them, everyone, but they only stare. "Why do people stare so?" she asks him.

"Well, look at you," he says.

She does look, in every window they pass, but she sees nothing remarkable. She's smiling and they aren't. She's dressed and they aren't, for the most part, with their toes exposed and their pantaloons cut off, way up at their crotches. In one window alone a whole row of women sit with their heads uncovered, hair hanging long and wet down their backs, right there where anyone could see them. She gasps as a man shears each one with his scissors. "I should stare," she says.

"Women don't cover up so much as you do." He only stares at a window full of dark blue jeans and pointy-toe boots in every kind of leather.

She tugs on his sleeve. "You said you'd take me where the books are."

"Today ain't all about you," he says. "I'm the one just got paid for working." He goes inside and she tells him she'll wait right outside. "I promised your ma I'd watch you," he says. "Don't go anywhere. Stay right there."

Amity tries to stand still, but the town moves her. Women push babies in carts so wide she has to jump out of the way and into the street, where cars honk and make her jump back. Big girls march by in high-heeled packs, spread across the sidewalk, and they must be run from, their pointing and laughing. And when she stops to look for Dust, she can no longer find his window. She can't find his stack of pants or boots, or mother, truck, or squirrel.

She walks in circles to look for help. She knows better than to speak to strangers, but when she finds a modest woman, her dress well below her kneecaps and a hat of straw on her head, she goes to her and takes her hand.

The woman withdraws it, sticky, and leans down to her. “You need something, sweetie?”

“The house of *The Grapes of Wrath,*” she says. And when the lady tries to leave, she sings out, “Library! Library!” remembering the old man’s name for it.

When she gets to the door, she knows it is the best of temples—dark and lit by small windows, where motes spin in shafts of light like tiny angels and the quiet hush of pages turning, soft as cloth on boards. A woman stands at its center instead of an oracle, with long purple hair and a silver star on her chest.

Amity walks to her and speaks in her bravest voice, loud and clear. “I have come for your *Grapes of Wrath.*”

“Shh,” says the woman. A slim silver ring in her nose wiggles when she smiles then, whispering, “Fiction’s in the corner.”

“Thank you!”

The woman frowns. “Shh.”

The walls and the dark shelves are lined

with books, old as the old man's, their spines in lines like a jiggedy rainbow. They are cool and slick in plastic sleeves when she touches them and when she pulls them out she can see their pictures: platters of meat and birds of prey, women bulging lustily from gowns and creatures wrapped in bandages. She presses on for a hand with grapes, setting the books down onto the floor.

"What are you doing?" The woman is beside her then, picking her books up and sliding them back onto shelves so she won't know where she's looked now.

"I'm looking for *The Grapes of Wrath*."

"Well, you're not even in fiction. You ought to be in the children's section anyway. You don't belong here."

"I know," she says. "Dust told me to wait."

The woman points her back into the corner and Amity moves her way toward it, distracted by dogs and soldiers and cakes, and when at last she pulls the book out, she gives a mighty "Hallelujah!" A shush comes from every table as she dances the book to the door.

"What do you think you're doing?" The

purple-haired woman catches hold of her book.

"I'm taking *Grapes of Wrath,*" Amity says.

"No, you are not."

"The old man says they're free."

"Well, they're not." The woman looks around the room, as if for help or divine intervention. "You need a library card to check them out." She looks at the book's cover. "This is *Viticulture for Fun and Profit.* What is this?"

"Those are grapes, ma'am. Grapes of wrath, ma'am."

"Does it say 'grapes of wrath' here?"

Amity looks up at her. "I don't know what it says, ma'am."

"Look, we have a section of picture books and easy readers. Let me show you where those are. Why don't you bring your mother back with you? Or your father?"

"Sorrow says he's coming."

The woman finally folds her arms around the book. "Young lady, this is no place to play games. Run along now. Go."

Outside in the sun there is no Dust waiting for her. There is only a peeling bench and a girl atop it, beside a giant stack of books. She knew how to get them.

"Hello," says the girl.

Amity flinches. The girl is smiling at her, not staring, not pointing. She looks—like Amity. Her dress is dark and her head is covered, not with a cap but with a crisp blue triangle of fabric, holding auburn twists back from her face.

Amity gives her a smile. "You're a modest people like we are, aren't you? I thought it was only us."

"We're Mennonite. What are you?"

"What's Mennonite?" Amity scoots closer. "Are there more of you?"

"Of course. My family and our church."

Amity nods. "How many sisters and brothers do you have?"

"Four brothers. No sisters. I wish I had a sister."

"You can have mine," Amity tells her and the girl laughs. "How many mothers do you have?"

"Why?" says the girl. "How many do you have?"

"Fifty." Amity looks at the girl.

"What do you do with fifty?"

"Well, I only have one father."

The girl leans in. “What’s it like to have fifty mothers? Do they all tell you what to do?”

It was getting harder to remember it. “Mostly, when we’re all in a circle and they’re spinning, it feels like the whole of the world is my mother. The whole world is spinning in love.”

The girl looks around them and whispers, “Aren’t you afraid you’ll go to hell—or to jail?”

“No. We’re the chosen ones.”

“We’re the chosen ones,” the girl says, straightening the pile of books between them. “What you do is most likely a sin, but it’s not my place to judge you.”

A long green car pulls up with plenty of empty seats. The girl grabs her books and skips to it as Amity calls behind her, “Maybe I could come home with you?” She pictures herself a Mennonite, her hair swinging out from a smart navy triangle. The woman driving wears a kerchief and she gives Amity a smile. But once her daughter points at Amity from the front seat, they both stare until Amity turns away from them. And then they go.

26
The Tiny Prophet

Sorrow doesn't want to leave the parking lot. In fact, she's not overly keen on leaving the car. No tug of the strap will dislodge her.

Amaranth studies the strip mall shops surrounding the parked cars: dry cleaner, doughnut shop, pet shop, nail salon. Nothing she wants, nothing she needs, but she wants to look at the things they sell, as if to pretend that they are a simple mother and daughter, like any who parked or walked past them, out for a day of frivolous spending. She tries to picture Sorrow with her lips around a doughnut or holding her nails out to be filed and painted pink. She watches the closed door of the bar where Bradley is and wishes she were in with him, then she thinks of Sorrow beside her, strapped around a bar stool.

"What are they looking at?" Sorrow points at a crowd outside a Korean barbecue.

"Let's go see," Amaranth says, desperate to see anything but the dirty inside of the windshield. They negotiate the parked cars together, strapped. She jerks Sorrow back as cars swish by, looking for spaces. She tells her to look both ways, as if she is leading a toddler or an alien.

Sorrow hurries toward the crowd, as if she can sense she is missing something, and Amaranth's heart sinks when she sees the plain, flat frontage and the sign beside the barbecue: THE HOLY CHURCH OF THE ONE TRUE LOVE. Only Sorrow could find a church in a mini mall.

The glass doors open and a purple banner, felt wheat spears on a satin cross, emerges. A bone-shattering organ chord comes from mounted speakers, accompanied by the jangle of metal tambourines. Sorrow looks at her mother, all smiles now.

Before the shop front, a congregation gathers, plain-dressed worshippers with paperback Bibles. A cheer comes from the crowd when a man steps through the doors, white-suited, in a cowboy hat. He lifts a hand in a blessing while before him, barely visible through the crowd, is a tiny blond boy in a shorts suit and a broad-brimmed black hat that's held up by his ears. The crowd surges forward, cars honking, people shouting, and a final organ-chord crash.

"Can I get a 'Hallelujah' from someone who believes?" the man calls.

"Hallelujah!" roars the crowd. Sorrow looks about her, eyes wide at their noise.

"We come together to praise the Lord!" the man shouts. "We praise Him in the churches and we praise Him in the streets. We praise Him in the fields when the crops come! Let us pray!" He whips his hat off and bows his head, showing off his scalp.

The little boy bows and his hat tips up. Sorrow does not bow her head but studies those who do, the crowd, the preacher, and his son, while Amaranth keeps a firm hold on the wrist strap, poised to yank her back.

"O Heavenly Father, we come to You from our harvests. We come to You from our fields. We come to You with nothing, as a people humbled, blessed with Your bounty, Lord, which we do not deserve. For we are miserable sinners."

"I'm a sinner, Lord!" a man cries out.

"Who's a sinner?" Sorrow asks her.

A car squeals past them and a spiky-haired woman rolls down her window to holler, "Get outta the road, ya Jesus freaks!" At that, the tambourines rattle, a chord comes, and the crowd begins to sing. "How is it that they know the same song?" Sorrow asks.

"It's a hymn," Amaranth tells her over the singing. "All churches probably sing it."

"All churches?" Sorrow strains forward now. "How many are there?"

"Far too many," says Amaranth grumpily.

The preacher greets the passing cars. "Are you ready for the final days, friends?" They honk in response or salute him with middle fingers. "Are you ready for God to take you away?"

Sorrow raises her arm to him, but the

man ignores her, sweeping his arms and saying, “Let’s hear from the Prophet. Speak, Prophet, speak!”

The small boy is scratching furiously, the back of his lace-up shoe hooked behind the other leg to work on bug bites. Hearing silence, he stops, puts his hat under his arm, and looks up at the sky. “I want to thank You, Lord-uh,” he chants, the end of his lines dropping off in a grunt. “I want to thank you, Jesus!”

“Thank You, Lord. Thank you, Jesus,” the crowd repeats.

“The Lord kept our rain from us and then He gave it back-uh. He took our crops and He let us reap-uh. But this is our final harvest, be in no doubt. The Lord will pull the righteous from their boots-uh, and cut the sinners where they stand-uh, like stalks with His sickle! For the Lord is a-comin’.”

“Praise the Lord,” the man calls.

“Fear God and give Him glory!” Sorrow calls back.

Amaranth tugs the strap. “Don’t.”

The man looks at Sorrow and puts a single finger across his lips.

"Mother," Sorrow whispers. "Can anyone build a temple?"

"It looks like it," she says.

But already Sorrow is turning back to the boy, then pushing through people to get closer to him, pulling Amaranth behind her. "Who calls you Prophet?" Sorrow calls. The crowd parts to get a look at her, this creature in the cap and dress, as Amaranth shuffles along like a string trying to keep up with its kite.

The man gives her a thin-lipped smile and reaches a hand out to greet Sorrow. "Hello, Sister."

She doesn't take it. "Who says he is Prophet?" She points at the little boy.

"Who are you, Sister, that you should ask?"

"I am the Oracle."

"The Oracle?" The man looks about at his worshippers and his strained smile stretches to a full-out grin of mockery. "What's that, then?"

"Have you no Oracle? How can he receive prophecies? How can he read the signs of God?"

The man guffaws. "Sister, we don't need

no Oracle. Everybody can read the Good Book for himself, can't they? Nobody needs to interpret God, 'less you're some papist. Our God speaks to all of us—if only we will listen—but the world has gone deaf!" He holds a hand up to the crowd and they cheer.

"How does God speak to you?" Sorrow calls to him.

"Well, through the Bible, Sister. You do know your Bible?"

"I should do. It is inside me."

The little boy looks at his father for reassurance, then squares up to Sorrow, turning his scuffed chin up from her chest to look her in the eye. "How is the Bible in you?"

"I see through the Father's eyes. I touch through the Father's fingers. I have His holy words running through me like water, all the time. It is all I hear and see."

"You can't see God," the boy tells her.

The man says, "It is foretold that in the final days false prophets will rise among us. And God will not spare them; no, He will not. He did not spare the angels when they sinned and fell! He did not spare the world from the might of His floods! The day of the Lord will come as a thief and the righteous will be stolen away!"

"The righteous have gone," Sorrow says.

The man falters. "So are you not among the righteous?"

"I was taken away from them." Sorrow tips her head at Amaranth, who mouths an embarrassed hello. "But the end is coming. It will come with fire."

The boy says, "Beware of false prophets."

Sorrow smiles. "You will know a prophet by his works and his gifts."

"That's the devil talking," the man says, gesticulating. "Only false prophets try to show you miracles; it's the devil making them boast."

"Our work glorifies God," Sorrow bites back. "What works do you do—what gifts have you?"

"He has the gift of tongues!" a woman in a wheelchair calls.

"Then speak, Prophet," says Sorrow.

"Speak!" the woman urges, and the crowd picks it up. "Speak!"

"You got nothing to prove, son," the man says, but the little boy screws his face up, throwing his head back and opening his mouth in a susurration of consonants, a string of long and sensuous vowels. A woman in a caftan falls to her knees, hands up to fondle heaven.

Sorrow flings her own head back then and roars her gift through clenched teeth. Where the boy's words are silken, hers come as stabs. Where his slip along a slick path, hers are a switchback of barbs and hooks, grunts and clicks.

"Listen to that!" the man calls. "Will the grapes of our Lord be gathered from thorns?"

The woman in the caftan struggles to get back up, grabbing hold of the wheelchair arms. "That's the devil's talk!"

"It is not!" Sorrow protests.

"You're making it up," the boy says. "Yours is a bunch of noise."

Sorrow pokes the boy in the chest. "You're making yours up."

"You are!" The boy's face goes red. "You're only a girl!"

"And you're too little to make Jesus!"

"Sorrow!" Amaranth grabs Sorrow by the shoulder as the man steps forward. They each put a hand on their holy child.

"I'm so sorry," Amaranth tells him, pulling Sorrow toward her. The tambourines rattle and pretty girls produce empty baskets, even as the cars honk and the crowd threatens to engulf them, and the music surges and the baskets fill up with dollar bills. She hurries her daughter between the parked cars and the idling cars waiting for spaces. She rushes her toward the bar, fearing the wail of sirens and police, someone coming to take her child away. She rips across the busy street, cars honking, fists waving, dragging her daughter by the arm, but Sorrow's head is turned back at the church and its people, even as she reaches the bar door and flings it open, calling into the darkness, to the smoke and the jukebox Elvis, "Bradley!"

27

The Plastic Box Oracle

Dust shouts at Amity. "You couldn't wait, could you? You want what you want when you want it. You're as bad as Sorrow. What if I lost you? What would you do? What would your ma do to me?"

She sits and takes it. She could take it all day, but once he's shouted himself quiet she hops off the bench and holds her hand out to him. "Can we go get the book now?"

"Oh, jeez," Dust says.

The purple-haired woman demands his library card, but when she sees it presented to her she says, "This is a children's card. *The Grapes of Wrath* is an adult book."

"What's an adult book?" Amity asks.

"One with dirty bits in," Dust says.

The woman tuts and Amity nods; the Joads were nothing but dirty.

Dust pulls a nylon wallet from his pocket. "I got ID. You can see I'm not a kid. I got a learner's permit means I can drive." And before Amity knows it, the librarian is stamping a new card and Dust is setting a book in her hands. "There you go. *Grapes of Wrath*. Happy now?"

Amity looks at the cover. "That's not it."

"It is. Lookit."

"Where are the grapes and the man's big hand?"

Dust looks at her. "You can't read."

She shrugs. "I don't need to read."

"You do," he tells her, walking her back to the counter. "People will take advantage of you. I could tell you anything and you'd believe it."

"You wouldn't."

"But I could. You can't trust people."

"Why not?"

"Because they're bastards." Dust hands the book to the woman and she stamps it.

"You could learn to read," he says. "I'll find you a site on how to do it."

"What sight?"

"Come on." Dust pulls her to a row of veneered study carrels filled with white plastic boxes.

"What are these, Dust?"

"Haven't you seen a computer before? Oh, man."

"What's a computer?"

"Here. You can read on it and look for things."

"Like an Oracle? Is it an Oracle?" She leans toward it as he sits and taps at keys. "Could it help us find Father?"

"Maybe," he says. "What's his name?"

Amity tells him all she knows, even secret things, but it isn't much. She knows his name is Zachariah and that he has fifty wives and twenty-seven children, more or less, including the first two, who were banished. She tells him about the fire. Dust nods and types the words she gives him: "Zachariah + church + fire + fifty wives." He also types in other words, "cult + polygamy," but he doesn't say them to her. Then there are lights and colors and symbols, a blue spinning circle. He pulls up pictures of churches on fire, buildings consumed in infernos, but none is their temple. The box shows pictures of black children huddled together and crosses burning, then a flock of young girls in bright, ruffled dresses being put on a bus. Their hair swoops and swirls. Amity shakes her head at it. “That isn’t us, but it looks like my cousin. Look at how pretty they are.”

“Are you kidding?” he asks her.

The screen fills up with symbols and Dust takes them all in. But she stops him when she sees it—a picture of Father, but not as she’s ever seen him. It was taken a long time ago, for he looks young and dark-haired, handsome. He holds a tray of symbols across his chest.

“This says he’s wanted,” Dust says, his voice full of wonder.

“Sorrow wants him.” Dust only stares at the screen. “Am I stupid?” she asks him.

“No. You’re ignorant. That’s not your fault.”

“What does it say, all those things?”

He hits a few more buttons and walks to the counter. He gives the woman some coins from his hard-earned harvest and gets a piece of paper in return. "I don't know what you know," he tells her.

"I don't know what I know."

"You better ask your ma, then. I don't know what she wants you to know."

Outside, Dust folds the paper into a tiny square and then Amity can see he is wearing a new pair of jeans, stiff and dark, creased from being folded. "Look at you, fancy!" He has a brand-new red kerchief around his neck and he smiles at her looking. "Can I wear it?" she asks him, pointing.

"Jeez, you're a pest. I only just got it." He fingers the knot.

She pulls her cap off. "I want to be a Mennonite."

"A Mennonite? I don't want your dirty old hat." He scowls, but he unknots the kerchief, begrudgingly draping it over her head.

She ties the kerchief firmly under her chin. "You don't want fifty wives, do you, Dust?"

"I don't even want one," he tells her. "I've seen enough of wives to know that. Bradley was married, you know. You should've heard them."

She nods to him, but she doesn't believe him. Everybody's married. It's only a matter of time. She tosses her cap in the first trash can they pass and she tries very hard to walk back through town as she thinks a Mennonite might.

BEFORE: *The Second Wife*

When the old, old woman died, the ground was too hard to bury her.

Amaranth and the women cleaned her and wrapped her in her linens, then carried her to a metal barn across the frozen field, because they were not yet forbidden.

By the thaw, she was only skin and brittle bones. Her husband dug a hole in the garden six feet deep. Onto the body they dropped down her photographs, her documents, any paperwork that bore her name. They dropped in the first of the year's shoots: kittentails, hyacinth, death camas. Her husband spoke a few words of her generosity and her capacity for love; he told them all that upon the soil and the rock of her they would build their church.

Amaranth couldn't grieve for her. She was too full of her own grief, for the baby her body had lost the year before—their purpose for their marriage—and the husband who left her, back to the roads to preach. "This is my work," he had told her as she clung to him, when she begged and then ordered him to stay. Her grief had skinned her raw.

The summer he was away, the old, old woman was failing. Her breaths came thin and she hovered over life like a hummingbird. Hope and the women carried on with the weeding, hoeing, deadheading, and harvesting, for their garden had to feed them through the hard winter to come. Amaranth moved like a ghost through the house and its rooms, weeping and waiting.

When her husband came home, the old, old woman came back to life, as if she, too, had been waiting. He went straight to her bedside, made up in the shadowed parlor, to pray. Coming to his feet, he announced that he had had a revelation: he and the old, old woman were to marry.

Amaranth raged at him, not caring whether the other women saw. "You are married. You can't just go away and forget you're married."

He spoke to her and to all of them. "When she dies, we have no right to live here. We treated her like family, but we are not."

"Fine," Amaranth spat. "Let her adopt you."

"All she ever wanted was a family," he said gently. "She hoped to be a bride. That is her ring you wear. She never wore it. There was no time to have a family once she had nursed and buried her parents. She was an only child." He looked pointedly at Amaranth.

"It isn't legal. It isn't right. You only want her land," she said.

"Yes, I want her land. Why should the government have it? What did they ever give to us? They will seize this land and then where will we go?"

Amaranth rushed upstairs, sickened. She had no idea her husband had been planning this—he must have been since the first moment he met the old woman and asked her if she'd heard the good news. What did he mean to do with Amaranth, then, with his first wife? Divorce her or disgrace her? Send her away, cast her out? She wept afresh for the baby she lost; if she had been able to keep it, none of this would be happening.

He brought her a china teacup of lemon balm and an old white sheet. It was threadbare and yellowing, its edges worked with spidery stitches that had been made by hand. When she examined them, she found the stitches made names: Eugenie, Martha, Leah, Ann. He showed her the name in the bottom corner and told her it was his great-great-grandmother, his ancestor who left Missouri with her family and had arrived, widowed and childless, on the Great Salt Lake. The names in the other corners were her sister wives.

"Sister wives?"

"My ancestors were among the first pioneers of Utah, the Latter-day Saints. She became fourth wife to a farmer on the trail."

"So you think it's normal to have more than one wife? You're genetically predisposed?"

"No," he said. "I left that church. It has

nothing to do with me or what I believe. I have seen how the Principle can unravel faith, destroy families. It happens all over the world. It always has."

"So does murder."

He looked at her, pained. "I had no idea that your love was so selfish."

She leaped from their bed. "Selfish? I'm your wife, for God's sake! Is it selfish to marry?"

"It is," he said. "This is why I thought I would not. But once . . ." He was looking at her stomach, at the flat front of her dress, and she hated him for it. She decided, in an instant, that she would leave him. She wouldn't wait to be told to go.

"God asks us to live in love," he told her. "He doesn't put any limits on love."

"Well, I do."

"Yes," he said. "I can see it. I will make her family, to protect what we've built here and to protect you. I have made you a vow. I will not lose my family, not again. I could not bear it." He wrapped his arms around her, so that she couldn't leave. She could not breathe. He held her until all the fight had left her, whispering, "Families aren't only given to you. The best of families are made by choice and made from scratch."

She told herself that it didn't matter if he married an old, old woman. It wasn't a real marriage; there would be no paperwork and no one would know. Only he felt it would give them legitimacy on the land, a moral right, and she could see the sense in the logistics of it. Why should the government profit from an old woman's childlessness? But it was hard to submit to preparing the house for an autumn wedding, hard to make a bouquet of the last of summer's flowers. It was hard to powder and dress the woman, lay her back in her bed, and see in her rheumy eyes that she had no idea she was a bride.

At the moment of the ceremony, Amaranth stood with the stitched sheet of his ancestors and the weight of her wedding ring in her fist, wondering how she would learn to share them. Her husband spread his arms wide, encircling the bed and the old, old woman. "Love asks us to make our hearts a home, big enough to shelter anyone. Think of all the women in the world with no one. Who will be their family, if we do not?"

Amaranth watched the gaze of each woman draw inward, as if remembering her own history of loneliness, loss, and betrayal. And she hung her head. He had given her a shelter, hadn't he, by marrying her? She was grateful to belong to a family and to have someone to try to love with her whole heart. Why did she begrudge an old woman at the end of her life the same?

She smiled at him, to show him she could put her selfishness aside, her fear, her anger. She shook the stitched sheet across the old, old woman, so that he could tell the story of his family. She took her ring off and held it out.

"This woman never wore this ring. She gave her own ring to me, so that I might marry." He took the ring and placed it on the end of the woman's twisted finger, easing it over her painful, swollen knuckles. "I take you for wife," he pronounced. "I take you for family."

"I take you for family," the women echoed.

"I take you for wife," Amaranth said, shuddering, trying to keep her smile intact.

He kissed the ring on the woman's finger. He kissed the woman's grizzled mouth. He took the ring and slid it back onto Amaranth's finger and kissed her, his lips already damp.

Amaranth waited for the three women in the circle to laugh then, to reveal at last that this had all been a painful joke, designed to dupe her, to mock her desperation to be loved. But they were silent, visibly moved.

Her husband held his hand out to her and the women filed to the kitchen, murmuring about cake. He sat on the bed beside the old woman and pulled Amaranth down to sit. He held her and stroked her, promised that nothing would change between them. Amaranth would be at the very center of his life and his marriage, come what may. Then he lay down beside the old, old woman. Amaranth tried to get up, but he pulled her down flat, a wife on either side of him. He took Amaranth's hand and turned to kiss the old, old woman.

He placed a hand on the old woman's sagging face. She covered her own face, her eyes shut, streaming, humiliated. He placed a hand on the woman's flat chest and he cupped Amaranth's breast. He slid his hand up Amaranth's skirt and she turned her head, afraid that he felt the old, old woman with his other hand. And then he was over her, staring down into Amaranth's eyes.

She heard the old woman take a phlegmy breath. He pushed Amaranth's skirt up to her waist and he moved himself inside her, shaking the bed frame, shaking the old woman by his side. He moved within her, pushing her head back into the bed. His breath grew rasped and loud and she prayed with each movement—give . . . me . . . a . . . child—until he hauled himself out of her, suddenly, and came in an arc across the stitching of the old sheet and the body of the old, old woman. He looked down, startled, into Amaranth's eyes.

And so a ritual was born.

In the morning she scrubbed the sheet and threaded a needle. She stitched herself down to him and his family, there, in the very center of the sheet. Two months later his second wife was dead, and when they buried her with all her artifacts, her husband said it was to keep them safe.

Amaranth only thought how it would make her disappear as if she never had existed, never lived or wanted or married or died there. Amaranth wondered if he would do the same to her when she died. Make her disappear.

28
News

Bradley licks his finger at the kitchen table, to flick a page of newspaper. He scans the page, finger poised and wet, searching the paper as he has the papers in the heap before him for news of a church on fire. He squints at the small print and she thinks of the kitchen drawer filled with eyeglasses back home, left behind at the death of a wife, picked up and worn again as younger wives aged.

There is a paper in Amaranth's pocket. It crinkles as she bends to scoop beans from the bins, less than half full now. Dust handed the paper to her in the parking lot.

"I didn't show Amity," he told her, but she could see from his face that he had read it. She could see how he looked at her now. She read and reread it when no one was looking, and when she finally showed it to Bradley, he went straight into town for a newspaper. Every day he buys one now.

The paper Dust gave her says that her husband is missing and wanted for questioning by local police. It does not mention who else is missing or if anyone else is wanted. It does not mention the number of wives or children missing. The police do not know who lived there, of course, which had been the purpose of their secrecy. "Multiple wives and children" is all the paper will commit to.

It does not say that Amaranth is missing or wanted, that she took her daughters and abandoned her husband, her family, saved her own skin. The paper doesn't know that she lived there or bore her children there. There isn't a scrap of paperwork for anything that anyone else did, but her marriage was his paper marriage. There will be a record of it, somewhere. They will want to find her, once they know she exists.

The police want to speak to her husband to investigate claims of molestation from "an estranged plural wife of the compound." She knows this will be Hope—it must be Hope—and that it means she is all right, somewhere, safe and still trying somehow to make everything right. It was Hope who had sent the police when she had first left, in the vain belief that she could help Sorrow. Hope couldn't have known that speaking to the police would lead to the siege, that her former family's fears would rise until they bubbled over into the fire that would destroy them. Even after all that happened, she still missed her friend, dearly.

Most of what happened is not in the paper. There is no mention of the siege at all, or of the days and nights of terror the police brought. It says that Zachariah is wanted for shooting at a police officer, though he did not, and for setting their temple on fire, which he must have done. The police take no responsibility for anything that happened. Their siege, undocumented, will be no Waco.

Down the side of the article, there are paragraphs in boxes on the history of polygamy and interviews with local townspeople. “Did you know there was a polygamous cult in your neighborhood?” they are asked. One local business owner is quoted as saying, “We knew they were strange, but we didn’t know by how much.” It concludes with the suggestion that their cult had a “death wish, common in splinter groups such as these—a desire to offer believers up as a kind of sacrifice.” She knows, at the end, no one wanted to die. They were afraid and exhausted, frightened beyond measure for their freedom and children, but no one wanted to die. No one but her husband wanted the world to end at all.

Every word that Bradley searches for serves to shame her. Here is proof of her betrayal, black-and-white proof of all their community did and failed to do. How could he want her to stay now, when the man she loved is become a monster, wanted by the police for arson, shooting, and the rape of his child? That word isn’t there, that hateful word, but she knows it is what he is looking for.

Who is this man she is married to, still? And why is there a picture of him, on Dust’s paper, that she had never seen? Why is he holding a rack of numbers across his chest and staring at the camera with the look of hatred he gave when the knock came at the temple door and he thought he would lose his family? It says he served time in prison, years before she ever met him, for setting alight a police car outside the Short Creek compound.

A pan boils over on the stove top, flooding scum across the burners, down to the floor. She makes a mess of everything, she thinks, dabbing the spill: beans, leaving, daughters, men. Who could want her as she was?

Bradley closes the paper and she looks up.

"Nothin'," he says. "Another lucky escape."

She thinks of her leaving and the paper in her pocket. She thinks of all she knew and allowed and did. Her every cell wants to run away from it. She wants to explain, or justify, or apologize, but she only says, "Soup?"

29

The Devil's Box

Sorrow builds an altar in the bathroom.

"Look," she says, proud and shy, opening the red dirt–marked door so Amity can see it, safe from the threshold.

Her altar is a bright blue wooden pallet, up on its end. Atop it is an armless rubber dolly, its hair burned into wiry coils. Its arm sockets are stuffed with stiff brown feathers and bits of colored string and twine, fluorescent blue and orange. Its legs stick straight out, and in its lap, wrapped like a baby, is the blue china shard.

"Anyone can build a temple," she tells Amity. "I've seen it."

Amity doesn't know why anyone would choose to build a temple in the dark of a bathroom, but then she thinks of the room below. She slides herself a step back, beyond the threshold, too far for Sorrow to reach. She doesn't tell Sorrow about the temple made of books and computers. She wants to keep that secret to herself, like the secret of what is happening within her.

The old devil hadn't been impressed by her *Grapes of Wrath*.

"What in Sam Hill do I want that for?" he said. "I got my own. It's a first edition. You'll have to take yours back, you know. You can't keep a library book; they'll send the police after you."

"I don't like the police," Amity told him. She looked at the devil's shotgun and thought of her Waco mother.

He was similarly unimpressed with Amity's tale of a paper with a picture of her father that she couldn't read. "Girl, we gotta sort you out," he told her. "We gotta learn you your ABCs." But he didn't. Instead, he worried about all he didn't know. "Why don't nobody tell me nothin'?"

"Nobody tells me nothing, too."

"That's 'cause we're youngest and oldest. We're the bread on a stupid sandwich. I reckon that's why they've got me watching you."

"I'm sure I'm watching you," she said.

He was impressed with the story of the plastic oracle, however. "Sort of like this one," she told him, pointing at the black box in the corner. "Except those ones switch on and you can see all these pictures on it. Yours just sits there."

"It does not sit there! Lookee here, you switch that TV on."

"What's a TV?"

"Go on and push that silver button."

When she did, the face of it was transformed. A fine white electric snow came, roaring a chaos of hiss and bee buzz like Sorrow's angel language but a million times worse. She put her hands over her ears. "Make it stop!"

"Hang on," the old man said, and he leaned over, nearly rolling out of his bed, to lunge at two silver poles on its top. "I can't do it," he said. "Go wiggle them rabbit ears. Go on."

She set her hands on the rods and the box went silent. And then, as on the computer, there was a picture, tiny people inside it, sitting on a sofa, moving, while invisible people laughed. It was better than the library's box.

"Look what your hands can do," the old man said. "Don't let go, now."

Amity looked at her hands on the metal rods. Yes, she thought. Look how they heal the TV.

Now she doesn't want to hear about the Joads. She wants to stand with her arms out, turning snow into pictures. She spins the dial and there is always a new picture waiting for her. Children eat soup. Men punch one another in the face. Once, a man stares out at her and tells her, just her, that they are still at war. "Still at war?" she hollers. "It's started—we didn't even know—the war in heaven!"

"War in heaven? Change the channel," he says.

She spins the dial, around and around. She knows that she is making the pictures. They are coming from her hands, through the rods, from God. She can't wait to tell Dust about it, this better, moving oracle, even if the old man wants her to stop.

"You wanna do some readin'?" he asks her.

She can hardly hear him to answer. She cannot move her eyes from the pictures, dazed by the light and the heat of it, the power in her hands.

"Your eyes'll go square." He gives a harrumph that becomes a mighty, chesty cough.

"But I'm making the pictures," she tells him. She holds out her hands to show him and the box makes snow.

"Bull pokey you are. Them pictures is whizzing about in the air. The antennae pull 'em down so you can see 'em, and the box sticks 'em all together."

"Is that so?" Amity looks at her hands again. Her hands are antennae. Now she knows their name, antennae, bringing down God.

"Open that book there now and turn that thing off," he says. "Show me where we were."

The screen pops and crackles without her. "Those Joads will never get to California."

"You can't read, so you won't know if they will or won't. I could tell you when they got there it was a land of milk and honey and they all had pie."

"I think someone keeps sticking more pages on the end of the book when we're not looking." She looks at him, suspicious.

"Turn that off," he says. He tries to swing his legs off the bed, lunging at the power button. "Damn legs," he says. "Damn old legs."

"What's wrong with them?"

"Well, they don't work, do they? Look at 'em." He pushes back his covers to show off the long and crooked bones of him, his kneecaps purple as prunes. She turns and pushes the power button off.

"I can heal you."

"You can what?"

She holds out her antennae-hands for him.

"I seen healers, you know," he says. "I seen tent shows and revivals and ballyhoos. All that dust left us wantin' miracles, but they never came."

Amity rubs her hands together. "Will I heal you?" She extends them toward his kneecaps. He watches her hands, growing nearer.

He stops her. "I might only get one crack

at your healing. Lookee here." He begins to unbutton his pajama top to show off his grizzled chest and she turns her head. She thinks of her father. "Fix this," he says, banging on his breastbone. He takes a breath that coughs and rattles.

"Okay," she tells him. "Shut your eyes now."

She rubs her hands together and places them flat across his plane of bone and skin. He takes a ragged breath and she can feel the air in him, under her hands, blow coarse as sand. She closes her eyes and she can see her hands slip into the skin of him, into his bones. She feels them slip through a gap in his Adam ribs and reach for the bags of gristle he breathes through. She feels the sacs cook in her fingers, ooze and bubble, until whatever is stuck inside him turns to liquid and runs clear, just as it did in Sorrow's belly when she touched it. She slips her hands back out of him and when she opens her eyes again, his skin is whole and clean, as if she hasn't touched him at all.

He takes an experimental breath. "I didn't feel nothin'." He takes another. "Did you heal me?" He breathes in hard and waits to choke on it. He breathes again. "Well, I'll be damned," he says.

Amity smiles. "I should hope not."

As repayment, he says she will learn her letters. She doesn't know what letters are or if there's a rule about them or not, and either way he makes her open his book and hold it.

"What's that letter there?" he asks her.

"Three sticks," she tells him. "Like a headless man."

"That's a *t*. *T* goes 'tuh.' You say it."

"*T* goes 'tuh,'" she apes. She thinks of all the things in the world that she might know if she could read about them, and she doesn't know if God wants her to know them or not.

"*T* goes in Amity, don't it?" the old man says.

"Ami-tee," she says. "There's a *t* in me."

"You start off with an *a,* like that letter there."

"*A,* like two hands up in prayer."

"And the next one's an *m* there."

"*M* like a mountain." She thinks of their driving.

"Come here and let me show you the next one," and she scooches close to him on the bed, to learn how to read.

30
Sheets

Amaranth boils beans while he flicks the newsprint, dwarfed by the yellowing pile of papers he adds to daily, nightly, all the shootings and swindles and explosions of the vast, sad world that he brings to his table, brings into his house. How can Bradley stand to look?

"He's not coming," she tells him. "He would have come by now. He's dead." He looks up at her. "I hope he's dead."

"It'd be reported. If he knows they're after him, he'll keep running. Wouldn't you?"

"I'm not running." She stabs at the beans. They spin and bubble, each trying to pull itself above the surface, only to be pulled back down by the water, or the other beans.

"You want me to stop looking?" he asks her. "Pretend nothing happened?"

Yes, she thinks. "No," she answers.

He finishes the paper and tosses it onto the pile, his inept haystack. "If you went to the police, you could clear this whole thing up."

"No," she tells him. Again.

"I don't know why you're still protecting him."

"I've told you. It's Sorrow I'm protecting."

He shrugs and gets up, bumping the table as he tries to bring his knees out. The stack of papers shifts and his arms go around it in an awkward embrace, to hold it together. But once he leaves, paper slides from the stack, fluttering down with pictures of storms and drowning houses, piles of bodies lying still. Paper after paper falls and flaps open, like a flood of paper sweeping through the house, and she wishes a great wall of water would come and wash all the pictures and stories away from her.

The kitchen is a mass of paper, all fire and famine and fluttering flags—but there is not a single picture of Sorrow. That is how she wants it. She won't have strangers knowing what her husband did, licking their fingers and flicking them past her.

Everything she sees is filthy now. The land and its dust continue their assault on the house. It is the end of summer and she can feel it like a frenzy, like back home, when wives were waiting, turning over the house and the rooms in anticipation of their husband's return. Here, she attacks dirty windows with vinegar. She rolls the old man from hip to hip to whip sheets from beneath him until he complains he's not a slab of meat, but it doesn't stop her. She rips Bradley's sheets from his bed and catches the scent of him, his skin and her skin, and she can't remember when she last reached for him. It is all those newspapers, coming between them like a dam, all those words and disasters. There are balls of socks and wads of underpants, wrapped with her long brown hairs. There are drawers half open, spilling their contents, and she shoves them in with hips and clogs, but the bottom drawer is set in crooked. When she yanks it to right and shuts it, she can see it is filled with magazines. Not *National Geographic*.

These are of women. All hair and teeth, bulbous breasts and shaved pudenda. She shoves the drawer back in, but it refuses to go. The women rock back and forth below her, plucked and perfect, licking paper lips. The bodies of home are imperfect and hairy. They harden with work and sag with children. She doesn't know what has happened to the state of women while she's been away, marrying and nursing, tending her family. Is this how women are meant to look? Is this what he expects or wants to see?

She throws the bedding and underclothes over the banister to boil in the kitchen, running water hot until it is scalding, hotter than her skin can stand, and forcing her hands into them. She misses the washtub and wringer of home, the many hands that squeezed sheets clean, the hands that pinned sheets to long lines strung in the garden, where children could hide in the wet, snapping maze of them. She misses her family, God help her. And she knows it is wrong now. She knows the damage it did, while she thought they had been healing.

Her children were raised to see bodies

as sacred, belonging to God. But they also saw how bodies were shared. They knew the chaste nature of their binding, the covered heads, but they had seen their father with a multitude of women, in and out of bedroom doors and tents. They will have heard about or spied, through temple windows, the unbinding that came as women were spun from wife to wife. Children were curious, even her children. How would they know where their own bodies stopped and someone else's began if everything was shared? Here, in this world, there were women on display, spread-eagled over paper, women who looked like whores but weren't, while her family, her children, were dressed like saints, like nuns or pilgrims, but were not and never had been. Their bodies were God's, for Him to do with as He wished.

On the black-marked dirt she builds a fire and she feeds it paper, all the paper of the house, the paper disasters, paper women and floods, the folds and open mouths, their heads flung back in burning. She stands in the face of the smoke and sees her family—how can she not? Burning and spinning, wild with fear, and she does not run away from it this time. She does not run from the fire she makes. She remembers how hard she had to pull Sorrow, to get her away from him.

Bradley comes down to her from the house, newspaper in his arms. He sees the fire but only asks her why the drawers of his room are all open and why his father has no bedding, and she remembers that the sheets are in the sink and none of her work has been done, when all she was doing was trying to make the whole dirty world clean. She swallows smoke.

He sees the ash of paper on her, white against her dark skirts. "You got to do something," he says. "I think you're crackin' up here."

"I know it," she says.

"You can't wait for him to come."

"He won't come."

"You know what he's done and you know no one knows it." He looks at her, no matter how she turns away.

"I know it."

"Then tell the police—"

"I know what we did to her, I know!"

“What he did,” he says.

“What we all did—what we allowed—what I allowed!” She walks in a circle, watching the fire. “I can’t tell the police, because I knew it was happening and I let it happen, don’t you see? If they take me away, who will care for her? Will you? Shall I leave her here?”

“No one’s taking you away,” he says. “He raped your daughter. You didn’t. I think he raped you all.”

“Stop it.” She stumbles away toward the field and her knees hit the dirt, then her hands. She cannot breathe for smoke. She saw it and did nothing. The light in her husband’s face was Sorrow; the fire in her eyes was he. That was what she saw and she turned her face from it. Like her children, she did not question it. She had told herself that Sorrow and Zachariah had a closeness that she had never had with her own father. She rejoiced in it for Sorrow. She thanked God for it, even envied it. But what he did with Sorrow had nothing to do with a love of God. She did not do enough. She did not stop it.

Even at the end, he was courting her,

wasn't he? His fifty-first wife would have been Sorrow if they hadn't run. And then would it have been every daughter?

She hears him behind her and she tells him, "She wouldn't have thought it was rape."

"He would."

"He thought he was God. She thought he was God."

"Bastard." He shakes his head at it. "Thing is, she ain't a kid now. She's older than you think; craftier, too. All kids are. By her age, I'd left school and I was running this place and there wasn't a thing you could've told me. She's old enough to pick her own way through this, if you treat her like you know she can."

"You don't have children," she says.

"No, I don't," he flings back.

"You don't, so you—"

"No," he says. His voice is hard now. "I didn't get to have children, but I've raised Dust as my own and I like to think I could make a better job of it than you all did. I like to think I'd at least have kept them safe."

"I took them away! I made them safe!"

"Did you?" He looks at her kneeling, crouching, the weight of the clothing she wears. She thinks of the weight of their faith and rules, their strange ways. She feels the binding they still wear, for no purpose now. Who was here to see it or know if they didn't wear it? No one, if they were all who were left. She has to dismantle every structure they have and she doesn't know how to begin. She doesn't know what to replace them with.

She stares into the dirt and tells him what the paper won't. "The police were looking at us before the fire. We thought they would take our children, because of what they thought he was doing—what he was doing. It's why he started the fire—I'm sure of it—to get us to run. So they couldn't take us." He would burn the world for Sorrow, but had he burned them all instead?

"They're his sins. They ain't yours."

Her shame is palpable. "Aren't they? You don't know what else I've done, how bad I've been. Before I met him, I used to wonder what it would be like if someone could see how bad you were, really see how dark it was inside you, and want you anyway. What would that feel like? I thought I knew, but—I don't know now."

"I see you," he says, but he does not touch her or bend beside her to help her up. He stands, looking out, and he lights a match. The world flames up around him and then goes dark. They are all of them dark inside. He blows smoke at her fire.

In the night, ashes will blow across the land and across the house, and into Amity's lap will tumble bits of paper, unburned circles of women's faces, women's bodies, hands holding breasts out as though they're blue-ribbon squashes. In the morning, she will think that God has sent them, pictures of women for her to see and know what is in store for her.

31
The Slip

Sorrow's altar is changing, all the dirt gone from the door. The sounds of the house are changed, with Mother and the farmer shouting conversations through the windows and the old man's cough gone silent. The Joads make it to California at last, but they aren't any nearer to the promised land they travel for, and Dust never leaves his barn.

Something is changing in all of them, no matter how they try to stay the same.

Sorrow scavenges the land and its cast-offs, fingering the wreckage piled between the gas station and the house. She uses her hands now, not to paint with dirt or stab things, but to dig and sort through what generations of people have discarded and forgotten, bits of dishes and rubber-baby parts, tiny metal cars and wheels. To her pallet altar she adds bottle caps and rusting wires, flower heads made from rotting plastic bags. From the trash she finds, she makes something strange, something beautiful. Something only Sorrow can see is holy now.

Something is changing in Amity, too. She has proof of it, there, at last. She should be spun.

When Sorrow first bled it was cause for celebration and ceremony. First girl born in the family, she was first to take the ritual spin, first to shed her little girl's dress and pinafore and be turned into a woman, with a wife's long skirts and bindings. The women spun her alone in the temple, no Father, no altar. A room filled with women, spinning, circling the temple's empty center.

Mother Hope brewed teas for Sorrow, floating leaves of raspberry, nettle, and motherwort set to steep by moonlight. The water was pale by morning. She watched Sorrow drink it, as though it were some magic potion that would transform her from within. And then it did.

No one is here to watch Amity transform. There is no spinning. There will be no new clothes for her, handed down from a mother, and no one to bind her. There is only one mother here now, and she is not looking at Amity. She is not looking at Sorrow. She is only looking at the man and all his paper, the paper parts of his women. And Sorrow isn't looking at Amity; she is only looking at her altar, at the things she stacks and strokes there.

Alone, Amity rips strips from her underskirt to wedge between her legs. And she doesn't tell Sorrow. And she doesn't tell Mother. She is a woman now and can keep her own secrets. But she thinks that—hopes that—when Dust leaves his barn he will see her and know her change.

The old man doesn't see it. To him, she is still just a little girl, one he can boss around and chivy. "Don't turn on that TV," he orders. "Bring me that book. Sit down there."

Or "Grab me a shirt from that chifforobe. Find me some pants. Where in Sam Hill have I put my shoe?"

She doesn't remind him how he threw it. She only looks at the dark face of the TV screen.

"Look in my son's room, will you? He's taken my pants so I won't walk around."

"You can't walk around," she tells him.

"Who says I can't? I've two legs, don't I?"

"I don't know if you do or you don't. They're always under cover." Amity slumps her way into Bradley's room, sees his unmade bed and a three-legged machine in his window, blocking any means of seeing Dust across the fields. She pulls it down to see it has a glass eyepiece and when she looks through it the sky zooms toward her, like a cloud attacking the house.

She sees no pants on the floor or the bed and knows she'll have to look in the man's drawers to find some. The old thought of rules comes to her and she bats it away. There were no rules left to follow now. His drawers hold socks and undergarments, short-sleeved and long-sleeved shirts. She finds a pair of his pants for the old man, but her hands keep pulling the drawers open and she finds, in the bottom drawer, more pictures like the ones her mother burned, ladies smiling with their open legs. Beneath them is something else, slippery and sliding. She pulls it out and she gasps right at it. She turns to look through the open door, in case someone can see.

It is a blue dress, deep and dark as the oracle bowl when it's wet, with two thin ribbon straps, two triangle cups, and a bit of lace up its front, and so shiny it practically leaps in her hands. She wants it. She rubs it against her cheek and smells its musk. This, she knows, is what women wore here. With no one looking, she slips it into her pinafore pocket and takes it.

"Ain't you found me some pants yet?" the old man shouts.

Once he's in his pants and his one shoe, he tells her he wants to go downstairs.

"You?" she asks him. But he needs more help than she can offer him. His legs are stuck stiff as a table's and when she heats her hands to set them on his knees, they only bend back and buckle.

"Will I get Mother to help?" she asks him.

"You will not. She shifts me around like I'm a side of beef."

"Will I get Sorrow?"

"Sorrow, in my bedroom?" That starts him laughing.

"Will I get Dust?"

"I don't want that half-breed in here, touchin' my things."

At that, she's out of options, as she won't talk to the man at all, with his spying machine and his naked women. "What does 'half-breed' mean?" she asks him.

The two of them spend what's left of the day in the heat of his room, he in his pants and she with her stolen dress, until he finally says, "Go on and get that boy of yours." She runs for him, the slip leaping in her outgrown child's pinafore, but when she finds him, he doesn't notice anything about her. He just says, "What?" She brings him back to the old man.

"Keep that half-breed away from me," he whines.

Amity looks at Dust, but he just sucks his teeth. "I won't touch you, old man."

"Then how will we get him downstairs?" she asks.

"He'll have to touch me, won't he?" He

crouches down beside the old man's bed. "You want down, you'll have to climb on." The old man mutters, but when Amity sucks her teeth at him, too, he hollers, "All right, you savages!"

The old man reaches his arms for Dust and Dust takes him onto his shoulders like a heavy scarf, like some hard-boned vest, and walks him to the landing. "What'd I ever do to you, old man?"

"Stayed, you freeloader." The two bump their way down the stairs, the old man calling behind him, "Bring that TV down with you!"

Amity cradles the TV down the stairs, rabbit ears clanging her kerchief, as Dust deposits the old man on the sofa. "Well, hello, living room," the old man says. He stretches his skinny legs along the length of it and grins. She sets the TV on the table, shoving the old stacks of paper aside. But when she punches the power button, the screen stays resolutely dark. She sets her hands onto it.

Dust jams a cushion behind the old man's head. "I'm no half-breed, old man," he tells him. "I'm Mexican, one hundred percent. It's you whites who're the mongrels."

The old man splutters. “My family arrived on the *Mayflower,* I’ll have you know. Why, they were here to meet the *Mayflower,* we been here that long!”

“Then you took the Indians’ land. Well done, white man.”

“We never needed wetbacks workin’ this land, not Oklahoma. This ain’t Texas, boy. You should’ve stayed in Mexico.”

Dust draws himself up straight. “I was born in this country. I’m legal as you. Mexicans are in every state, working your land, doing the work you won’t do. You remember that.” And with that, Dust stomps out the door and Amity wishes she could follow, even if he has no time for her anymore.

The old man chuckles. “Well, I’ll be.” He tells Amity to plug the TV in and she stands until he points at the wire coming off the back of the box, and he tells her to find a socket. She stands there holding the wire until he tells her what a socket is and how she should stick the end of the one into the other.

“Like when you make Jesus,” she marvels. The old man stares until she jams the end in, and then the TV is on with three big gold letters.

"Gimme them letters, girl," he commands.

She raises her arms to make a *W* shape, then points her arms out to make an *E*.

"What's it say?"

"Wee?" she says hopefully.

"Wrong again. It's World Wrestling Entertainment." The picture comes on with a roar as two men, big as cows in shiny suits, spin onto a stage lined with ropes. "Hallelujah!" the old man hollers. "It's Saturday!" The men slap their chests and bark. "Don't you worry. Got sumpin' to show that you'll like, come Sunday."

"What?" she asks him, doubtful.

"Sunday's when the preachermen are on. Go and tell your sister."

Her hands go into her pocket, to feel the fabric that waits there. Sunday, she tells herself.

32
Do Drop Inn and the Mesa

He drives Amaranth down a thin road between cut fields that runs between the highway and the hog farms. "This is the old road," he tells her. "The one that used to bring folks to the station when I was a kid. It ain't Route Sixty-Six, but we got cars enough."

"I don't like highways," she says. There are no street signs, no lights, just their headlights on the dark road and the hiccup jumps of jackrabbits into them.

"Then you're my kind of girl," he says.

She'd found him in his room, looking up

through his telescope at stars. He'd only nodded when she asked if they could drive. She'd walked past her daughter and his father on the sofa, watching TV like some ordinary family, and she'd shaken her head at how resilient they all must be.

"Where you wanna go?" he asks her now, his face dark. The dashboard lights have burned out, from Sorrow's fire.

"Not into town," she says. "No papers. Take me where you'd go if I weren't here." He pulls her up before a yellow neon horseshoe and a sign: DO DROP INN. The parking lot is half filled with dirty pickups, parked against a set of hitching posts that flank a saloon door. The trucks are laden with gun supports, their beds full of chains and tools, boxes and barrels, bumper stickers about God and beer. He turns the engine off.

She can picture the bar inside, sawdust on the floor, maybe, a wooden counter lined with farmers and cowboys, their pale mugs of beer, college football on a screen. She tries to picture him walking in with her beside him or behind him, to hide her skirts and her cap. She pulls it off and pops it into his glove compartment when he opens his door.

"You comin' in?"

She pictures him drinking too much, too fast, coming back to her on his dirt in the kitchen garden, how he drank when he thought he saw his wife. She pictures them inside, together, sees herself drinking too much beside him, trying to be someone else, shaking her limbs to music she doesn't recognize, trying to fill up all that darkness with noise and liquid. She shakes her head. "No. Take me somewhere you've never taken anybody. Not a soul."

He thinks for a minute, then pulls the door shut. "Women," he says, giving her a smile.

He turns them back to the dirt road and goes past the turnoff for his farm, driving her west. He stops at a shop for cigarettes and a six-pack and when he doesn't bring a paper back, she is grateful. "Have one," he tells her, and she pulls a can from a plastic ring, pulls it open, and holds it, guilty as a child, between her skirted legs. He turns them north, up a blacktop road, and they gain elevation. She can feel her ears pop, see the dark scrub in the headlights change to pine and piñon. The air is cool and she rolls down the window, smells juniper and smoky mesquite.

"You keep driving, you'll hit Four Corners," he tells her, "where four states meet. You could go anywhere from there."

"I don't want to go anywhere."

"Well, you're goin' to Black Mesa." He tells her it was named for the volcanic lava that formed its tabletops and valleys, that it adjoins two reservations, Navajo and Hopi, and if it were daylight she'd be able to see the cholla and the pines, maybe spot an eagle, a pinyon jay, or a bear. But it's dark, so she only sees darkness, the dark shapes beyond them. He turns them up a road, rough and rocky, the truck jostling along a length of barbed wire and metal snow markers. He parks and takes his cigarettes, grabs a flashlight from the glove compartment, and takes the beers by their ring. "Come on," he says.

"What, we're walking?"

"End of the line," he says, whistling his way to the barbed wire and taking his shirt off before it. He lays it over the wire to help her lift her skirts over, snagging and ripping. When she laughs he shushes her. “This is private land. Prob’ly dogs,” he says.

“Is this legal?”

“What do you care about legal?” He pulls her by the hand in the dark, over sand. His flashlight sweeps a dry creek bed, lined with boulders and tufts of dry grass. The sky above them is frosted with stars, thick in a twisted band of galaxies, close enough to pull down. “There,” he says. He points his light at a hole in the ground, saucer-shaped, the size of a dinner plate. “Dinosaur tracks,” he tells her.

“Come on,” she says with a laugh.

“What, you don’t believe in dinosaurs?” He sweeps the light up a row of tracks, staggered along the creek bed, lined up like the gait of an ancient land beast.

“Of course I believe in them,” she says. “Just because my children are ignorant doesn’t mean I am.” She stops and bends to look at it, to put her fingers into the fossilized edges, like doubting Thomas probing a wound. “I saw some bones in a museum when I was a kid, strung together with wire. They were probably plastic. Still, the size of them, I couldn’t believe it.” Most children were fascinated by dinosaurs. Not her children. “Is this really a footprint? How do they know?”

“Everybody wants proof,” he says. He opens a beer and guzzles it, the beam of the flashlight wandering while he swallows.

“Not my children,” she says. They have faith, proof of nothing. “We should bring the girls out, show them proof of dinosaurs, real proof that the world is older than the Bible teaches, older than four thousand years.” What would they make of the tracks? How would she begin to take apart everything they knew and believed? Could she?

He hands the can to her and her lips go over the teardrop hole. She tips the drink back and looks up at the swirl of stars, hoping one will fall so she can wish on it.

“When I was little, I wanted to be an astronaut,” he says.

“Sure,” she says, handing the can back. “Why not?”

“Ma gave me the telescope. Grew up lookin’ up for men on the moon. Just kept extendin’ the legs. I wanted to see their boot prints up there, like it would prove that they'd been and I might go up. Pa'd just say, 'Nothin' up there, boy, ain't no wheat on the moon.'"

She takes the crook of his arm and squeezes it, pulls her collars up to her neck.

"Cold?" he asks her, reaching to rub her sleeve with his other hand.

"No, I just—did you never bring anyone here? Not your wife?"

"She didn't like getting dirty," he says, and he starts to laugh. "Should've never come to Oklahoma then."

"No," she says. "She must have been miserable."

He nods, the laugh falling. "I guess she was. She never did want to plant or work things. Don't know what those seeds were about. She was always tryin' to get me to tell her things'd be okay, but, you know, I didn't know if they would be. Every year I think I'll lose this farm. Every harvest will fail me. Every child we had, well . . . We had some bad luck."

She nods. She knows.

"Life is just seeds," he says, shrugging. "You know, you plant in the dirt you're given. It's all you've got. You water, you tend, and sometimes seeds don't take. Sometimes it all goes away from you. She didn't want to hear about that. She wanted promises, and you can't make promises. They're just what you want to happen, not what will."

She thinks of all the promises she's made, all the times she's said I do and I will, over fifty ceremonies. She thinks of the promises made by her husband and how they turned to threats. What she wanted to happen, what they wanted to build, wasn't what they made in the end. Bradley was right. "What would happen if we stayed? With you?"

"Well," he says, rubbing his face, "it'd probably be much the same. But winters are hard here. You can't imagine it, this heat, but you couldn't keep to the porch unless I could box it in. I suppose someday Pa'll give his room up and the girls could have it, 'less he decides to live forever just to spite me."

"What would happen—with us? I'm not looking for promises, but—"

"I guess it'd be like this." He swallows. They stand in their silences, in the dark of night, with the shards of light above them, flaming. They may have died when the dinosaurs walked here, those stars, but the light is still there.

Everything seems simple. Possible.

"I want to tell you something," she says.

"How much more can there be?" He crushes the beer can beneath his boot.

"A lot," she says.

He turns to her. "Well, I don't need to know it. That's all your business, back there, and you'll deal with it. I don't need to know what you done. I just want to know what you're gonna do."

She thinks that there is only dirt and sky, Bradley and her. It is all she has and all she wants. She can let go of her husband's family and the family they tried to make, but then she realizes she can't let go of the children they made, her children, who her children have become. If she never tells him, he will never really know them. He will never understand her darkness or their fears. But she tells him nothing, as he wants.

He smokes and they drink and they speak of nothing together, not families, not histories. Just stars and seeds. No promises, only wishes, until the dark sky pinks behind the mesa and his cigarettes are gone, and the sun rises over them to heat the land where dinosaurs turned and walked away once.

33
The Sunday Preachermen

Sunday, and Amity spins the dial. Sorrow won't walk into any man's house, so she stands, glowering, at the doorway, coaxed from her altar with the promise of glory. Her folded arms say this had better be good and Amity wiggles the rabbit ears for all she's worth.

The old man strains to watch Sorrow over the back of the sofa. "You ever seen a real preacherman, girl?" he asks her. "Not that scrabbling 'round you folk do. I mean, the real Holy Ghost deal?" Sorrow will not speak to any man, but Amity can see she is listening. "Stick your hands on 'em, like a healer would," he shouts at Amity. "Give it some gusto."

Sorrow huffs a breath out, which tells Amity she'd better make the TV snow turn into a temple and fast. When she grips the antennae, fit to strangle them, a man's great finger flies out from the TV, pointing at all of them. "Are you Rapture-ready?" he calls.

Sorrow leans her torso into the house to watch.

"Have you made your peace with God, your Father?"

Sorrow's arms stretch against the door frame and the old man crows, "Didn't I tell you? Didn't I say?"

"Hush," says Sorrow, and Amity looks at her. She does not even notice her rule breaking. She slides a clog into the room.

"The Lord is coming to take you away, and it is up to you whether you follow Him up or follow Satan down. Either way, God is coming for you. He is watching you. He sees every step you make, bringing you closer to Him, or taking you further away. It is no one's doing but your own."

"Is the preacherman behind that box there?" Sorrow whispers.

Amity chortles at that. “No. He’s coming through the air in pieces and the rabbit ears make him come into the box.” She points at the old man. “He said so.”

“Where is that preacherman?” Sorrow asks the old man, straight out.

“He could be anywhere. He could be clear across the country or right down the street. There are preachermen everywhere, girl. It ain’t only your pa.”

Sorrow’s eyebrows arch up to her cap. “Everywhere?”

“Watch this,” the old man says, and giggles. “He’s gearin’ up to start speakin’ in tongues. Holy crap, I love this part.”

The preacher holds his hands out to them, as if he can reach right from the TV and grab them. “God the Father can see you,” he says, his voice all syrup now, and then he’s speaking in tongues, right there on TV, for believers and nonbelievers, as if every house is a temple. And as he speaks the words that only God and Sorrow know, she is drawn toward him, drawn in close to the back of the sofa, then around it and toward the box until her very face is up against the screen.

“You’ll go blind,” the old man calls.

Sorrow watches the preacher's every move, mimicking him with a twitch of fingers and shoulders, the way he raises his hands to the sky and to his heart. She smiles when he smiles, big and wide as she can. "How does he know?" she wonders.

"Girl, everybody knows it. Your father didn't write the Bible."

She looks at him. "Not all of it."

"Girl, he didn't write any of it. Not one snip. That Bible was written thousands of years ago and I ain't a bettin' man but even I'm bettin' he ain't that old."

"He didn't say that he wrote it, Sorrow," Amity says.

"No," Sorrow says. "He said we would write a new Bible. He and I, from what I saw."

"A new Bible?" The old man laughs. "You can't just up and write a whole new Bible. That's like makin' a new God up."

"That's not what Father told me." Sorrow crosses her arms and Amity looks at her. Wasn't it exactly what they were trying to do, make new Gods, all of them?

Sorrow relents. "Whose God is this preacherman's God?"

"He's everybody's God, girl. Your God and mine. There ain't but the one God, whether you got a hat on your head or three heads. God is big enough for everybody."

"Show me these other preachermen," Sorrow says.

Amity spins the dial and there's a slick-haired man at a podium, reading calmly from a Bible. She spins and finds a pack of people in robes, clapping their hands and singing while a man kicks his legs and dances before them, like he's having a holy fit. Sorrow's eyes never leave the screen. She only asks, of each one, "Do you like those preachermen? Do you like that one?"

Amity watches Sorrow settle herself onto the sofa beside the old man. And then it is Amity who has to stand behind it to watch.

"It's theater, girl," the old man says. "It's all for show. It's how they make their money."

"Money?" Sorrow blinks at him.

"Preachers need money. Churches need money. Why you think they're on TV?"

"God doesn't need money. Money is man's."

"You had a church, didn't you? All them mouths needed plenty of money. Didn't you shake bags and boxes under the noses of the faithful?"

"No," Amity says. "They brought whole carloads of things. Tea sets and cans of food."

Sorrow glares. "Can anybody be a preacherman and go on TV?"

"No. You gotta have money to get on TV so you can ask for money. You can't just start there, you gotta do the rounds first, earn it. Make a name for yourself. All them preachers started out on the tent circuit, like they always done."

"Where is this tent circuit? Will you take me there?" Amity watches Sorrow lean toward the old man, locking his eyes with hers so that they are the only two in the room, in the world. She's seen it before.

"Here's how it works. You start out on the road, drumming up crowds in fields and parking lots. Then maybe you can get yourself a tent and some musicians. From there, you might rent a town hall or a little theater. You can't just jump from a dirt farm in Oklahoma straight to TV, that's for sure! I tell you, I seen 'em all." The old man hardly stops for breath. "I seen the devil scared straight out of a crazy man. I watched the devil hop out, little red imp he was, run 'round the inside of the tent, and fly out through the flap. He left a burn mark, right there on the grass. I saw a whole family stick their hand in a box of massasauga snakes to prove their faith."

"What else have you seen?" Sorrow purrs.

The old man doesn't give Amity so much as a glance now. "Things that'd make your hair curl, if you had any under that shower cap, but none of that matters. Thing is, you need your own gimmick. Everybody's got sumpin' special. Back in the hungry times, we was lookin' for miracles. We was lookin' for rain. We was waitin' for somebody to tell us that God had not left these lands, wrung 'em out like a dishcloth, and headed to California Hisself. There was many a pretty rainmaker makin' money here. There was cloud seeding and soothsayin' and rain dances, white people all up and out dancin' 'round poles like prairie chickens. We started to think that maybe

God sold us out, and the devil had a hold of our Panhandle, so's he could hold it over his fire. You gotta find what people want to hear and when you give 'em that, then they'll give you money."

"I don't want money," Sorrow says.

"Well, you will. Money ain't an end, it's a means. Means it gets you where you want to go and I'm bettin' you wanna go somewheres."

Sorrow considers this, leaning her cap against the sofa cushion. "But this is the end of time. This is the time of false prophets. No one will listen to me."

"Preachers been talkin' about the end for years and we're all still here. We're all still stumpin' up cash for 'em, too. Lookit."

"Even with how they live here?" Sorrow points to the TV, where a woman slides her oiled breasts across a car, waiting for the preacherman to come back and shame her.

"Well, don't look at that," the old man says, coughing. "It ain't all wicked like that."

"I see what I see."

The old man looks at her until her smile fades. "You don't, girl; you see what you want to see. Your folks kept you stupid and that's their fault, but it's your fault if you wanna stay stupid and I don't think anybody ever told you that before. Nobody told either one a you. That you could choose who and what you wanna be."

"I'm not stupid," Sorrow tells him. Amity says nothing; she isn't sure herself.

"Right, then. Tell me what you got."

"What I've got?"

"Tell people sumpin' new about the end of time. Stop wallowin' in what they already know and tell 'em what they can do about it. We need a rainmaker. Give us some hope. That's what sells."

Amity thinks of home and shakes her head. She can't remember anything of hope but the mother who left with Adam and Justice, and none of them had anything like hope then.

Sorrow studies the ceiling, deciding. "There is no hope. The end is near."

He points at the TV now, where a woman has joined the man, sitting beside him and crying as symbols flash below them both. "They're not selling good news. You wanna cry like that at folks?"

The TV woman begins to howl then, pointing at the numbers, her padded shoulders jerking up and down. "No," she says. "Why isn't he crying?"

"Give him time. Look at 'em, Sorrow. You see them numbers getting bigger? People fork out cash for misery. People love to watch sufferin'. You can sell that, if you want to."

She shakes her head. "We don't believe in suffering. We worship and we love. We don't want to cry like that for people." Sorrow sits up straighter now. "I don't want to have to dress like that and I don't want that black stuff running down my face."

"What are you selling, then?"

"Father tells us that there is a family of God and all can belong to it and be loved, forever. That's what makes women come."

"With their tea sets." He shoots Amity a wink.

"I wouldn't cry if I was a preacherman," Sorrow says. "Father never cries."

"You could be a preacherlady," the old man says. "But you'd have to study. You'd have to learn to read and write. You gotta know your Bible and what people want to hear of it."

"Father says we must have the Bible inside us. We don't have to read to find God."

"Well, I'm tellin' you that your father is wrong. And he's on the run now, ain't he, so what does he know?"

Sorrow starts to snap back at the old man, then her shoulders droop. "I thought he'd come by now."

"I don't think he'd dare," the old man says. "God wasn't never scared of police. Think of Jesus. Did He run from the cross? He did not." He lets Sorrow think on that, then he tells her, "Anyways, you're forgettin' the biggest part of preachin'."

"What's that?"

"Well, you need sumpin' flashy to wear."

At that, Amity backs to the screen and the porch. She's tired of God and she's tired of her sister. The old man was hers and Sorrow took him. Even the TV was hers first, but Sorrow gets everything. Sorrow always takes what she wants. She slips away, while no one is watching, to the gas station to open the door to Sorrow's altar. There, in the darkness, she takes her clothes off. She looks at her dark shape in the room's wavy mirror, but she sees nothing but ghostly skin. And onto this skin, she slides the inky fabric of the blue dress, slippery on her body, loose and flowing where she has only known ties and straps. And then she puts all of her clothes back on over it, to wear her dress like a secret.

She finds Dust in his barn, kneeling before his motorcycle, worshipping it with oil. She watches kittens roll in straw and swishes her hips to feel the blue slip slink beneath her skirts until Dust looks up. "You need the bathroom, go," he says.

"I don't need the bathroom," she says, cross now.

He cannot see her secret. She will have to show him.

He swings his leg astride his motorcycle and pulls the choke out, turns the key. The engine fires and stalls, filling the barn with an oily blue smoke.

"Is it supposed to do that!" she yells as he restarts the engine.

"I'm still fixing it!" he yells back. "Piston ring!" He switches the engine off and she pushes open the barn door, kittens scattering, to let out the blue smoke and breathe. "Piston ring's sticking." He slaps the seat, as if disciplining a child.

"When will your bike be ready?"

"Soon. Real soon."

"And then will you go?"

"Once the harvest's done," he says. "I wouldn't leave him my work."

Amity kisses him, square on the cheek.

"Hey," he says and he wipes the spot, embarrassed.

"Will you show me your scar?" she asks him.

"You've seen it."

"I healed it. I want to see it healed."

He gives the scar a rub beneath his shirt. "You are so weird," he says.

"Am I? How am I weird?"

He lets his shirt down off his back. His scar is red and upraised, just as before.

"Your scar has come back," she tells him.

"Where do you think it went?" He tries to pull his shirt back on, but her hands are already inside it, rubbing at the knots of his scar. "Stop touching it."

"But I healed you."

"You can't heal people. Nobody can. Let go." He buttons his shirt up and she undoes her pinafore. "What are you doing?"

"Don't look," she says. When he turns away, she tugs the round collars from her neck and wriggles out of the too-short sleeves. She drops her dress off her arms and removes the underblouse to expose the deep V of the blue slip, its billowing cups and the bones of her chest. She thinks of the girls she saw in town, with their legs out and their hair down, and she pulls the kerchief off. “You can look now,” she says, and she lets him turn. She lets him look. And because he has nothing to say and his mouth is open, she moves toward him, fastens her mouth upon his.

She looks at him, blurry, close-up, and he pulls his mouth away and wipes it with the back of his hand. She reaches for his belt buckle.

“Amity!” He scoots back from her. “What are you doing?”

“It’s all right,” she says.

“It isn’t. You don’t do this.”

“I do,” she says. “I’m bleeding.”

“Jeez,” he says. “Oh, jeez.”

“I watch things. I know what to do.”

“Well, I don’t. You’re just a kid. Put your dress on.”

“I’m old enough to make Jesus now. Look at me.”

Dust slaps her hands away and does his shirt up, buttoning it all the way to the top, as if to keep her out of it. "There's something wrong with you, isn't there? There's something wrong with all of you. Why isn't anybody doing anything?"

"I don't know," Amity tells him. This is all she knows and all she wants, and her hands are outstretched, empty. They reach for something to heal.

But Dust is running away from her. He sprints from the barn and she follows him, cutting across fields for the house and the gas station. She trails behind him, blue slip fluttering, sticking to her skin in the heat, and she wonders if it's a kind of game, some prelude to Jesus-making, a step in the process she's never seen, despite her watching. Maybe they do things differently here.

She watches him reach for Sorrow's door, bang on it and shout like a man possessed. No one can resist Sorrow, not even Dust. When Sorrow opens it to him, he reaches for her, puts his hands right on her and shakes her, and Sorrow doesn't yell. She doesn't pull away or shove him back, as she should. She lets Dust touch her and she lets him speak. She listens to him—she actually listens—and when she sees that Amity is watching, she pulls him into the bathroom, into her secret place with her secret altar, where she takes no one but Amity. Amity wonders what he'll find in there, what he'll make of the things spread across her altar.

She wants to fling the door open and pull Dust out. He knows that Sorrow is dangerous in darkness—he saw how Sorrow cut her—but he doesn't know everything Sorrow can do in a dark room. And if he didn't want to do it with Amity, would he with Sorrow? Would Sorrow let him? And if he didn't want that, what on earth was it that he wanted from Sorrow? What would anybody want?

Amity pulls the blue slip off over her head and buttons her dress up. She stuffs the slip into a pile of trash. The door stays closed and she knows then that Sorrow has taken her Dust, taken him like the TV and the old man. Taken him, like Father. Taken him, like God.

34
Buds

Amaranth listens to Sorrow laughing. A noise that lifts her heart and tells her all things are possible now. There is nothing more she need wish for. On the other side of the house she stands, easy in conversation, speaking out loud, as any ordinary girl might. It is a far cry from last Sunday, when the television boomed preachers all day, robed men in glass churches, hellfire preachers on polyester settees, all hand claps and hallelujahs, while her children stared in silence.

Sorrow is changing; she can change.

The kitchen garden is a lush green from

watering, a ragtag oasis of leaves and stems and fisted buds in every color: orange, fuchsia, violet. The storm moved the seeds from their ordered rows and floated them into untidy masses and clumps. Still, it will be a sight when the plants unfold and show their faces.

Another high-pitched giggle bursts from Sorrow and she cannot keep from grinning herself. When there is time, she decides, they will talk about Sorrow starting school, making friends her own age, girls who will teach her what normal girls are like. She will come to see how bright she is, how capable, once the fog of her father has cleared, once she has forgotten.

And chickens, she thinks. Chickens for Amity, who likes to take care of things.

Bradley comes back to her, shaking his head. “They’ve got my pa on the porch playin’ dress-up. I don’t know what they’re plannin’.”

“Well, whatever it is, go with it. Enjoy it. Sorrow’s laughing. Did you hear her?”

He strokes stray hairs back from her forehead, hairs that would have been kept by a cap. “Know what you’re growin’ out here yet?”

"I thought they'd be herbs." She thought these would be healing herbs, actually, black haw and blessed thistle, squaw vine and lady's mantle. It's what she would have grown, if she were his wife. She was relieved to see no angelica, pennyroyal, calamint. If his wife's seeds had grown emmenagogues or abortifacients, she would have felt compelled to tell him, so he would have proof of the reason his wife had miscarried, proof that the world wasn't randomly cruel, that it wasn't God but a woman who had chosen her own fate. These were herbs their community knew well, despite their constant desire for children.

"I hoped they'd be food," he said. "Ma had carrots and beans out here."

"They aren't," she says. "They're flowers. Just flowers."

"Flowers! What good are those?"

She laughs. "They'll be beautiful."

"Just like my wife," he says. "Growing somethin' nobody needs. Ain't worth the water."

"Beauty is its own purpose."

"That so?" He squats down to look and shakes his head at the folly of them. "Flowers. When you plant seeds next time, make 'em somethin' we can use."

She laughs as he walks to the house, calling jokes to her daughters. It's the closest she'll get to a promise.

35
Shattercane

Sorrow rehearses, so that she will be ready.

"Stop spinnin' around," the old man calls from the porch. "You're makin' me seasick. Put down that old bit of bowl."

Sorrow tells the old man about the little boy prophet. He tells her that the tent circuit is full of boys and men like him, prophesying disaster, telling the fortunes and futures of the faithful. "That's the devil's work," Sorrow says.

"What else is prophecy? Just tellin' the future, Bible-wise."

Sorrow listens to him as if he is the first person ever to look at her and to see her and not want something. Amity watches them both, but there is no role for her in Sorrow's show. She sits in the shade beneath the scabby tree, writing her name and Dust's name, all the letters she knows in the world now, over and over on top of one another in the dirt with a stick.

"Do you believe?" Sorrow spins and points her arm out.

"I can't hear you," the old man cackles. "Speak up! Stop wiggling! Sock it to me, sister. Give it to me straight!"

Sorrow spins and laughs out loud.

Amity can only think of Dust and all that Sorrow won't tell her. "I showed you the TV," Amity said. "I took you to the old man. We don't have secrets, you and me."

"It's nothing to do with you," was all that Sorrow would say. Nor would Dust tell. He kept his distance from her, wouldn't meet her eye, ashamed as he seemed to be of her. "I'm just trying to help, Amity. It's stuff you don't need to know," is all he would give.

She wishes she had hidden somewhere, even inside the horrible room, so that she could see what they did and how they did it, so that she could see what it was that he wanted and make herself be it, if she could.

The day of Sorrow's debut, Amity makes a handbill of sorts, following the old man's instructions. Her name had to be written up large across a sheet, he told her, so people would know when to come and where. They tie his bedsheet to the front of the porch and she writes the letters as big as she can across it with old paint, running back and forth to look at his version of the word in the dirt. Even so, some of the letters don't turn out like his. CMIN SOOON, she scrawls. SOROW.

Amity sweeps the porch for Sorrow. She drags kitchen chairs into the shade and gathers plastic-wrapped foodstuffs from the man's small shop by way of refreshment; the old man insisted that there were always refreshments at entertainments, to bring in more cash. The old man finds a tie in his chifforobe and puts it on, dampens down what's left of his hair, while Sorrow practices, daringly, in the bath upstairs, splashing and chanting for hours on end.

She gathers Sorrow's audience, helping the old man to a chair, hectoring Mother and Bradley to come in from their hoeing and spraying. They sit in the shade and fan the backs of their necks in the last of the day's heat. Dust wouldn't come.

When Sorrow appears from the house, she is transformed. She is magnificent. She flings back the screen door and glides onto the porch, a shimmering vision in the old man's silken robe from the Far East, a black tasseled sash pinching in her tiny waist. She turns her back to display a red satin-stitched dragon, teeth bared and claws curled. She has even removed her cloth cap to show pale, clean braids pinned into a halo. Her cheeks blush from the bath and all their looking.

Mother and Bradley elbow one another when they see her and the old man bobs his head in approval. And then Dust is beside her, settling onto a chair. Amity turns to him, to thank him for coming, and she watches his eyes widen, his mouth go slack. He cannot keep his eyes from Sorrow. No one can.

"Do you believe?" Sorrow asks. She starts to spin and stops herself, wavers. Then her arm shoots straight out, pointing at every watching face. "Do you believe?"

"I thought we were getting a show," Bradley mutters. Mother scolds him as Sorrow bolts for the screen door. "Sorry," Bradley calls. "Come on back."

"Everybody gets hecklers," the old man calls out. "Suck it up."

Sorrow straightens the placket of the shiny robe and steps back to the edge of the porch. She makes a ball of her hands and flings them upright, as if she has thrown something hard at God. The black sleeves pool down onto her bony shoulders, showing the white sticks of her arms. "God the Father asks that we believe in Him, even when He's hard to find, even when it seems He's gone. God the Father asks us to believe in the unseen, to wait and watch for His signs even when we're sure they'll never come to us." She drops her arms and the sleeves flow down to smother her hands. "God the Father is not here, but He is coming. Do you believe?"

Mother hisses as the man shifts in his chair. "How will this help her?" he lashes back.

"Go on, girl," the old man calls. "Stick to the script."

Sorrow stares stonily at her feet, but

when Dust calls out, “Come on, Sorrow,” she gives him a rare smile that fires her face. Amity slumps in her chair and wishes the ground would take her in for comfort.

“The Lord will give you such a show,” Sorrow says. “A holy show that will shake you to your core. Are you ready?”

“Shoot,” Bradley says.

“I prophesy that the Lord will come like a storm from the north. He will pour out seven bowls of wrath onto your soil and ruin it.” A pink rash climbs up her neck. “Can you feel how He bakes your land?” Sorrow points out to the harvested fields. “This is the time for seers and prophets. They preach from the devil’s box with their hands out for money and a face full of tears, but the Lord says, He doesn’t need your money. He doesn’t want your clapping or crying. He wants your blood and your bodies. He needs the whole of your minds and your hearts, for there is nothing but Him. He is all there is. There are false prophets at work in the world who’ll say that you’re saved if you pray enough or pay enough, but they are wrong. I tell you I am the last, true prophet. I have seen the wrath of God! I will be His Second Coming!”

"Jesus," Bradley says, and he stands up. "Will you listen to her?"

"Please," Mother says. "Let her finish."

"I can't," he says. "Will you tell her? Will you tell her she was raped and the whole thing she's doing here is wrong—just—"

"Stop it, please," Mother begs.

He turns to Sorrow, hands out. "Look, I know what happened to you and when they catch him, I hope they lock him up for a long time, but somebody's gotta tell you it's nothin' to do with the world ending or God. He's your father, Sorrow. And he raped you and it's wrong."

Sorrow's hands press to her chest. "This is holy work."

"Sorrow!" Mother's hands fly to her mouth and Sorrow turns on her.

"You didn't want me to be the Mary. You didn't think it would be me, but the Father saw it."

"Your father isn't God, Sorrow," Bradley starts.

"But you can't be the Mary without the child," Sorrow carries on. "So you took me away and you took me from him and you killed it, here, on this man's cursed land! This wicked land!" Sorrow swings to the man, even as he's turning for Mother, telling her to say something. "Don't you think I can hear you upstairs, profaning with my mother? I hear your rutting, and so does the Father. They can hear you both, way down in hell. I see that your land will turn to sand in your fingers for wickedness. All you grow and want will blow away!"

"I'm not listening to this crap," Bradley says, starting for the house.

Mother slides from her chair to the dirt as she babbles, "It's my fault, mine."

The old man struggles up from his chair, his voice a rasp. "Sorrow, girl, you ain't the Mary. That ain't how the Second Coming works and whoever it was told you that did so for his own purposes, but you can't read the Bible so you don't know any better. And that makes you a fool." With that, the old man runs out of breath and takes a rattled one back in.

Sorrow shakes her head at all of them. "I'll tell you who's the fool," she says. "I never wanted to be the Mary, no matter what he did to me. I wanted to be the Father and I will be."

The old man hacks and clutches his windpipe. Amity rubs her hands, to charge them for healing, as he bangs on his chest and gasps for air.

"Repent while you can, for the world is ending!" Sorrow shrieks. "I can see it! God the Father will come and strike you down, one by one!"

"Shut up about your father, girl." The old man coughs and splutters until he's squeezed out. "Aw, git me on back to my bed. What am I doin' out here, anyway?" Bradley puts an arm around him, half carries him into the house.

Mother reaches up for Sorrow. "This is my fault."

Sorrow looks down at her. "When you killed the baby, you made this happen—when you killed the Messiah, you tried to stop the world ending—but it will end. It is ending!"

"No," Mother says, struggling up in her skirts. "It's my fault for indulging you and not seeing—not stopping—not stopping my husband—"

"Your husband? My father!"

"Stop it, Sorrow, please."

"But I don't need the baby. I don't need the Father and I don't need you! I will be the holy one! I will make it come!" Sorrow leaps off the porch and past them, black robe rippling.

Dust stands, knocking his chair backward. “She’s mad, isn’t she?”

Amity can only shake her head at the furniture, her mother sobbing, the sign sliding down the front of the house. “I don’t know what to do.”

Dust pulls her away from the porch. “Something bad’s gonna happen. Why won’t anybody do anything?”

“Because it’s Sorrow! Nobody ever does anything about Sorrow!”

“Well, I’m taking her home.”

Amity yanks her arm from him. “I don’t want to go home.”

“I’m not taking you. And you can’t tell anyone.”

“She won’t go. She won’t go anywhere without me.”

“She doesn’t care about you,” he says. “You should hear the things she says about you.”

“I don’t care,” she flings, stung. “You can’t take her. She’s my sister. She’s mine!” Amity rushes after Sorrow, following her into the fields, where she moves across the dark, seeded land and the rape stubble.

Sorrow zigzags between giant sunflowers, heads nodding as Amity follows, the coarse hairs of the leaves and stems scratchy on her face, her hands, and arms. Dust pounds the dirt behind her, chasing Sorrow, chasing her.

Sorrow shoves her way through the plants, but they snap back upright, hitting her full force and getting even, the stems weeping milk everywhere Sorrow has been.

Amity hears a match being struck. "The end of the world will come with fire!" she hears and she waits for smoke, for a sunflower to catch and go up like a mighty candle, but she only hears it sizzle and die. Sorrow kicks it.

"They're too green," Amity calls.

"Stop following me!" Sorrow turns on her.

"I always follow you."

"Well, don't!" She lights a match and holds it out to Amity, flame dancing between her fingers. Amity watches, wondering what the end of the world will look like when it comes at last, as Dust catches up. He runs past Amity and right to Sorrow. He takes hold of Sorrow by her slippery arms. "Stop this, Sorrow. I told you I'd help."

"Help?" she says. "I know what you want. I know what you all want." Sorrow whips her robe open to show, beneath it, her pantaloons and apron. Amity gasps at her in her underclothes. Sorrow puts her hands into her apron pocket and bulges it out, to make a belly, looking at Dust and laughing. Then she pulls her hands back out, holding the paring knife. She twists it to catch the sun on its blade and Amity's hand throbs in response. She swings it halfheartedly at a sunflower.

"Give me the knife, Sorrow." Dust holds his hand out.

Sorrow gives a thin-lipped smile to Amity. "Shall I, sister, give it to him?"

"Don't you hurt him!"

Sorrow sneers, "He doesn't care about you."

"Shut up, Sorrow," Dust says. He takes a step closer, his hand outstretched. "I promised I'd help, didn't I? Leave Amity alone."

"Everyone leaves Amity alone. That's why she's always watching." Sorrow looks at Amity. "All she does is watch."

Dust grabs hold of Sorrow's wrist and shakes it. "Drop it," he says.

Amity watches Dust holding Sorrow and

she thinks of them together. “I do more than watch.”

Sorrow leers at her. “Oh, do you?”

“I heal with my hands,” Amity tells her. “You know I do.”

“I know no such thing. I’ve never seen it.”

“I do more than heal. You think it was Mother, but it was me. I put my hands on your baby and I took it.” She rubs her hands together, to show her, to remind her what she did.

Sorrow lunges at Amity with a cry, but Dust has too tight a hold on her. He squeezes her arm until she has to throw the knife down, but when he bends to pick it up, she slips away between the dark stalks.

“You okay?” Dust asks her.

Amity cannot look at him. “She hates Mother for what she did. But it was me. She should hate me.”

Dust only puts his hand over her mouth. “Hush,” he says. “Listen.”

They hear Sorrow’s feet running and stopping, changing direction. They hear the rustling of stalks. He points across the field and they see a flash, a match flaming up. “She’s in the rape!”

• • •

Sorrow stands in the snap of the knee-high stubble. She lights a match and throws it down. They watch a patch of stubble catch.

"Burning won't hurt it," Dust says. "Nitrogen's good for the soil." But even so, he watches, to see what she will burn next. Flames lick from the stalks and a column of smoke rises like a sea beast from dark water.

Sorrow sees Dust's barn, just as Amity has the thought of it, and runs for it, Dust and Amity on her heels. Sorrow gets to the door first, opens it, and rushes in. Dust flies behind, kicking the stand up on his bike and rolling it out as Amity claps for kittens. She bends for a kitten, for two, and shoos them outside. They slink around her ankles and she has to kick at them, frighten them into running, and she calls for the mother cat.

Sorrow sees her. She screams and rushes toward Amity and Amity must grab hold of the barn door, to slam it shut on her sister, trapping her inside. Dust helps, pressing the door shut with his whole, straining body. They hear Sorrow gasp for breath on the other side of it and stop, panting. “Sorrow?” Amity breathes. Sorrow gives a tiny, tinkling laugh, like something breaking.

“Don’t open the door,” Amity says, thinking of the kitten, of what Sorrow did. They hold it closed together. Then they hear a cackling and a crackling, like paper being balled.

“Don’t open that door,” Dust says, but Amity cannot help herself. It is Sorrow. She pulls the door back, and air rushes in to feed the smoke. There comes a fiery ball of flame. Amity beats her way in, sees Dust’s bed and the hay bales on fire. Dust pushes past her, shirt up against his face, and Amity follows until she cannot breathe. She cannot see him or Sorrow and she thinks that this is how the world will end, in the choking smoke of an angry God. She gropes her way back to the door, shouting into the dark for help, for rescue, and finding the light as Dust bursts free from the barn, coughing. He drags Sorrow by her waist. She swings in his arms to be free of him, and they collapse onto the ground together, coughing, clinging.

Amity sees it first: the plastic container in Sorrow's hands.

Dust grabs at it. "Gas—for the bike," he says, but Sorrow is too quick for him. She leaps up to dance back across the fields. He gives a hacking cough and rubs smoke from his eyes. Amity looks at the barn, at the smoke pouring out through the door, and she thinks of the gas station, of the fuel there, all a sister would need to end the world. "Come on," Dust says.

Sorrow stands in a faraway field, dark down a row of sorghum, where the plants stand tall as rows of corn. Their blade-long leaves curve down from their stems like skirts. Bright green by day, they darken as the sun sets, the sky going orange. Sorrow moves between them, twitching them. Amity sees her take the cap off the container and splash it about her.

"No, Sorrow!" Amity calls.

Sorrow begins to spin in place, holding the container out and letting the gasoline go in an arc, like a skirt flung out to bell in prayer.

"Sorrow, don't!" Amity sees Sorrow

release the container, so it flies away from her. She hears her strike a match. "Sorrow, no!"

The gas in the circle around Sorrow lights in a snap. Blue flames rise around her and she lets out a gravel-tongued roar. Sorrow spins and in her spinning the silky fabric of the old man's robe threatens to catch, to make of her a whirling tempest, a wheeling chariot of fire. The field around her catches, row after row, as stems spark, radiating from her like a spinning dance passed hand to hand.

Amity hears shouting behind her, hoping Mother will have seen the fire, will have found a way to get some help. She scans the fields, left and right, for Dust, but she cannot see him. Her heart plummets for him and her abandonment, but she cannot blame him for it. Maybe no one can help her sister but she. She is Sorrow's keeper and this work can only be hers.

Amity runs to her, hands out over the band of her fire. She feels Sorrow take her hands, forgive her, and spin her, around and around—or maybe to try to pull her into the fire itself. Amity sees the edges of her own skirts catch. Sorrow throws back her head and roars her prayer as her robe flames. Amity's hands burn on Sorrow's skin while Sorrow's fire burns Amity, and their heat becomes one heat, her hands fuse onto Sorrow's hands, and they are one sister, one being, and Amity can feel for herself the rage and want within her sister. She can hear the language of angels, the swarm of bees in Sorrow's head. She can see her sister with her Father, as she had seen them both, but now she can see Him as if from within her sister's eyes, His eyes on her, His body on her, in Her, like God, setting her alight. Amity tries to pull the fiery robe from her, but Sorrow won't release her hands.

"His word is like fire!" Sorrow shouts. "Listen and let it take you!"

"No!" Amity yells, and even as she spins she knows this spinning will consume her. And that is what her sister wants. Amity rips her hands from Sorrow's. She can feel the skin on her palms tear and split as Sorrow grabs hard for Amity and misses. Amity leaps back from her sister and Sorrow's arms flail, empty. And then Sorrow spins herself, crashing across the flaming sorghum, her hands swatting unseen demons and angels.

Amity is pulled to the ground. The man Bradley throws himself on top of her, pats her to put her out while Mother wails, "Sorrow!"

"It's okay," Amity tries to say, but she chokes out smoke. Her lips feel hot, blistered as sausages. When she can, she will tell them she has fireproofed Sorrow. She has brought Sorrow's fire into herself. Sorrow can spin, but the fire will not consume her. The fire will not want her, now that Amity has touched her with her healing hands.

She hears the man say he'll get her to the hospital, hears him tell Mother it's his fault, there's weed killer on to kill the shattercane. "It's an accelerant," he shouts. But Mother only sobs, "It isn't your fault. It was always mine."

"It's okay," Amity tries to say again, and her mouth fills with blood. She reaches her fingers up, to clear it, and she sees her hands are dry and brown and stiff as two small Bibles. Her mind moves her fingers, but her fingers do not.

Bradley takes his shirt off and she flinches from him and his nakedness, but he only wads it, to put it under her head. “Don’t move,” he tells her. “Hang in there, kiddo.”

She lifts her head to look for Sorrow, but the man pushes her down, saying, “You have to keep your hands above your heart. Keep them up!” So she holds her hands up to the sky, to watch the smoke between them. She can hear shouting and crying, the choke and thrum of a motor. A motorcycle, she thinks, taking her two best loves. Dust is taking Sorrow away from her, just as he said he would, and no one stops them. No one can stop them. Before her hands, upraised before the heavens, she sees a stream of blue smoke. He is gone. And Sorrow is gone.

BEFORE: *The First Wife*

There was no veil, no organ. There was no cake or Champagne.

There was no confetti, no rice, no guests. There were no invitations.

There was only Amaranth and a retired justice of the peace, his wife for a witness. A cassette tape played one of Vivaldi's *Four Seasons* on an endless loop.

There was a preacher beside her, solid and sturdy in a pale linen suit, his graying curls pulled back. Amaranth married him. She was nineteen.

She wore a full-length lemon-colored dress from a Salvation Army shop in the small town where they married, off the highway, headed north. Someone's cast-off prom dress, she figured, though she had never been to a prom. It had long gauzy sleeves and a fitted bodice covered in daisy-chain lace. It was a little too short. Her hair was scraped back in a ponytail, just as he wore his, and there were wild-flowers jammed in the rubber band, picked from the cracks in an empty parking lot.

It wasn't the kind of wedding a little girl dreams of or plans for, but she was not that kind of little girl. She had never played dress-up, never wore her mother's over-sized gown, draped Kleenex on her head, or practiced the step-together-step of the "Wedding March." Her Barbies had no wedding gowns—not a one of the eight Barbies who lived with the single Ken in their plastic house, on their cardboard beds, in sin. No one she knew was married; her parents hadn't been. She had never even been to a wedding, but she understood the rituals from TV shows. She knew there should be a dress and a bouquet. She knew there would be a ring and a kiss and a promise to be faithful and eternal, 'til death did them part.

His hand was warm in the crook of her elbow. The gauze of her sleeve was damp and clinging. When she turned to look at him, she felt dizzy, dazed, and thirsty. She felt stripped and exposed. She felt beautiful, but sick to her stomach. She didn't know that love could make you sick.

He gave her arm a squeeze and she felt all the eyes of the room on her.

"I do," she said into the expectant silence. "I do."

After the ceremony, her husband drove them northward. All she owned was balled in a duffel bag in the back of his van, beside the cardboard boxes filled with tracts and pamphlets. She watched the world roll by through his van window and curled her fingers around the heavy gold ring he had placed on her fourth finger. It was too big for her and she had to make a fist to keep it on, for she had a habit of losing things.

She had grown up in the high desert, down sand roads from a town of a hundred, a stretch of the Mojave where flat land met the San Bernardino Mountains, snow-covered in winter and clouded by dynamite blasts from the quarry in summer.

Her grandmother's bungalow sat squat on a hundred acres of hard-baked sand, Joshua trees, and creosote bushes. It was hard land that yielded little. It was a land to leave behind, as her mother did, as her father did, but it was all that Amaranth knew. Her life was her TV and her bedroom, the sand and the fruit trees, the abandoned houses and rock formations of the mighty, empty desert, where she searched for land turtles and roadrunners, collected red ants in a jar, and waited for her father to come home.

Her father always came back, as her mother never would. "Wanted the moon," was all her grandmother would say of her, the dark-haired woman in the black-and-white photograph who had borne her, named her, and left. "Wanted the moon and ran off to marry it." When she was a little older, Grandmother would tell her that it wasn't her fault. She was a victim of Free Love, the kind that hippies had before babies were born, but she couldn't make of her father a hippie in her head. Old TV shows were full of hippies, all fringe and headbands, women with long, straight hair like her mother had. "Don't you believe that love comes free," her grandmother said. "You're living proof of it." She didn't like the name her mother gave her, but Grandmother said she was lucky not to be named Sunshine Ladybug or Diaphanous Lampshade. "It could've been a lot worse," she was told. Either way, her father called her Amy.

And when he came home it was Christmas, Easter, and the Fourth of July all at once. When he came there was honky-tonk on the turntable and groceries in the fridge, fresh milk and butter and potato chips, Cactus Cooler and Delaware Punch, hot dogs and tamales and jars of hot sauce and salsa. Bottles of liquor would come out of the pantry and there would be canasta and three-card stud and laughter around their table, just like on TV. It seemed to be the only time her grandmother smiled.

When he came home there were trips into town, down the sand streets to the asphalt street in his car, to the parking lot that was town, lined with all the shops they had: Grandmother's hairdresser, where she got her blue rinse, the grocery store, and the coin-op Laundromat. There was the bar called Buzz, where her father would lift her up to a bar stool to drink glass after fizzy glass of Shirley Temples, rims festooned with mermaids and parasols. Best of all, there was the mobile library, parked in the parking lot, where she had already read the whole of the children's section and was working her way through young adult to gothic and historical. The librarian let her take out a brown paper shopping bag of books at a time and never scolded when they were overdue. After all that, she would drive them, for her father and grandmother did not drink Shirley Temples. Seated on her father's knees, turning the wheel left and right, she would get them home.

When her father was home to tuck her in, she wasn't afraid of the dark. When he was home, the closet didn't make noises and coyotes didn't howl. Sometimes he would sit and smoke in her room and tell her stories about how he ran away to the circus, how he ran away to sea. But he never wanted to tell her how her mother ran away.

On her first night of marriage, she slept in the back of her husband's van, parked along a dark stretch off a two-lane highway at the state border. She had never left her own state before. He lit votive candles and set them across the dashboard, like some makeshift altar. He told her they would be home by tomorrow night at the latest. He took off his suit, draping it carefully over the back of the driver's seat, and knelt on the futon mattress on the van's floor. "Pray with me," he said.

She wished she had a bottle of something—anything. Her dress felt tight, suddenly, cheap and childish. She wished she had something frilly on beneath it, something lacy and white, or the blue that tradition said she was meant to have worn for the wedding. She yanked the zipper of her dress down and stepped out of it. She kicked it away to stand in her old bra and underpants, their elastic frayed. She took those off, too, as he watched her.

"Come, wife," he said, and smiled, as if the word was sweet in his mouth.

"Husband," she said, trying it out.

He patted the futon. He held his arm out to her and she knelt, desperate for alcohol. It was all that she could think of. She shut her eyes against the want for it. She felt his hands find her skin. She breathed in the scent of his van, its gasoline and upholstery, and of him, wood smoke and the patchouli-oil smell of his hair. She told herself that this was home now, wherever he was. He would be home.

"I thank God for you," he told her. She swallowed, thirstily, and let him pray.

She loved his van, as she had loved her father's car. She loved anything that could take you away. She knew that was what her father loved best about his car, too. There were a number of rituals that let her know when he was going. Grandmother's Deepfreeze would be stocked full of TV dinners. Library books would be swapped by the bagful. Just before he left, there would be some trip away for them, just the two of them, to the dry lake bed where the turkey shoots were, or into Barstow to look at the trains. Once, he took her to a ghost town's silver mine and laughed when she said they should go in and steal what was left, so he wouldn't have to go away to work. "Millions of dollars, just sitting there," he said. "And it'd cost more to mine it than it's worth."

"That's not fair," she had told him, and he had laughed at her.

"Life's not fair. That's one thing you might as well know now."

It wasn't fair that she got left behind, and when she was ten, she decided she would go with him. She knotted her clothes and her Barbies in a pillowcase. She snuck into his backseat to hide. He was nearly to town, hard rock on the radio, before he reached around for a can of Coors and found her. Then he slammed on the brakes and spun the car around, back for home.

"I want to come with you," she whimpered.

"I want a lot of things," he said. He dropped her off and watched until she had trudged to the house, checking each step for scorpions. When she opened the door, he sped off again, wheels churning sand. Then she jumped on her bicycle and pumped hard on the pedals to follow him, skidding into the ruts he'd made, where packed sand had given way. She thought if she could reach him before the road turned to asphalt, he would have to stop and let her in. She rode as fast as she could behind him, following his taillights.

The asphalt road was just ahead. He stopped and swerved, jumped out of his car. “Go home!” he shouted.

“I hate it here.”

“You don’t know what hate is. You don’t know what I hate.”

She held her breath. If he hated her, the world would end. It would stop its spinning. It would be snuffed right out.

His voice came soft then. “You can’t take kids where I’m going.”

“I’m not a kid,” she whined. “I’d be so quiet. You could just leave me in the car. No one would know.”

“I’d know,” he said. “And I need you here, to take care of your grandmother. I need you here, waiting for me. Now go.” He waited until she picked up her bicycle. Then he slammed his door and drove.

The sky above her was inky black, punctuated by stars and planets and constellations, a sickle of moon. A whole world above her, around her, that told her that the whole of her life wouldn’t be this small and mean, this rocky, this sandy, this quiet. The Milky Way twisted above her like a road made of diamonds. It told her she would leave, too, as soon as she could.

• • •

On the first day of their marriage, they drove out of California, heading north for Oregon, for Idaho. She had only seen desert and freeways. She had never seen such unbound green, such an expanse of old trees, of silent roads and forests, where waterfalls tumbled beside the van and nobody stopped to photograph them.

Amaranth was accustomed to things being fake, being mocked-up and make-believe. She had lived for the last several years in a world of fantasy lands beneath a fiberglass Matterhorn, which towered over the city and its acres of hot parked cars. For Amaranth, the structure guarded a privileged and secret world, hooped by the elevated concrete track of the futuristic Monorail, alive with the sounds of a steamboat's lonesome whistle and the nightly crack of fireworks exploding in the sky. It was a world she couldn't afford to visit, surrounded by cheap, worn-out streets where everything was themed. Motels were alpine, space-age, or Polynesian. Diners served triple-blob pancakes in the shape of mouse ears. Each and every business added “land” to their names, to join in on the fun, to flog their wares and services to unsuspecting tourists in such locales as Camperland, Liquorland, and, Amaranth’s workplace, Tacoland, a Mission-themed stucco building in a cracked asphalt lot lined with palm trees, whose packets of salsa made her think of her father. Vents poured out heat and the scent of grease. Her car smelled of deep-fat-fried tortillas and her arms were sticky from pouring jumbo Cokes into fiesta-striped bucket-size cups. She thought she knew what boredom was in the desert, but she didn’t know about the mind-numbing tedium of fast-food service and a three-dollar-an-hour job. She was seventeen and it was the best job she could get.

She had been working for two years before she met her future husband. She had served every item on the combo menu, in every combination. Employees had come and gone in a loop as endless as the restaurant’s mariachi Muzak. Zachariah had leaned into the tile-arched ordering window and asked her where the nearest church was. He laughed when she told him it was the circus tent next door called Melodyland. "Have you heard the good news?" he asked her.

"Here?" she scoffed. "You want good news, go find a happy hour."

He had laughed and told her she was cute. She called him a letch and he'd laughed again, delighted by her. They got all sorts at all-night fast-food establishments like Tacoland. She had seen it all—college boys on spring break from the Midwest, hoping to score with a California girl; middle-aged sleazeballs, thinking she could be bought with cheap wine and a meal. Sometimes she could.

She found him asleep in his van in their parking lot when she arrived to open up and fire up the fryers. "You can't sleep here," she told him, but a few months later, she would be sleeping in the parking lot herself, having run out of sofas and fast friends made over a cheap bar buffet.

A year later, when he came back to the parking lot, he would find her in her car, the doors open and her purse gone. She had been drunk again, drunk out of her mind. "Have you heard the good news?" he asked her, and then, leaning in to her, said, "My God, are you okay?" She was not okay. Not at all.

When they reached his land, he turned up a gravel path, tight between white pines at the base of a gray-rock mountain studded in conifers. Three women stood before a house, rough-hewn wood with hay-bale foundations. It was painted a bright, fresh yellow. There were raised beds overflowing with bean plants and vines in full flower, lettuces, and bushy herbs.

She looked at him. Who were these women?

"You must be Amy," the first woman said with a smile, pulling open the van door and holding out a freckled hand to help her down. Yellow paint striped her arm. "I'm Hope." The other two women had gone straight to his driver's-side door and squealed like girls to see him. They were not girls. They were older than Hope and significantly older than Amaranth. They were bone-thin, in faded overalls, and their teeth, when they smiled their hellos, were long and brown at the gums. She watched them each kiss his mouth.

Hope took Amaranth by the arm. "Let's

get you inside. Such a long drive you've had. Come and meet Mother."

Amaranth looked back at him. Whose mother? He had no family. It was the one thing they had in common.

Hope opened the door and took her through a piney entryway into a gloomy parlor, the small windows hung with heavy curtains. "Here's our Amy," Hope called into the murk.

An ancient woman sat shrunken in a needlepoint chair, dwarfed by a tasseled lamp. Hope switched it on above her and the light made the white tufts of her hair glow in a holy aureole. She lifted a knobby-knuckled hand, veined and spotted, and Amaranth took it, warmly. She thought of her grandmother and her final days in her bed, when she seemed to shrink into the rind of her own skin. She thought of how mean her grandmother had become.

The old woman's fingers explored her own, twisting the loose band she wore. She held her hand out, palm down, as she had seen other women do when showing off their rings. Before she knew it, the old woman had snatched it off.

"Oh," she said to Hope, embarrassed. "She's—taken my ring."

"Has she?" Hope said. "I'll get her pills." Her husband came in with the two other women and she told him how the old woman had taken her ring.

"It's her ring," he said. He held his hand out for it. The old woman cocked her head, opened her mouth, and slid the ring into it. Amaranth grimaced: the horrible vision of her wedding ring in the sagging, wrinkled mouth of the crone, the sound of it clicking against dentures. "Is she mad?" she heard herself whispering. He glared at her. "She'll choke on it, is all."

Hope entered with a handful of pills and a glass of water. "Come, Mother," she said.

The old woman shook her head and pursed her lips, but no one shouted or threatened, as Amaranth would have done. Her husband only put his hand on her, his bride, and smoothed the fabric across her belly, as if he could show them all the tiny bean inside her, though she was not showing yet. The five women each made a noise: Hope a gasp, the two women tandem "oh"s, Amaranth an embarrassed laugh, and the old woman a pop as her tongue slid out with the ring on it, wreathed in spittle. He dried the ring on his trousers and slid it back onto Amaranth's finger, still slightly damp.

He took her up the stairs and along a landing to a back bedroom, sloping under the house's pointed roof. The gray mountain hung in the small frame of the window. They sat, back-to-back, on opposite sides of a small double bed heaped with the quilts that spoke of hard winters and no heating.

"Who are these women?" she asked him.

She heard the bed frame squeak as he bent to unlace his shoes. He slid them carefully beneath the bed. She kicked her own shoes off and slung them under the bed, knocking something hard. When she bent over, she found a porcelain chamber pot. She sat back up and tried to pull him around to her by his shoulder. "You told me you had no family. Who are they?" Someone had put wildflowers in a jam jar by her bedside. Was it her bedside? Where did all the women sleep? "Did you lie to me?"

He turned around to her. "What?"

"What's going on here?"

"I did not think I should take a wife," he said.

Her eyes stung. "Fine," she tossed out. "Take me back."

"No," he said. "You misunderstand. I thought it was selfish, to raise one woman above others. To raise you above all."

When she spoke, her voice was small. "Then why did you?"

He came around the bed to kneel beside her. "I never thought to have a child."

"Then you shouldn't have slept with me." She wanted to hurt him.

"But I loved you and I wanted you. And I could see how lost you were."

She choked on a sob. She had nothing and no one and he had been her one last hope. He promised her a home and a new, clean life. If she left, she would be going back to nothing: no job, no car. She had sold all she had for money she had already spent on a dress and secret liquor. And then there was the pregnancy. "Who are those women?" she asked him again.

"Women who were lost like you," he told her. "Women I love, but not like you. I love you, Amy. I always will. My heart has set itself on you."

She thought of her mother, who married the moon. She thought of her grandmother, dying. “Not the moon,” her grandmother said. “I never said moon. I said Moonies.”

She looked down at him and made her choice. She knew that she could run away, as her parents had, and raise a child alone in an absence of family, of love, or she could stay. She could just stay, to see where his love would lead them.

Part IV

SEPTEMBER

36

Driving Back

Mother drives, but there is no looking backward, no scanning behind to watch what they have left. She stares ahead, hunched and humming, and it is Amity who looks back now, turned around in the front seat of the burned truck to watch the gas station and the road recede.

Mother jostles a tire in a pothole. “Okay?” she asks.

Amity nods and faces forward. Her hands are bound and outstretched before her as if she is holding an invisible tea tray. “Oven gloves,” the old man called her. Whenever the road is rough and her hands hit the dashboard, Mother cries out, but Amity says nothing. She cannot feel it. Her hands are two boiled hams on the hocks of her wrists.

Four days they will drive, to get where they're going. Home.

There are no signs to look for now. The end has come.

37
Ash

Amaranth slows to watch for their turnoff, the thin path between the pines that is so easy to miss. Deliberately, intentionally so. The red firs stand, heavy with cones, and the tamarack turns golden, ready to throw down its needles for fall. She brakes and puts her arm across Amity, to hold her back as the truck swings off the road and into the dip that leads to their land. Headlights sweep the bark. Gears grind. She thinks of Bradley.

"I could come if you wanted," he said as she was leaving, standing over her, head resting atop her own. "But who'd mind Pa?

Who'd put rape in for winter? Take twice as long, with Dust gone." He turned his head to kiss the parting between her twists of braids and then her forehead. "You'll come back, if you've a mind to."

She nodded. She wanted him to tell her to stay. She wanted him to promise her that it didn't matter, all this damage they had done to his food stores, his land, his crops. She wanted him to tell her it didn't matter how crazy her daughter was. "I'll have your truck. I'll have to come back."

He turned away when she started the truck and belted in Amity. Only when she pulled away from the gas station could she see him looking after her, then waving behind her, waving as the red dirt road stretched between them, taking long, loping steps to walk behind them to wave some more. She wanted to slam on the brakes, fly out of the car, and run back down the road to him, to ask him if he would be there if she came back—when she came back. Because she was certain that as soon as she was gone, he would pick his house up, tuck the fields into his pockets, and vanish. She would follow the red dirt road back to find a red dirt hole.

It had been a hard, hot summer, undoing the work of Sorrow. Bradley harvested the shepherd's-crook stalks of the sunflower seed heads and turned over the remnants of the sorghum, unharvested and ruined. He worked in silence and alone while she emptied the rest of his food bins, rubbed menthol into his father's chest, and salved Amity's burns. In the kitchen garden, flowers bloomed and no one saw them.

Now, headlights urge them through the dark and the lodgepole pines. She can smell them, hear them scrape the truck's sides. Goats bleat, far across black fields. Up the path, high beams catch what is left of the temple, surrounded by a fluttering of faded yellow caution tape, marking it out as a crime scene. Her daughter stirs and she drives past it, so she will not see.

The front of the farmhouse is black with smoke. Beds that once stood filled with beanpoles and edible greens sprout dried weeds. A lacy curtain waves through a broken window like a white flag.

She unbuckles Amity and takes the flashlight, lighting their faces like moons in the cab. She cuts the truck's engine and all the world about them is dark.

"She will be here," Amity says. "Won't she?"

Amaranth reaches across her to open her door, and Amity slides down off the seat to land.

The front door of the house stands open.

"Hello?" she calls into it. She shines the flashlight on the entryway, across the blackened walls and the sodden quilts and tapestries that hang there. "Hello?"

"Sorrow?" Amity calls behind her. "Dust?"

Amaranth moves into the house, one arm reaching back for Amity. She shines the light into the parlor, its scorched walls and moldy needlepoint furnishings, the split cushions, the velveteen sofa erupting with springs. She moves around the newel post of the stairway and down the hallway. Glass crunches under their clogs.

In the kitchen, the floor has been flooded. The icebox door is open, dripping, reeking of milk gone off. Each cupboard door stands open and emptied. The walls are smeared with dark shapes, blood or feces, molasses. She steps on a china saucer and sees that the floor is covered with bits of china, gold-rimmed with tiny pink flowers, from the old, old woman's trousseau, as if there has been a one-room earthquake, as if every cupboard has vomited.

She opens a drawer for storm candles and safety matches and lights them, setting them into broken cups. She makes a ring of light for Amity. "You stay here," she says.

"Don't leave me," Amity whimpers.

"I just want to look upstairs."

"Please."

Amaranth looks at her daughter, her pale face, her outstretched bandages, the dark rings below her eyes. Her daughter is half a head taller since they left this house; how has she not noticed her growing, how her wrists jut from her sleeves? But her face is as taut and frightened as when she was made to run from all she had known. "We can look in the daylight," she tells her. "I'm not leaving you. Okay?" She gathers up a few of the candles and places the flashlight, gently, between Amity's two bound hands. "It will all seem fine, come morning. You'll see." She leads her child back through the house, their shadows rippling across the walls.

She settles Amity back into the truck.

The interior dome lamp is burned out, but she turns the ignition key half on to switch the headlights to full bright, telling herself it is for Amity. She is not afraid of the dark or the things flapping and flitting in it, catching the corner of her eye. It is only a bit of plastic bag blowing or a Styrofoam cup, caught by the wind.

Amity stares out into the light. Her hands reach like a zombie's. "What happened here?"

"The fire? You remember."

"No. Before. What made us all like this?"

Amaranth turns to her. "It started with love. It started with your father and his wanting to help people, to make a family for them—and with them."

Amity's head whips to the side, distracted. "Look!"

A flash of white runs across the headlight beams.

Amity's hands flap uselessly at the door handle, to get out.

"We mustn't scare her," Amaranth says.

"Sorrow," Amity whispers.

They peer through the window, but they see nothing more.

• • •

When Amaranth wakes, Amity is stretched across her, sprawled across her lap.

In the dawn's light, it all looks much worse. The raised beds before the house have been trod in and flattened. The goats have been in them, she figures, eating the spring buds and summer weeds, once there were no humans to bang buckets filled with peelings to feed them.

She turns the ignition key off with a groan. She tries to start the car and finds it won't. The headlights she left on have drained the battery. She'll have to check the barns for jumper cables. She'll have to find another car with power.

The house in the daylight is worse, too, and Amity stays in the car, as if she doesn't want to see the damage. Walls are polka-dotted with black mold. Amaranth mounts the stairs to search the rooms above and her foot goes through a stair tread, as if the house itself will pull her down into it. She clings to the handrail and hauls herself up to the landing.

Each bedroom door stands open. There are small things dropped and scattered along the floor. A sodden ribbon, an ashen strap. The plump, headless body of a rag doll bears the tread of a boot print. Inside bedrooms, dresser drawers are open, their contents spilling. She finds blond baby curls and bobby pins, a damp brown envelope filled with translucent milk teeth, and her heart aches for the children who lost them, the mothers who nursed them, the blur and chaos of the family she loved and left.

And then she tells herself no. The love she longs for is a lie. She must remember.

In her own room at the back, her drawers and cupboards have been opened and searched. She reaches between the mattress and the springs to find what she has hidden, the proof of her life that she left behind: the black-and-white photograph of her mother, her marriage certificate, and the brittle paper of Eve's death certificate, a reminder that this was never Eden. She takes a last look at the ransacked room and jams them all into her apron pocket. This is all she has to show for her life here.

The hatch to the attic is open, but the ladder has been pulled up. She stands beneath it, calling up into the hole. "Sorrow?"

Back outside, she finds that Amity is not in the car. Heart pounding, Amaranth rushes to find her beside the temple steps, kneeling before a huddled pile of trash, a soiled, makeshift altar of stuffed teddy bears, a Virgin Mary votive candle, a single faded American flag.

The temple looks as if it has only just been abandoned. But when she looks more closely, through its shattered windows, she can see that the floor has blackened and buckled from the heat. It is studded with debris from the fire. Her husband's temple, stilled from the spinning of women, silent from the gunshots and the shouting and Sorrow's rasping tongue, burned now and ruined.

She thinks of the food in the room below and how hungry Amity must be, how hungry she is. She looks at the thin ribbon of caution tape and wonders what the police found before they unspooled it. She wonders what they took away.

Amity looks at her. "It doesn't look safe," she says.

It isn't safe, Amaranth thinks. And it never was.

38
Goodwill Industries

Mother walks her away from the house and the gardens, over their land to count and inventory the cars and campers parked beneath trees. She names the wife who drove each one. She opens trunks and glove compartments, looking for paperwork, looking for supplies and jumper cables. She inserts keys into ignitions, all jangling from the one big key ring Father kept, while Amity follows tire tracks on grass and gravel, looking for the single track that will tell her where Dust's motorcycle was, bringing Sorrow.

Amity hears her mother scream and

she rushes back to find her inside a car, her head down on a steering wheel. The ring of keys has been flung onto the dirt. "It's dead," she says. "They're all dead."

"Who's dead?"

Mother lifts her head. "No, Amity, the cars. No one's dead."

"How do you know? Where are all the mothers? Where is everybody?"

Mother leans over to pick the keys up. "This is the seventh wife's car. She drove it across the country to get here. I need the car of a later wife, a newer wife. . . ."

Mother wanders toward the fields of alfalfa, heavy with purple blooms, no longer forbidden. Amity follows. They hear the drone of bees. Mother claps her hands for the goats, to see if they will come and be milked by her, but they are used to their freedom now. They stare back with their slit-iris devil eyes. Beyond, the barns are fallen, collapsed under their metal roofs. Amity remembers when she saw them on fire, but Mother only gives them a quick search and says there is nothing for them inside.

Mother finally gets Wife Forty-Eight's car to start, though the tires are flat on their rims. She tells Amity they'll drive into town to buy some cables.

"Will there be food?" Amity asks her.

Mother steers them toward the temple. "I thought there would be food left here." She idles a moment beside the sag of the caution tape. Then she moves them down the dirt trail, driving them to a gas station and to town.

Mother unwraps her bandages at the pharmacy counter. Amity looks at the spinner racks of glass jars, balms, and unguents. She looks anywhere but down at her hands, being slowly revealed. The pharmacist in his white coat takes a quick look at them and then he runs away from them, into a small glass room, where he speaks to another man and points at Amity, and she turns away from them to stare into a corner filled with wooden legs. And then there are two men, staring into her palms. They ask her to wiggle her fingers.

"What are you putting on these hands?" the man asks.

"Comfrey and honey. Ash from the fire," Mother says. "I mash a poultice. I hope—"

"You've done very well," the pharmacist says, taking in her dress and Amity's. "Under the circumstances. You've no eschars. You'll keep these scars, of course, but they'll fade over time." He flexes Amity's fingers back from her palms and she can feel the skin stretching. She fears it will rip. "Keep these wrappings off now. The skin needs to breathe."

"We do a burn balm," the other man says. "Better than honey. I'll get you a tube."

"But is she all right?" Mother asks. "Will she be all right?"

The pharmacist smiles at Amity. "You might have considered skin grafts, but this is how she is now. And such a pretty little girl."

Amity pulls her hands from his. Liar.

"Try to use your hands, child," he says. "They'll forget what they're made for."

At this, she looks up at him. She is forgetting what her hands can do, too.

People stare in towns here, same as Oklahoma. They walk and laugh and buy too much, just like there. She can see the signs of the shops up and down the street, now that she isn't being told to hide or stay down, and the windows piled high with baked goods and ice creams, women swinging shopping bags in wide, proud arcs. There seems to be so much that people want in the world.

Seeing a sign, she spells out the letters in GOODWILL INDUSTRIES and she thinks that's what they all need, some goodwill. She looks inside at the clothing, hanging and stacked, and thinks of the day when Sorrow ran and Mother sent her to buy something that she could make into a wrist strap. How surprised she was to see all the manner of ways that a woman could dress back then, when she exchanged a coin for a white belt that had lost its dress.

"We don't need anything," Mother says.

Two girls walk past then, seeing Amity's dress and pinafore, her mother's dress and apron, the raw skin of her outstretched hands. They bend their heads together and, once past, they let out loud guffaws, exaggerated and oversize laughs, butts swinging. Amity curls herself over her hands. She wishes Sorrow were there. She misses her wrist strap.

Mother shifts the brown bag on her hip, the apples and cheese, the squishy loaf of bread. "Perhaps we could afford something."

The thrift store is filled with garments and housewares, racks of clothes and stacks of furniture, tables on sofas, chairs upside down. There are shelves of old books and crockery, china, and crooked-heeled, foot-worn shoes. Amity brushes by a rack of blue jeans, faded and ragged-hemmed, as Dust's were, while Mother flicks dresses across a metal rod: flowers, polka dots, stripes. She rubs fabric between careful fingers and reads labels. "These are man-made. Cotton and wool is what you want. Nothing that says 'Keep Away from Fire.' "

Amity stares at a rack filled with slippery fabric and elastic straps, breast-shaped and crotch-shaped. In a fire, they'd be the first to go and quite rightly, too.

Mother takes her into a curtained cubicle to stand with her arms out, so that Mother can untie and unwrap her, pull dress after dress over her head. The full-length mirror shows her, shows all of her. She has never seen all of herself, all at once, and she steps close to it, closer, until she hits her nose on it. The mirror shows a dress, short, exposing her knees, a pleated riot of burgundy roses in blowsy bloom. Mother cinches a satin bow, pink and shiny as her unwrapped hands, about her waist. “Lovely,” she says.

“Will this stop people from staring?” Amity asks.

Mother looks in the mirror and at herself in her own long skirt and braided hair. Her eyes tell Amity that people will always stare at them, no matter where they go. She pulls Amity’s sash open and unzips her.

Amity whispers, “I just don’t want people to look at me.”

“I know,” Mother says. “Me, neither. You go and choose something.”

She follows Amity over to the denim and her hands stroke the jeans and tops, uncertainly, fingering labels as if she suspects more fires are coming.

Once Amity is dressed, Mother counts the modest fold of bills in her apron pocket and pays for Amity’s clothing. She folds Amity’s old dress and pinafore and slides them toward the young girl behind the counter. “Perhaps someone can use these,” she says.

Amity rubs her legs together, each clad in its own denim tube. She bounces on the rubber soles of her new secondhand sneakers and looks down at her T-shirt-covered front, where cartoon fruit sits. Her hair is in two looped braids beneath Dust's kerchief. She wishes he could see her now.

The girl leans on her elbows and snaps her gum. "You all from that cult that caught fire?"

Mother frowns at her and snatches a long dress from a rack, dark and plain. She says nothing as she hurries into the cubicle with it, stopping only to snatch a handful of those slippery, flammable undergarments.

Back home, Mother makes them a picnic, slicing apples, cheese, and bread to eat on a patch of weeds in the afternoon sun, where goats watch, from a distance. There is nowhere to sit inside that isn't damp or smelly. Mother doesn't eat. She pushes her food about and stares at the house. She pats the coil of jumper cables and tells Amity that when she gets the truck going they might as well go, and Amity can only stare at her then. How could they go without Sorrow? Why wouldn't she come out?

Amity thinks of all the things that Sorrow loves and how she has none of them here now. No bowl, no Bible, no Father, no hellfire on TV. No one to watch her spin or pray. Of all the things Amity has to offer, she decides the best thing is herself—and sandwiches. She folds bread over cheese into awkward, spongy half-moons. She forces her hands around an apple.

When Mother bends over an engine, Amity creeps into the house. She trembles in the entryway, in the cool and the damp. "I know you're here," she whispers. "I just want to see you." She thought Sorrow would be waiting for them, arms crossed to scold them from the front door. She thought Dust would be there, waiting for a lift back to Oklahoma. "What took you so long?" he'd ask and hop in the back of the truck. "Get me out of here," he'd say.

But he is not here, not waiting for her. His note said he was taking Sorrow. She could read those letters, the ones spelling Sorrow and home. But when she looked at it, checking every letter, she knew she wasn't in it. She couldn't find the letters of her own name. He hadn't written her goodbye.

Still, it wasn't Sorrow's fault. Everyone moved heaven and earth for Sorrow. Why shouldn't Dust? Her hands drop the apple. She sits on the bottom stair and sets the fold of bread down, which springs open to display its cheese. Either she or the sandwich will lure out Sorrow.

39
The Temple

When Amaranth looks up from the car's engine for her daughter, she is not there. Amity is gone again. "Amity?" she calls toward the house and the gardens. She calls to the fields and the goats.

At the temple, she sees someone has broken the caution tape to enter it. The ends wave like arms. She looks up the concrete steps and into the temple, but the room is empty. Undisturbed, but filthy. Sodden lumps dot the wooden floor.

"Amity?" she calls. She stretches a clog to nudge one. Almost uniform, the debris is, spread across the floor like low hummocks on a lunar landscape. She taps the lump with her toe to find it is fabric, heavy cloth, stuck hard to the floor, the rucked boards that were once planed and smoothed by the turning of a hundred wooden shoes. Amaranth bends down to find it has a waistband and gathers. The piles are skirts, dropped where each wife stood, spinning, and she thinks, my God. Rapture. Her husband was right.

Wives had been taken, pulled to heaven from their skirts. And she ran away from it, ran her own children from Rapture. Her final test of faith and she has failed it. She lost faith in her husband and his vision, and now she has damned them all to a hell on earth. No God could ever forgive her for it. There can never be repenting enough.

She lifts the skirt, as if it could reveal the wife who wore it, so that she might be mourned. But she sees no clogs beneath it. No stockings, blouses, or undergarments. And then she knows that the skirts were not shed in Rapture. They were dropped, on fire.

God did not take them, none of them. They ran away, as she did. They all ran away and she is no worse than any other wife, running to save her skin and her children's. She chides herself: how quick she is to believe and to judge. They are only skirts in tidy piles, like Lot's wives burned for turning, all turned to ash instead of salt.

Across the temple floor she sees the altar table, carbonized, lying on its side. It is clear of the hatch, which stands open. She can almost hear the shouting, hear the hatch being closed. She can hear her husband screaming, "I will open the seals!"

"Amity?" she calls. "Are you down there?" Would she go down there? "Amity?" She looks back at the house and the land around the cars for her daughter. Where is she? And then she is afraid. Has Sorrow found her?

She kneels at the burned mouth of the room below. It is dark below, down where the temple foundations are. There are no windows or doors and only the shaft of light through the hatch hole. "Daughter?" she calls down. "Daughters?" She hears something. A scratch and a moan. And then she fears that Amity has fallen in—or been pushed. She swings her legs into the hole. She kicks at the air like a child on a swing, thinking of the flashlight, there in the truck, but she reminds herself that she is not afraid of the dark, not afraid of the room below, or of ghosts.

She drops down into it, feels herself falling to the floor of it, lumpy, soggy. Blankets are there, warmth for the end of the world, damp now from whoever had tried to put their fire out. Her clogs trip over the bedding. Knees bent, her arms swinging before her, she gropes her way forward, out of the hatch's light, to feel for the wall. It reeks of rot, of decay and waste, worse than the inside of the ruined house. "Amity?"

A scratching comes and she thinks of the metal shelves with their foodstuffs, the sacks of grains and rice. Rats, she thinks, and shudders. Only rats.

She kicks something hard on the floor and she crouches, thinking shelves will have fallen or been pulled down. She might be walking on all of their food. She freezes, so as not to destroy any more of it, whatever the rats have left her. Her fingers feel through cloth and find stitches, the spidery stitches made by wives of many generations. Stitches made by her.

Something is breathing. She holds her

own breath and decides in the silence that it must be her. Her daughter is not in the room below. She is weak with relief, but still she can feel her heart slapping her chest from within.

She creeps forward, slowly, clog step by clog step, until her hands find glass jars, stacked and whole. Safe. Her hands find bags of grain that are soaked, no doubt sprouting, and sacks of apples rotting, fermenting. She finds the carboys of water they took turns to fill and haul down.

The room is Rapture-ready, but Rapture never came. Still, God hates waste. In the dark she fills her arms with Mason jars, beets in vinegar, tomatoes in molasses, whatever her hands can find. She waddles them over the lumps of the floor to pass them up through the hatch hole, to shove them across the temple floor, where they topple and roll above her. Then she creeps back, to gather more.

She hears the scratching again—a twitching. Something heavy, moving against the metal shelves. "Amity? Is it you?" She hears a low, ghostly moan and she thinks of the old, old woman, buried beneath the temple, inside its very foundations. She wishes for the flashlight.

And then her feet are caught. Her heart pounds and she bends to the stitching. She feels the shapes beneath it then, and she cannot place them or imagine what they are, and she can only remember how wives dropped their children, down through the hatch, and how she pulled her own children free, running them away, while the children of forty-nine wives were shut in for safekeeping and the altar table slid across to hide them. So that they could not be taken. She remembers how the flames took hold as she ran.

Had wives run without children? Had the children not been taken at all, but left down here?

Her hands leave the sheet. She cannot bear to lift it. She clutches at her skirt.

She has to get out of here. She no longer cares about the food they stored or the sheet that might prove to the outside world that they had lived and loved there, one family all. Everything is tainted now, by all that has been done. She reaches up for the hatch, to pull herself up, and then she hears it.

The voice that stops her. The voice that haunts her.

“Wife,” she hears. “Amy.”

40
Spinning

Amity plays hide-and-seek with Sorrow. Sorrow wants Amity to find her. Amity knows it by the apple core, lying brown and dainty on its side. She knows by the cheese crumbs, leading her up the stairs.

She looks and listens for Sorrow. She hears doors slam and follows the sound to the top of the landing, where she is struck by the emptiness, by the absence of family. The house is too big without them, spilling out of bedrooms, bustling by with hands full of linens and babies. The house is too quiet now.

She sniffs the air for Sorrow. She thought

she would only have to follow the smell of her fire, but all the house smells of Sorrow. She peers into bedrooms, sees their empty, unmade beds. She calls down the corridor. And then she watches as the long legs of the wooden ladder are slowly lowered from the attic, inviting her up.

She looks up the length of them, up into the eaves of the house, expecting Sorrow's grin or grimace. "Sorrow?" she calls up to the roof and the silence.

She hooks her elbows around the rails and climbs up, her clawed hands unable to catch hold of the rungs. She moves, one sneaker at a time, up into the smoked A-frame of the roof. Her head pokes up through the attic floor and she can see their giant bed, made for all the children, the floor covered with air mattresses, cushions, and blankets where they all slept together in a tangle of limbs.

"Sorrow, I'm here." Amity shuts her eyes.

Across the room she hears clogs shuffle over floorboards. She smells Sorrow's acrid smoke. "We just want to see you."

"Don't you look," she hears back, breathy.

"We won't hurt you."

"You couldn't hurt a fly."

Amity nods, her eyes shut, and waits until she feels two bony hands cover her eyelids. She feels tears squeeze out from beneath them, as if they pour from Sorrow's palms. "Are you okay?" She knows better than to ask about Dust.

"Don't look at me," Sorrow tells her, and Amity nods.

Like blindman's bluff, Sorrow leads Amity through the house, eyes shut, her arms tugged and pulled as if by their missing strap. Amity winces, waiting to be smacked into a wall as her sister walks her. Sorrow pulls her down the stairs and at every step she expects to put a foot out and find the tread is gone beneath her, that Sorrow has walked her off the edge of the world.

When the heat of the sun hits her face, she knows Sorrow has walked her out the front door. Her eyelids flicker open and she catches, for a moment, the sight of a shape in a dark skirt and dirty blouse, cap jammed tight as muslin on a jar. She looks like any wife or mother. She feels Sorrow's hands slap back over her eyes.

"I told you not to look," she says.

"I'm sorry." Amity bites her lip, afraid of what Sorrow doesn't want her to see.

"You will be sorry. Come on."

Amity feels herself dragged over dirt and up cement steps to floorboards. Her sneaker slips over lumps and bumps and Sorrow's hands dig into her face, but she trips. Her ankle twists and her useless hands fly out to break her fall. She sprawls across the temple boards, arms sliding over fabric. Dazed and flat, her eyes open. She looks up at the dark skirted shape of her sister, bending down to scoop her up. She sees Sorrow's face.

"Don't!" Sorrow shoves a hand out and turns away, shielding herself with her other hand, but Amity has seen her. She is beautiful, beautiful as she ever was. Amity has taken the fire from her and into her hands, just as she had hoped. She had healed Sorrow after all.

"Sorrow," she says. "Look at me." She holds her boiled hands out. She waits for Sorrow to pinch them or kick her, to exert her revenge at last, but Sorrow only drops her own hands from her face. "The fire didn't get you."

"No," Sorrow says, as if she is sad about it.

Amity closes her eyes and she can see the fire rise up about them. She can hear how Sorrow shouted, from the field and from the altar. She can see all the fires she started. Then she feels Sorrow take hold of her wrists and pull her upward, walk her forward, and she is afraid.

But Sorrow says, "When you pass through the waters, I will be with you." The promise and threat of their prayer.

"Through the cities of war, I will be with you," Amity finishes. She feels herself walked in a circle. Her heart leaps for Sorrow.

"When you walk through fire you shall not be burned."

Amity finishes the prayer. "And the flame shall not consume you!"

And then Sorrow spins her, faster and faster, at last. Her eyes shut, the room wheels in her head and all about her. She feels herself spinning with the stars and the sky. She feels herself in a circle of women, visible and invisible through all of time, family eternal. They are there in her body, there in her blood. She knows they are waiting for her, reaching down from cloudy heaven. And Rapture, when it comes, will come as a vortex, twisting the faithful up to God with the dead. That is what they are spinning for—they are spinning to feel how the world will end. When Sorrow releases her, Amity spins free in an orbit about the room as the wives did, flinging her body in a whirlwind as she has only witnessed, whipped like the spinning top of God. And she is embarrassed by her jeans and her sneakers then, rubbing and squeaking over the floor. She should be dressed for spinning, in a woman's skirts and cap. She has forgotten who she is. She has been vain enough to think that people have been looking at her, when she should only be staring at God.

And then it is all she wants—to be who she was.

From below her, from beneath them both, she hears a voice. She hears a scream.

Amity looks at her sister and she is only smiling.

"Father," Sorrow says.

41
The Room Below

"Wife," he calls her.

Through the dark of the room below, she hears his voice with a jolt that shakes a scream from her, and she knows why he didn't follow them, why the cars that pursued her were never his, why the police couldn't find him or question him, why he hadn't come for them after all. He was down below.

He had been here all along. He was the one who stayed, finally, and waited for her return. And then she is sorry to have come back, Sorrow or no. Her eyes strain in the darkness, but she cannot see him. No husband, handsome, the white suit of his wedding days. No husband as she found him, lost and bewildered in his haze of drugs, nor the beauty of him, lost in prayer, beyond any of their reaching. He would be wasted away to nothing, she knew, living on the scraps of the room below, or scavenging the house as she thought Sorrow must have done. He might be only skin and bone, much as his second wife was now.

"I knew you'd come."

"Not for you."

"Help me up," he says. His voice comes clear and strong. She can afford him no pity.

She steps back into the square of light from above, making it harder to see him or find him in the room below. She hears him moving, following her into it. "I'd have bolted the hatch if I knew you were down here."

"To bury me?" He gives a laugh that becomes a long, wet cough. She can hear the fluid in his lungs, from the damp and chill of the room below, even in summer. The cough doubles him over, the slim shape in the darkness that moves closer, comes toward her.

From above her, she hears footsteps, the sound of wooden clogs turning on boards. "Daughter?" she calls. She looks up.

"Daughter," he says, and then his hands are on her and he is pulling her to him, away from the light, and all she wants is to get out, grab her daughters, and go. The slim bones of his fingers shackle her wrist, reach for her face, her mouth and nose, to silence her once and for all, and she shoves him away. He catches her arm and pulls her into a filthy embrace, and then she must scream.

The footsteps stop above her. "Daughter!" she shouts.

From above, from the light, a face pokes in. Amity's face, her dark braids dropping down. Then Sorrow's face beside her, pale and frowning, beautiful.

"Sorrow!" she cries.

"Sorrow," he echoes, and she turns to him, there in the light. His tunic is stained and greasy, dark stripes marking sweat and waste. His hair hangs in rats.

"Don't you say her name—" she shouts.

"I only wanted—" he falters.

"I know what you wanted."

"I never wanted—Sorrow—"

"You shut up." She pulls away from him, flying backward, toppling back, stumbling over the blankets and the sheet, where arms reach down from the light for her. Two sets of arms. She reaches up to let hands grip her forearms and elbows hook her to lift her, even as he comes for her. She feels her two daughters draw her up, save her, pull her from the room below, even as his hands are in her skirt, around her ankles. She gives one good kick with her wooden sole and feels it connect with bone with a crunch.

And then she is in the light of the temple and her two girls are there and it is all she wants in the world, her two girls safe, and she is sorry to have wanted more. She thinks of Bradley for a moment, an ache and a loss, then she holds Amity to her, fiercely, breathing her in. She holds an arm out for Sorrow, her own Sorrow, but she does not come. "Daughter, you're safe now," she says.

"Am I?" Sorrow turns to the hole in the floor and bends down toward it, as she did when the fire started, and Amaranth is afraid of what she will do and what she has done. She is afraid of what Sorrow wants.

"Come away from there, Sorrow." She follows to draw her up by her shoulders, away from the hole and the room below. "We've come back for you."

"Go away!" Sorrow snarls. Amaranth puts her hands on Sorrow's shoulders and Sorrow squirms away from her. "You threw it away. It's mine now!"

The skeletal bones of her husband's hands reach up from below, for Sorrow to take. The nails are dark and split. Sorrow only smiles at them.

Amaranth bends before her daughter. "This is wrong, Sorrow, what you want. Can't you see it?"

"You don't know," Sorrow says. She takes hold of her father's hands and Amaranth pulls at her, to pull her back from him. Sorrow shouts, "Let me go—you don't want him!"

"I want you, Sorrow," she says.

"You never wanted me," Sorrow snaps back.

"Oh, daughter. That's not true." Amaranth can remember how that felt, not being wanted, left behind and abandoned.

She remembers how desperate she was for someone to want her, anyone. Wasn't that how she came to be here? She holds a hand out to Sorrow and Sorrow looks at it with disdain, like the pathetic thing that it is, offered too late with too little.

Sorrow reaches down for her father's hand. "Behold, the Lamb," she says.

Bradley's truck and the car of Wife Forty-Eight sit, bumper to bumper, clipped together with cables. Amaranth turns the key of the car and watches the temple. "It'll take a few minutes to charge," she says. "Goddamn it."

"We can't leave without Sorrow," Amity cries through the truck window, straining against her seat belt.

"No one can leave if I can't start the truck."

"But we will take her? We won't leave her here?" Amity's voice breaks with a sob.

Amaranth thinks of the bodies in the temple, the bodies in the room below. She thinks of her husband and of Sorrow, their bodies entwined in the room below, and how she did not want to see it. If the temple were on fire again, right now, she would let it burn to the ground and make it disappear.

Sorrow and her husband step from the temple. He is bent and scrawny. His face is a skull, dark sockets for eyes, but Sorrow is strong beside him. She looks strong enough to carry them both.

Amaranth jumps from the truck to them. “Ask him what he is hiding from, Sorrow. Ask him why he hides from what he did.”

“Wife,” Zachariah murmurs. “I didn’t—I never meant—”

Sorrow holds a hand up to him and he cowers from it, as if he is afraid of Sorrow now.

Yes, Amaranth thinks. It is Sorrow who should mete out his justice, for all that he took from her. But instead, she sets her hand upon his filthy head. She raises the other in benediction, in forgiveness. “Give him glory, for the marriage of the Lamb has come.”

He covers his eyes and turns his head away from the two of them.

“Come away from him, Sorrow.” Amaranth stalks back to the cars.

Sorrow smiles. "Behold his bride, the New Jerusalem."

"My God. Forgive me." Zachariah crouches into a kneeling prayer.

Amaranth throws off the jumper cables and slams both hoods. She sees Amity trying to open the passenger door, and she gets in the truck and starts the engine. Amity tries to push past her, to scramble out for Sorrow, but she shoves her daughter back and jams the truck into gear, grinding, and drives them toward the temple. She idles to hold a hand out for Sorrow, one last, desperate hand, but her daughter and husband only take hold of one another. She sees them flame to life in one another's eyes. She can see there is an invisible strap between them, tying them together, stretching across the whole of the country. There is nothing she can do to pull them apart, no matter how he protests now or how her daughter smiles.

She slams the truck into drive and hauls toward the path, tires spitting gravel. In the rearview mirror she watches, to see if he will move to the other car, try to follow after, to explain and protest his innocence. But if he has the thought, he doesn't act on it. Sorrow holds him still and fast, beneath the flat of her hand.

Amity cries out, “Mother—we can’t just leave her here!”

But Amaranth does. She steers between the thin white pines to drive them from Sorrow’s New Jerusalem, the smoldering, moldering ash of her heaven and desire. And Amity can only scream for Sorrow, soundless in the glass of the cab, until the house and the temple and their family are gone again.

42
Home

Amaranth parks outside the police station, finding a dark spot away from the streetlamps. She grips the steering wheel with shaking hands.

"But we don't talk to police," Amity whines. "We can't tell them anything."

"That was your father's fear. Everything is changed now."

"I don't want everything changed. I want everything to go back!"

Amaranth pulls the key from the ignition. The sooner she gets Amity back to Oklahoma, the better. "He has broken laws, Amity. Think how he hurt Sorrow. Think of the room below—"

"I know."

"No, you don't know. You don't know everything. You think you do."

"I do know. I saw him. I saw Sorrow. I know what fathers do."

"No, Amity." She shakes her head.

"You think he killed everyone, but he didn't."

Amaranth grabs her daughter, a hand on either shoulder. "What did you see?"

Amity turns her head away, toward the police station. "He didn't start the fire and you can't tell them he did. I saw her, at the hole with Father shouting. I saw her, when he said he wouldn't let the police split us up and how we should hide. I saw Sorrow start the fire."

"No." She gives Amity a shake. She tries to picture Sorrow, bending mid-prayer in the frenzy at the hatch, while Amaranth pulled at her, trying to make her run. "It was him—he wanted to kill us all. That's why he brought us all into the temple."

"It was Sorrow," Amity insists, turning

back to her mother. “So that hers would be the only holy child left of his.”

Amaranth swallows bile down.

“But family is eternal,” Amity carries on. “It doesn’t matter if you’re dead or not, it doesn’t matter if you leave them or you go. Even Sorrow’s baby—it’s still with her, even though I killed it. She’s forgiven me, Mother. She spun me. I’ve been spun!”

Amaranth pulls Amity in to her. She holds her and rocks her, grieving for the two of them. Grieving for the hope that was born and lost, grieving for the faith that turned to poison. She grieves for her husband and her daughter, lost, for the living and all of the dead below. She grieves for every name on the sheet and she grieves for Amity; she grieves for herself, until Amity wriggles free from her.

She drives them away and through the night until she can stop at a bank of pay phones and drop two quarters into the slot. She asks for the Do Drop Inn in Oklahoma and she dials the number, watching her daughter in the truck’s front seat moving her scarred fingers against the glass. The woman who answers tells her in a bored voice that she does know Bradley and yes, she'll take a message. What does she want to say?

"Tell him we're coming home," she says.

When she gets back to the car her daughter asks her, "Can we go and get our old clothes back?"

Driving south, she phones the bar every time she stops them for gas or the ladies' room, every time they stop to eat handfuls of bread and cheese or sleep, hunched together, in a dark corner of a grocery store parking lot. The sun swings over them. Amity asks when they can stop to spin and pray.

At the border, she rings the bar again.

"Yeah," says the lady. "He's here. Sittin' up like some kinda dog."

"Hello," Amaranth breathes, the receiver hard against her ear.

"Bought a cell phone so you could reach me," Bradley tells her. "Forgot you wouldn't have the number so you could."

She laughs and he laughs. "How are you?"

"Much the same," he says. "You?"

"Tell me how you're the same," she says. In the car, her daughter flies her hands through the air, swims them like Sorrow did. She turns away.

"Sorghum's coloring, what was left. Got the wheat in, so I'll have somethin' to grow for next year. Pa's taken to his bed. His cough's bad now. Says his lungs need Amity, whatever that means. Prob'ly just means he's lost what's left of his mind."

Her throat catches and she pulls the mouthpiece away, lest she make a sound.

"You find Sorrow?" he asks her.

"Yes." She cannot bear to tell him all of it. Perhaps she never will. "No Dust."

"No, I picked him up over in Oklahoma City. He hitched that far when his bike gave out, tryin' to get back. I could skin him for taking your girl back home and skin him again for leavin' me all that rape to drill on my own."

She laughs and finds she is crying. She can see him and Dust together, watching the land, side by side, and she wants only to stand between them, watch the land grow beside them.

"Spent the last of the money on seeds," he says. "Amaranth."

"Yes?" Her heart pounds. There is something he needs to tell her—he has found someone new, or his wife has returned. He has learned the truth about her at last, all the darkness within her, all she has done, and he does not want her to come back. She will have to leave the truck somewhere for him, make some new plan for what to do next, she and Amity. Find somewhere safe to go.

"Amaranth," he says.

"Tell me." She steels herself for his bad news.

"It's amaranth. The seeds. What I'm fixin' to plant. Amaranth."

She breathes all her fear out. "Is it a good crop?"

"It's a new crop to me. Still tryin' to figure it out." She hears him breathe in a lungful of smoke. "You gotta set the share pretty high so you don't kill what's growin'. You think it won't come to much, but it's all there, workin' beneath the surface, settin' down its roots. And when it comes time to bloom you see it's bloodred, like blood in the fields."

She looks across at the truck and her daughter, waiting.

"That okay with you?" he says. "You still there?"

"I'm here." She understands her name then, feels its claim on her. She can grow on his land and be planted. She can learn to root herself and hope to flower. She can plant what was sacred and see what would grow. She knows his planting is his asking her, to stay. "That's okay with me," she says, and her heart bursts wide, past her daughter, past the weight of what was.

Even he, down in Oklahoma, must hear it.

Mother fills the tank and says they will be home soon.

Their lives are waiting to be picked up, like stitches, but Mother has forgotten where home is. Home isn't made or chosen, like she says it is. Family isn't handmade or reworked like cloth. Family is the family that God gives you, the family He wants you to have, even if it hurts you. The hurting is what He is teaching you. That hurting is your family.

All the world is shouting this truth, but Mother cannot hear it. She hasn't seen what people do on TV. She doesn't know how lonely an empty bed is or how bare an unstrapped wrist can feel, no sister to bind you to anything.

"Not long now," Mother says every few miles. "Look, there's a sign."

The writing at the border says OKLAHOMA. "I know. I can read it," she says, and Mother looks at her, all surprised.

Amity thinks of Dust and she thinks of the land. She thinks of the fields and what she could do in them, and then she knows that she is the strap, stretching between what Sorrow is and what her mother wants, and between them is Amity, looking forward, looking backward, head covered, but wearing jeans.

She looks into her hands and wonders what they will do next.

See how they twitch and they want.

Acknowledgments

I would like to thank everyone at Little, Brown: my editor, Judy Clain, whose clarity and concision helped to make *Amity & Sorrow* a leaner, better book; her assistant, Amanda Brower; publisher Michael Pietsch; Liz Garriga; Jayne Yaffe Kemp; and everyone in the art department. Many thanks to Tinder Press in the UK—to editor Charlotte Mendelson for her support and encouragement throughout this twisty process, her assistant, Emily Kitchin; Samantha Eades; Vicky Palmer; Yeti Lambregts; and all the team at Headline.

Grateful thanks to my agent, Joy Harris, for taking a leap of faith with me.

Thank you to New Writing South and director Chris Taylor for their support during the writing of my first draft. Not only did they provide a grant so that I could take up a place at Arvon, they also supplied a free read by the Literary Consultancy. Many thanks to Hilary Johnson for her manuscript assessment and for introducing me to writer and editor Caroline Upcher, who helped me see my book with fresh eyes.

Thank you to Sara Maitland and Susan Elderkin, authors who were particularly generous with their time and their feedback.

Thank you, early readers and dear friends: Tim Macedo-Hatch, Monique L'Heureux, Sue Bickley, and my great friend Katherine May, who twice read drafts in a hurry, when I needed her most. Thank you to the coven and to friends and family, near and far.

Thank you to the writers and readers on Twitter and to the #amwriting online community for their generous support. You provided good company and solace during many a draft.

I would like to acknowledge books that were particularly helpful while putting the world of the book together: Jon Krakauer's *Under the Banner of Heaven* for its consummate history of Mormon fundamentalism; *The Worst Hard Time* by Timothy

Egan, a history of the Dust Bowl and the Oklahomans who stayed; and John Steinbeck's *The Grapes of Wrath,* which casts a grand shadow over any book about Oklahoma, farming, drought, or road trips.

Finally, many thanks to my husband, Graham, for building me the Blue House and for making a home for my heart.

Peggy Riley is a writer and playwright. Her work has been produced, broadcast, installed, and published in magazines, anthologies, and online. She has been a bookseller, festival producer, and writer-in-residence at a young-offender prison. Originally from Los Angeles, she now lives in Britain on the North Kent coast. *Amity & Sorrow* is her first novel.